"I'll get answers out of you eventually, Isabel."

Lord, he was persistent. Give him some hope then continue to whittle away. "I am quite sure you will but not this eve." She gracefully smoothed her skirts, lowered her voice—hid behind her lashes. "I'll not ask again. Share with me, Devin. I would really like to know what disturbs you so."

Devin's low chuckle warmed her insides. "You think to get answers from me by flirting? Good luck, lass. I invented that method."

Isabel's eyes flew to his. Insolence! She almost faltered at the devilish twinkle in his gaze, the languid way his come-hither eyes roamed her face. Indeed, he did flirt well. She squelched the lop-sided grin she felt beginning to erupt. "I see no reason for your secrecy." Isabel again leaned close and whispered in her best co-conspirator tone, "Then you really are a spy."

His thick-lashed eyes fell to her lips and he leaned closer as well. "In my own way, that is exactly what I am."

Now she was getting somewhere. "Ah, I knew it."

"Did you?" His gaze slowly slid down her neck and she'd swear his finger grazed the soft skin. Goose pimples rose on her flesh.

"Yes, I did." She continued to follow his gaze, could almost feel how he saw her…feminine…enticing. "It makes perfect sense."

"Aye." Devin's gaze fell to the swells of her breasts peeking out from the top of her dress. "You found me out."

A deep inhale, then he exhaled slowly, his hot breath flaming across her chest. Nipples tightened.

Searing warmth flooded between her thighs. Isabel inhaled sharply. His eyes met hers, knowing. How did he do that? What exactly had he done without moving an inch?

"What did I find out?" she murmured, her mind swimming in pleasure, relaxed, not nearly as sharp as it had been moments before.

A ravishing grin crinkled the corners of his eyes, made enticing sweeps of his dark eyelashes. "That I'm not quite who I seem to be."

The Georgian Embrace

Calum's Curse: Acerbus Lycan

By

Sky Purington

Dear Reader,

Thank you for purchasing The Georgian Embrace. The characters and concepts in this story completely engaged me and I hope they will you as well. For the first time ever, I wrote about a werewolf. Always a fan of the supernatural creature, I enjoyed crawling into its mind. How it might think and act. How it might love.

Devin O'Rourke is one of four paranormal investigators who have made this series shine. Irish, with a great love for cooking, he became a character unlike any other. No doubt, he was the most light-hearted of the bunch and had to rediscover that about himself through this book. After all, he'd inherited some unusual gifts that he'd rather not possess.

Isabel is like most of my female characters, a strong woman. Her journey begins at a young age in a time when women were not nearly on the same social scale of men. But I think it was her very upbringing that made her able to handle all of the things that The Georgian Embrace threw at her.

The love between Devin and Isabel was one of my more passionate tales. I loved how their perseverance allowed them time to develop feelings for one another. Had either not been determined to fight, this novel would not have been possible.

Regardless, it is with the full participation of all the dynamic characters in this series that it becomes so amazing. Leathan, Devin, Seth and Andrea make up The Worldwide Paranormal Society. The curse laid upon their ancestor, Calum, creates the wild journey they all become part of.

Start at the beginning with Leathan's story, The Victorian Lure (Calum's Curse: Ardetha Vampyre) and finish the series with Seth's story, The Tudor Revival (Calum's Curse: Ultima Bellum).

Best Regards Always,
Sky

What They're Saying....

"I literally could not put this book down. Every twist and turn left me wanting to know more, read more. What starts out as a fictional ghost story, transcends into a truly believable story of love and its ability to weather any storm. The Victorian Lure has been one of the most fulfilling, moving books that I have ever had the pleasure of reading. With an ending I never could have imagined, Sky Purington has proven "Nothing is ever as it appears to be" ~S Siferd- Night Owl Reviews

"The Georgian Embrace is a wild, twisty ride for both the characters and the reader.... another excellent installment in Ms. Purington's Calum's Curse series." ~Author Shelley Munro

"Just when you think that this series can't get any better authoress Sky Purington manages to throw readers another literary fast ball that is destined for "out of the park" status. Just as in the first two books of this wonderful romp through paranormal wonderland, you will find a few ghosts, a beautiful time shifting back drop, romance, toe curling sex...and so much more. Watch Seth and Alana put love to the ultimate test in The Tudor Revival." ~WTF Are You Reading Reviews

PREVIOUS RELEASES INCLUDE…

~The MacLomain Series~

The King's Druidess (MacLomain Series- Prelude)
Fate's Monolith (MacLomain Series- Book 1)
Destiny's Denial (MacLomain Series- Book 2)
Sylvan Mist (MacLomain Series- Book 3)

The MacLomain Series Boxed Set

~The MacLomain Series- Early Years~

Highland Defiance. Available Autumn of 2012.

~Forsaken Brethren Series~

Darkest Memory.
Heart of Vesuvius

~Calum's Curse Trilogy~

The Victorian Lure (Calum's Curse: Ardetha Vampyre)
The Georgian Embrace (Calum's Curse: Acerbus Lycan)
The Tudor Revival (Calum's Curse: Ultima Bellum)

CHAPTER ONE

Devin drove down the long, desolate road and again contemplated the previous year. What happened in the old Victorian both repulsed and fascinated him. Though paranormal investigators, he and his cousins never could have imagined what it had in store for them. Time-travel of a sort, vampires and of course, ghosts.

That house and everything in it had changed them irrevocably. Devin didn't like it one bit. Unlike his cousins, he didn't embrace the 'gift' they'd inherited there. Who wanted to be part of Calum's Curse?

Now he was en route to Andrea's new house. While she too investigated the paranormal and had been at the Victorian, she'd avoided their fate. Lucky her! But he was grateful. She didn't deserve it any more than they did. Now she felt her new house was haunted and needed his help. No problem... if he could find her home.

He pulled over and hopped out. Legs crossed, leaning against his pickup truck, he whipped out his cell phone and texted, "K, officially lost. Did you have to move to no man's land?"

After hitting send he sighed and tilted back his head. Tall, stoic pines swayed in a light breeze and spit down random needles. The air felt different here, deceptively fresh. Devin wasn't sure why he thought it wasn't as pure as it could be.

He pulled from his pocket the picture Andrea had

sent him and stared at it. Without doubt, a woman stood beside Andrea and her husband. Gently rubbing the side of his thumb over her face, Devin once again felt mesmerized, sucked in almost. Though impossible to make out features, her slender frame and long curling white-blond hair were arresting. He wanted to reach into the picture and run his hand through its thick, inviting length. Wrap his arms around her tiny waist.

His phone rang and he answered, "What, you don't like texting?"

"You know I don't," Andrea said. "Why not just call?"

"I dunno, habit not to I guess."

"Where are you?"

He almost snorted. "The forest."

Her chuckle bubbled through the phone. "Vague."

Picture tucked in his pocket; he opened the truck door and slid into the vehicle. "You tell me how else to describe a long paved road with nothing but towering pines on either side."

"What's your GPS say?"

Devin rolled his eyes and started driving. "Turn right at the slumped pine tree. Drive a mile until you reach the really tall pine tree. You have reached your destination."

A smile in her voice, Andrea replied, "Come on, what road are you on?"

About to speak, he yelped when the phone turned flaming hot. Ouch! He tossed it away, blew on his fingers and frowned. What the hell? The GPS flashed, its pixels scrambling, before it said over and over, "Turn left."

What left? Devin banged the GPS with the pad of his hand. The truck leapt forward. He fell back. Damn! Though he slammed the brake, the vehicle bucked and swerved. Hands on the wheel, Devin tried to bring it under control. Regrettably, it hit forty miles per hour in short time. Though he pressed the brake to the floor, something else had power over the gas. Grunting and groaning, the pick-up's back end started to fishtail.

Remain calm. He started to pump the breaks. Pretend he was on an icy road. C'mon baby. Bloody truck didn't like it. Slamming from the right to the left side of the road, dirt and rock spit up in his rearview mirror, pummeled the truck bed.

The GPS sputtered—the feminine voice, though slurred and dying repeated, "Turn to the left."

Hell. Devin continued to struggle with the out of control truck. I'll be damned if I die like this. Suddenly, the vehicle slid to a stop. He lurched forward. His body hit the steering wheel. The airbag released. Whoosh. He slammed back. Plastered against the seat he eyeballed everything.

This wasn't good.

They weren't kidding. Airbags really could kill. Or so it felt like it. The thing had him pinned, head turned sideways. Devin felt inside his pants and pulled out a pocket knife. He punctured the airbag and breathed deeply.

The bag deflated. What the? Devin's mouth fell open. Was that a dirt road jutting off to the left? I need to relax. Think clearly. He took a deep breath. Why go searching for the paranormal when it found him first. He'd better perform a quick EVP (electro voice phenomena) session.

He pulled a tape recorder from the glove compartment and pressed record.

"Who are you?" he asked.

After waiting the appropriate amount of time for a spirit to answer into the recorder he asked, "Why did you do that to my truck?"

Once another minute passed, he hit rewind then play. Nothing had answered his questions. Figures. Putting the recorder back in the glove compartment, he sighed. Some might be afraid at this point. Some may see all this as completely freaky—a good reason to leave the truck, run hard as heck, and never look back.

Not him.

Truck in gear, he turned left. Two minutes after he started down the forgotten rocky road it opened up. Devin almost stopped when he saw what loomed beyond. Look at that. He pulled up in front of one of the most impressive houses he'd ever seen.

Andrea, tapping her cell phone against her hip, grinned and walked his way. Devin smiled and hopped out of the truck. Before she made it much further he scooped her up and spun her. She laughed and hugged him.

"It's been far too long, cousin." He set her down and grinned. "Look at you!"

"Just the same." Andrea smiled.

He didn't comment on the fact her smile seemed slightly forced.

"I'd say, not hunting the paranormal suits you." He nodded at the mansion she'd moved into. "It's incredible."

She offered it a haphazard glance. "It is, isn't it?"

He squeezed her hand. "You called only me.

Can't help but find that curious."

Andrea sighed. "I didn't want to call everyone if I'm wrong."

With her long wavy brown hair pulled back into a ponytail, Andrea appeared more beautiful than ever. But he saw the faint lines around her lips, the worry between her eyebrows. "I don't think you're wrong," he murmured.

Her eyes met his. "Something's already happened to you."

"Aye, let's just say my truck went a little nuts." His eyes wandered back to the imposing stone Georgian backed by deep green pines. Symmetrical, three stories tall, with four massive chimneys and numerous multi-pane windows, it seemed to be a living, breathing thing. "But I've no definitive way to know if it's connected to this house."

Andrea's eyes widened briefly at the limp air bag sagging from the steering wheel. She looked to the house. "I'd be shocked if it wasn't. You okay? Did you get in an accident?"

"I'm fine. Just a ghost having some fun." Devin reached into the cab of his truck and pulled out his duffel bag. "I think we should get Seth in on this as well."

"What about Leathan?" she asked.

"He's still on his honeymoon. I say we call him only if—" his voice trailed off and he grimaced.

Andrea watched him steadily. "Only if it proves to be part of the curse?"

With a grave nod, he walked with her toward the house. "I'm sure it's not. Don't worry, lass."

Visibly shivering, she shook her head. "This is my new home. That'd be terrible."

Devin stopped before he walked up the steps to the front door. A shiver slithered up his spine. Had someone been standing in the window above? He could have sworn. "We'll figure this out. I'm sure it's just your average haunting. Calum never said the curse would necessarily continue after the Victorian, did he?"

"No, but you know as well as I that his journal heavily implied it."

Devin once more contemplated Calum's journal and the terrifying Victorian where his cousin Leathan had met his current wife, Dakota.

Andrea ushered him into a small breezeway decorated with blue velvet upholstered benches on either side. The main foyer hosted a pale marble floor with a huge area oriental rug that mixed various shades of pale blue-gray together. A staircase ran up to the second floor. Andrea led him into the living room. "You want a tour of the house now?"

"No, I say we sit and have something to drink. Catch up a little first."

She nodded. "Sounds good to me. Make yourself at home. I'll go get some tea."

Devin shot her a look.

Her brows rose. "Whiskey?"

"If you don't mind."

"Of course not. Be right back."

While he waited, Devin studied the room. The walls were wood paneled to Dado height then wallpapered in sage green printed with repeating trefoils. Mouldings were intricate and the furnishings wing-backed and delicate, upholstered with burgundy glazed cotton fabric designed with small sprigs of flowers. Long curtains had the same fabric with pagoda styled pelmets on top.

But it was the fireplace that caught his attention. Huge and elegant, flanked with classical pillars, it had basket grates, a cast iron back and decorated fonts featuring swags, urns and medallions. A firescreen with a trompe l'oeil painted in a similar sage green as the walls sat in front of a crackling fire.

When Andrea returned she handed him a cup. Devin sat and took a deep swig. "You definitely kept with the era in this place, eh?"

She rolled her eyes. "Don't you ever read my emails? I told you this place came fully furnished. Now I'm starting to wonder about that."

"Ah yes." He took another sip of whiskey and pulled the picture out of his pocket. "You must be referring to the period clothing the woman in this is wearing."

Legs crossed beneath her, Andrea sat in the opposite chair. Her eyes widened. "How many times have you looked at that thing? It's nearly threadbare!"

"Not that much," he replied defensively, but couldn't help but glance at it once more. "Are you sure she's a ghost?"

"Of course she is. When my friend took that picture, there was no one there but the three of us." Andrea set her tea aside. "But I think you know that. I think you sense it."

Naturally, the conversation would have headed in this direction. "Honestly, I haven't really...experimented with my new gift the past year."

"Yeah, I know. I heard."

His eyes flickered to hers. "Seth can't keep his

mouth shut. Then again, sounds like he's dived headfirst into our, "new state of being.""

"I'm surprised you haven't," Andrea murmured. "What's up?"

It seemed he'd had to answer this question a hundred times in the past year from both Seth and Leathan. Since they'd learned they were warlocks—whatever that meant. "What purpose would it serve? It doesn't apply to my life."

Disturbed, she responded, "How can you say that? Chances are the Victorian was only the beginning. Hasn't it occurred to you that we started there because the haunted houses after it might be more vicious?"

"More vicious than that place? Are you serious?"

Andrea cocked her head. "You seem different, not the jovial Devin I've always known. What's going on with you, hon?"

Good question. He'd been asking himself that for a while now. "Nothing. Just trying to get on with life."

He clutched the picture possessively and stared into the fire.

"Devin," Andrea said softly.

When his gaze met hers, he saw clearly her concern. "I'm okay. Really." Devin mustered up his brightest grin. "When do you expect Tim home?"

She studied his face for a few moments. When she spoke her voice seemed strained. "Regrettably, not for a week. He's away on business but sends his love."

Were they already having marital problems? "Well then, I suppose my timing is good. You won't be alone here."

Andrea nodded absently. "Your equipment in the truck?"

"Of course." He gulped down the rest of his whiskey. "I should probably unload and set up."

"I agree. But don't think you're off the hook. I'm keeping my eye on you, cuz. I want to know what you've been up to the past year besides hunting ghosts."

Devin was about to answer when a telling cool breeze blew through the room. The temperature dropped. Andrea obviously felt it as well because she pulled out her cell phone and started to snap pictures.

"This happen often?"

"Lately, yeah," she responded. "But I never catch anything."

Typically, a sharp drop in temperature indicated a spirit. A cool hand brushed his where he held the picture. "Something tells me you might now."

Andrea looked at the picture she'd just snapped and froze.

Devin took a deep breath. She was near. He knew it with every ounce of his being. "Do you smell that?" he murmured.

Andrea didn't respond, eyes wide.

He turned his head slightly and inhaled deeply. "Spicy, fresh."

Help me.

Gripping the picture, Devin whispered, "Who are you?"

As quickly as the spirit came, she fled. Devin stood, suddenly desperate. "Come back. Please."

Andrea snapped a few more pictures. "She's gone, sweetie."

Crossing to her chair he held out his hand. "Let

me see what you caught."

Andrea clicked to a picture and handed him the phone. Though difficult to see, something had definitely stood by his side. With a few clicks, he sent the picture to his phone and handed Andrea's back to her. When he sank into his chair, Devin felt distracted, edgy—eager almost. "Have you researched this house?"

"Naturally, but I found no record of a young woman with blond hair living here."

"But she did. I know it," he muttered, his mind spinning as he planned his next move. He lurched from his seat and headed for the door. "I'm getting the equipment."

Andrea followed. "I'll help."

When he exited the house, the sun was setting beneath the line of trees. It cast orange prisms of spiked light over the fresh, green lawn. Desperate to catch this ghost in any way possible, Devin took long strides. Her words haunted him. Help me. Was she somehow trapped?

"Did she ever speak to you?" he said over his shoulder.

"No, never," Andrea responded. "She talked to you. What did she say?"

Almost to his truck, his phone beeped. He'd received a text. Andrea did as well. They stopped and looked at one another, pulling out their phones.

Devin pulled up his message. It was from Seth. "Stab me with a pine tree and put me outta my misery."

What?

Andrea laughed. Screech. They looked down the drive. It couldn't be. Sure as heck, as they watched the tree line, a black Mercedes broke free and peeled up the drive. It had to be traveling at fifty miles per hour. Well-timed, its driver slammed on the brakes soon enough that a cloud of dirt kicked up behind and managed to not hit the back of Devin's pick-up by mere inches. A loud base thrummed a steady beat from inside as the dust settled. Across the top of the windshield, in thin gothic words, Worldwide Paranormal Society became visible.

The door opened and a tall man with black hair and even darker sunglasses stepped out. Andrea wasted no time but flew into his arms. "Seth!"

As he had, Seth spun her, laughing. "Sis, are you really that surprised to see me?"

"Truthfully? Yes!"

Devin approached with a smile. "Cousin. Good to see you."

The men embraced, patting one another on the back. Seth shrugged. "What can I say? Had a feeling you guys might need me."

His attention turned to the house and he released a low whistle. "So this is it, huh?"

"Thought you were covering the haunting in Delaware?" Devin said.

"I was. I did." Seth shoved his glasses on top of his head, blue eyes challenging. "Easy fix. Spirit just needed to say goodbye. Besides, that—" he nodded at the Georgian, "requires immediate attention. Am I wrong?"

When his gaze found Devin's, he knew his cousin already knew more than he was admitting. "Seems so," he replied carefully.

Seth turned, popped his trunk and started pulling out equipment. "So, how goes Ireland this time of year?"

Devin started to unload equipment as well. "Wet."

"Your damn country's timeless forecast." Seth smiled and shut the trunk. "Hasn't been the same investigating without you these past few months."

"How's Dakota done with it?" he asked.

Seth's eyes met his, dark. "Good, she loves it."

No fool, Devin knew what he was thinking. Why was Dakota there when you should've been? Where have you been? What's your problem?

Andrea grabbed a few more bags and headed for the house. "Seriously, not that I'm not grateful, but what brings you this way, Seth? I haven't told anyone about what's going on here but Devin."

Seth chuckled. "Didn't you get the hellish memo—Haunted Victorian House 101— I'm a warlock."

Tapping her forehead with the palm of her hand she responded in a lightly sarcastic tone, "How could I have forgotten?"

"You mock!" Seth grinned and entered the door after her. "And I shouldn't have said it that way as you both know I've embraced my new role."

Had he ever. Once again, Devin wondered…should he have? No, definitely not. It could only lead to trouble. After all, he didn't seem to possess half the power Leathan and Seth did.

The faint smell of roasted potatoes and corn beef filled the home. Good old fashioned Irish-American meal. Andrea took one of the laptops from him and shot a sheepish grin. "I thought it would be you and me. I dared to challenge the best cook ever."

For a split second, looking into her smiling eyes,

he almost felt like the man he'd once been. "A lot to take on, lassie." He sniffed. "Must admit, smells delicious."

Andrea preened. "Come, both of you, to the kitchen."

"Grabbed some take-out hours ago, at the border of this desolate state, but must admit, bit hungry again." Seth entered the kitchen in front of Devin.

As elegant as the living room, the only difference in the kitchen were all the modern day appliances. But even they were masked discreetly behind wood paneling and soft subtle colors so nothing appeared intrusive.

Andrea shut off a crock pot on the counter and nodded to Devin. "Plates are in that cabinet, silverware in the drawer. Help me set the table. We'll eat in the dining room. Sound good?"

In the past year, Devin had avoided this. Anything that reminded him of who he was before…what had happened. Staring around blankly he said, "Sure, Seth, help out."

Seth and Andrea gazed at him for a long moment before they swung into action. Seth started pulling out plates, Andrea silverware.

"How about at least setting the table?" Andrea asked.

"Sure." He took the handful of utensils from her. The kitchen table was simple and wooden. Almost carelessly, he plunked the pile in the center and turned back.

Seth and Andrea stood, aloof, and stared at him with matching frowns.

"What?" he asked.

They shook their heads and kept to their

business. "Nothing," Andrea responded. "I'm glad to have you guys here. This is great."

"Quaint place," Seth said. "Never would've figured you for it."

Spoonful by spoonful, she filled plates with corn beef. "Kind of fell into my lap, you could say."

Silence descended.

"Sorry, I didn't mean it like that." A weak smile vanished from her face as she carried the plates to the table. "More like it was meant to be?"

Seth stood in the doorway, frowning. "We all know how Dakota found that Victorian. Andrea, if there's a chance this house came into your hands in a way you found unusual we should have already known about it." He frowned. "But we're willing to hear the truth now if you held back before."

Devin met Seth's eyes, then Andrea's. Seth was right. Nothing but the truth had a place in their lives, most especially in any haunting they investigated.

Not after the Victorian.

Hands braced on the counter, she shook her head. "No, no. It wasn't like that."

"What wasn't like that?" Devin felt a sickening sensation in the pit of his stomach.

Andrea blinked rapidly, as though something fell into place in her mind. "There's no way this house is—"

"Is what?" Seth said.

Devin put his arm around her shoulder. "Tell us now. Let's not have to research it on the internet. What's this house's story? Why did you buy it?"

The same chill he'd felt earlier passed over him. Seth stood straighter, eyes narrowed. Andrea hung her head.

Devin clenched her shoulder harder than intended and said through clenched teeth, "Andrea, what's going on?"

The room grew colder. "Her name Is Isabel," she whispered.

The picture in his pocket burned against his thigh. Devin laid it on the counter and pointed at the picture of the ghost. "Her?"

Andrea nodded. A tear escaped.

Seth leaned forward and studied the picture. "Why didn't you tell Devin? Any of us?"

Andrea swallowed hard. "Because I had no choice. I couldn't."

Before Seth could slide the picture his way Devin pocketed it. "Why?"

Andrea shook her head, eyes hollow and vacant. "It's got Tim."

It felt like a tidal wave crashed over him. "What the bloody hell are you talking about?"

"We need to eat," she urged absently and headed for the dining room.

He and Seth exchanged a look of confusion before following. Her brother spoke first. "Who has Tim? What's going on, Andrea?"

After she set a plate on the table, Andrea crumbled into a chair, sobs wracking her slender form. Seth knelt and put an arm around her shoulder. "It's okay," he soothed.

"No, it's not," she mumbled through tears. "You don't understand."

"Help us too." Devin sat in the chair next to her. "Please."

Andrea shook her head and said nothing.

"You have to," Seth urged, brushing hair away

from her forehead.

She took a shaky breath. "Leave, both of you. Now."

Devin frowned. "Figure the odds. Talk to us. What happened?"

When she stood abruptly, they leaned back. "This." Andrea made a wide sweep with her hands. "This place."

Seth stood. "So I was right."

"Right enough," she said, voice strangled. "I should have never," Andrea's mournful eyes locked with Devin's, "brought you here. Can you ever forgive me?"

"For what?" He grabbed her hands and pleaded. "What's happened, lass? Where's Tim?"

Though she made to speak all that resulted was a heavy, cheek-streaking tear escaped from her right eye. "I love him so much," she whimpered.

Three phones beeped at once. They had all received a text message. When he released her hand, Andrea sunk back into her chair, and cried harder.

He and Seth fished their phones from their pockets.

Devin knew they had the same message...sent by Leathan.

It read... "The curse is back. I'm coming."

CHAPTER TWO

"How could you?" Leathan ranted. "We've been down this road before. You should've been honest from the start."

Three hours from the time of his text message, they sat in the dining room. It was as though the past year hadn't existed and once more, they fought a nameless evil together.

Andrea held up her head, chin jutted out. "I'm done saying sorry because, God knows, I am. Tim is at stake here. I had no choice but to do it like I did."

"Hmph." Leathan shook his head, fuming. "So if this house had had its way Devin would've been its soul victim? Drawn to a woman who haunts it?" Fists clenched, face red, he continued. "And you were okay with that?"

Her chin jutted out further, eyes narrowed. "You twist things. Tim is my husband, my love. Tell me, what would you have been capable of had it been Dakota?"

"He's your cousin!"

"Tim's my—"

"Enough," Devin interjected. "Enough," he said softer. When he had every eye on him, Devin said, "Fighting with one another isn't going to solve a thing. Again, Andrea, tell me why it is this house wanted me, why Isabel wanted me."

"I think it was clear the first time, lad," Leathan said. "Through her, whatever nasty creature is trapped in this house wants you."

"Still the same prickly bastard; would've thought marriage agreed with you," Seth muttered.

Leathan shot Seth a look that could kill. "Callous as ever, eh Seth?"

Seth bristled and sat forward. "What's your—"

"Enough." Devin repeated. Damn his cousins to hell. If Andrea could be any paler, she'd match freshly fallen snow. "Fighting isn't helping Andrea. What's happened to us? We never fought like this before. Now everyone shut up. Let Andrea talk."

Leathan mumbled to himself but nodded.

"Sorry, Andrea. You have the floor," Seth said.

She squeezed Devin's hand. "Thanks, Devin. You're being better to me than I deserve." After a heavy swallow, she continued. "As I said before, it all started about two weeks ago, the day we started renovating. As we all know, making the slightest adjustments to a house has the ability to cause spirits to act up. In this case, it was fast and furious. I thought I could handle it on my own. Everyone's been so busy the past year and Leathan and Dakota were going on their honeymoon. I mean seriously, I've been a paranormal investigator for ten years. I really thought I could handle this."

Devin understood. He would've done the same. "Go on," he urged when she paused.

Andrea nodded. "Two entities immediately made themselves known. The first, Isabel. I know her name because I caught it during an EVP session. I know little else about her. The second, and far worse, is a dark presence. It hasn't identified itself but it's been extremely active, much more so than Isabel. I'd be inclined to say the dark presence is overwhelming her, but her spirit almost strikes me as...rebellious?"

"Explain," Leathan said.

"Well, for example. One night Tim and I were sitting in front of the fire in the living room. Suddenly, there was a loud, inhuman roar. The fire leapt from the hearth and spread over the carpet. Instantaneously, a bucket appeared as though held by something unseen and dumped water over it, dousing the flame. We heard another roar, a woman's cry, and then everything went silent. The carpet was as it had been before. It'd all been an illusion! We couldn't help but think she was defying the dark presence."

"Certainly sounds it," Devin murmured. A strange feeling washed over him. Isabel. What other traits did she possess?

Leathan's gaze once more focused on the worn picture in Devin's hand. Their eyes held for a moment. His cousin already gathered he had become somewhat infatuated with this spirit. But for some reason, she felt real to him, important to him.

Andrea continued. "A few days ago everything spun out of control. And believe it or not, I'd even managed to get a priest here to bless the house. Nothing worked. In the end—" She put a hand over her mouth and shook her head, eyes filling again.

"In the end the house swallowed Tim," Seth stated.

"I've never seen anything like it," she whispered. "It looked as though the wall enfolded him. It was terrible. You couldn't imagine. The fear on his face, the pain he must have felt."

"You said there was a tape, that you performed another EVP session immediately," Leathan reminded. "We need to hear it."

Devin wanted to smack him upside the head. Of them all, Leathan and Andrea had always been the closest. While he understood his cousin being upset…where was his compassion?

Andrea nodded toward the hutch in the corner. "There."

Seth scooped it up, set it on the table and hit play.

Andrea's voice could be heard first. "Give my husband back! Please! Who are you?"

A masculine voice clearly answered. "Set me free and I will. Who I am matters naught."

Andrea's voice. "How do I set you free?"

Silence.

Andrea's voice again. "Please. Tell me. I'll do anything."

"Devin," he whispered. "Get only Devin O'Rourke here. I will give you back whom you seek."

It took a lot to scare Devin. This did. What did this spirit want with him? But he already knew. This had to be the second creature trapped by Calum's curse. And he must be the warlock it wanted.

Andrea's voice again. "Why Devin?"

Silence. This time—though Andrea prodded—there came no response.

Seth clicked off the recorder. "I suppose the question now is did the presence know that Leathan and I would show up?"

"Of course," Leathan said. "As I told you before, Calum visited me and said the curse was once again upon us. I needed to get to Andrea. Why are you here, Seth?"

"Strong feeling." Seth looked pointedly at Devin. "You'd be amazed at what we're capable of as warlocks."

Devin ignored him. "Have you looked for the journal, Andrea?"

In the Victorian, they had read what was said to be Calum's first journal. It told of a curse that had been laid on him hundreds of years ago. Three creatures of the night were sent to destroy his descendants—them. Using time-travel, he had built three houses and trapped the creatures. Trapped until the day the talisman connected to the creature was found. This would begin the unraveling of the spell he'd cast. Calum, naturally, had ensured that three of his descendants, Leathan, Seth and Devin, would become warlocks upon the reading of the first journal, a boon to aid them in fighting the dark curse.

Andrea shook her head. "No journal. I've looked extensively."

"What about the talisman connected with this creature?" He glanced at Devin. "My guess is it has to be a crimson stone. One that matches your aura."

Devin took a deep breath. In the Victorian they'd learned that Calum had hidden three separate stones in various parts of the world. Three that matched each warlock's magical aura. Dakota had found the blue one. It had ended up matching Leathlan's. He'd fought the vampire. They still didn't know what the other two creatures were. "I've come across no stone. I would've contacted you immediately."

"We know." Andrea nodded and wiped away another escaped tear. "But someone did, must have. I just wish I could find that journal. It'd be so helpful right now."

"Without doubt." Leathan finally sat beside her. "But it's here. I'm sure of it."

"I can't think where. I've torn this place apart."

"Why the hell can't Calum tell us where it is?" Seth asked.

"Because he's a bloody trickster of a ghost, that's why," Devin said.

"Anyone heard from Adlin?" Seth asked.

Adlin was a ghostly wizard whom had helped them a great deal in the Victorian. A friend to Calum's long deceased parents.

Leathan shook his head. "No. And as far as Calum goes, you know as well as I that it's all part of the curse unraveling. As before, Calum's spirit can only contact us when possible. Never quite know when that'll be."

"You would've at least thought he'd tell you where it was when he contacted you," Seth said.

"Nope, he told me the curse was upon us. That's it. No matter, we're all here. We'll find it and we'll find Tim," he assured. Leathan took Andrea's hand. "I'm sorry I was so upset, lass. This can't be easy for you. Forgive?"

"It's okay. I don't blame you for being upset with me. I've endangered everyone, especially Devin."

"You had no choice," Devin said. "Besides, I'm meant to be here."

Seth cocked a brow. "So tell us cousin, what's going through your mind when you look at the picture of Isabel?" He leaned forward and squinted. "What we can see of her that is."

Devin pocketed the picture. "For lack of a better word, familiarity. I feel like I know her." He clenched his fists. "The feeling's so strong. I feel like she's been with me somehow, since I saw this picture in Ireland."

"But she didn't contact you until you got here I assume?" Leathan asked.

I wish. "No," he said uncomfortably. "But I hoped the whole time she would."

Leathan's lips drew down. He sat back. "This is new to me. Then again, I expected little else."

"How do I get him back?" Andrea asked, heart in her voice.

Everyone looked at Leathan as though he had the answer. Devin knew full well he didn't. None of them did. "We start to investigate."

Seth and Leathan looked at him.

"He's right," Leathan agreed. "What choice do we have?"

"None," Devin responded. "The bigger question is…where in this house do we start?"

Andrea shoved a plate with a freshly toasted bagel in front of him. "How about you eat?

The smell of it made his stomach curl but he understood what they were looking for. The 'Devin' they remembered. "Sure." He brought it to his lips.

When he bit, it tasted like cardboard. Still, he chewed. What else could he do? They all stared at him as though he were an experiment. "Good." He nodded and swallowed.

Unconvinced, clearly seeing he struggled to eat it, she said, "I baked that fresh, with raisins, your favorite." Andrea shook her head. "It's a homemade bagel. Everyone knows the work that goes into that!"

"Sorry," he responded. "It's great. Really."

"Unreal." After buttering another slice Andrea said, "I know they're an odd addition to the meal, but…well, I thought to cook your favorites. Guess I had a really guilty conscience."

Devin took another bite and smiled. "No worries. Thanks again, sweetie. You outdid yourself."

Thankfully, everyone switched to idle conversation after that. Had he needed to explain his new personality at length right now, Devin would've managed to choke on his bagel. Instead, he finished it and excused himself. It was time to explore the massive home. He climbed the staircase to the second floor. Had Isabel lived here? Had she walked down the very hall he now did?

Devin flopped down on a bed in the first room he found and stared at the ceiling. He knew it foolish to obsess over someone he'd never met. Never mind a ghost!

Still.

All he'd fantasized about for the last week was her. He envisioned her face—wanted so much to know the color of her eyes, the feel of her skin. How many times had he already touched her slender, narrow shoulders in his dreams?

What was he thinking? This was nuts. Women weren't a problem for him. This girl, spirit, whatever she was, shouldn't affect him so profoundly. He sat up and frowned. None of this made sense. Then again, most hauntings didn't.

He left the room and continued wandering. Nothing relieved him from restless musings. This house didn't welcome him. Why would it? Honestly, he almost wanted it to. Walls, rooms, furniture, that's it. There existed no recognition…nothing that drew him inexplicitly.

Except her.

Everyone was busy bringing the dishes into the kitchen when he returned downstairs. With an overwhelming need to escape, he went outdoors. A purple twilight had descended, casting the wood line into deep, rich shadows. A southerly wind ushered in chilled air. Mere miles from the Canadian border this desolate corner of Maine struggled to embrace summer. It occurred to him Andrea had failed to mention why she'd bought this place.

Though he intended to bring in more equipment from the truck, Devin suddenly found himself less than eager to start investigating. His sole gift—the ability to hear what no other could—made him stop walking. Water trickled in the distance. Someone whispered, the voice almost lost in the clicking of tree branches overhead. Primitive and low, an animal growled.

Danger.

Anxiety stiffened his spine. Another gust of wind blew. It carried scent. Spicy. Fresh.

Isabel.

His reality shifted. Something changed. Although he felt slightly aware of the transition, it didn't matter. Sprinting forward, Devin flew across the lawn into the trees. Though darkness fell fast and the moon new, the forest brightened. Every stone and stump discernible—every twisting path, easy to navigate. Eyes to the night, intent on his destination, Devin coasted around tree trunks, leapt over boulders, desperate to reach her.

Isabel.

The low growl grew stronger. Time was running out. Her heavy breathing mixed with the wind. Thump. Thump. Her heartbeat mixed with his. Petrified and fast, pounding so hard and thickly it filled his throat.

He burst free from the trees and skidded into a clearing.

A woman knelt by a stream, her long curling blond hair a delicate fan over her back. Bright orange blossoms decorated the ground around her. He inhaled.

Spicy. Fresh.

"I always wondered why they grew here." She fingered a blossom at her side without turning. "Butterfly Weed, my favorite flower."

Devin tried to respond but couldn't.

"Don't be afraid. Come closer. I won't hurt you," she whispered.

Hurt him? Unlikely. Why would she say such a thing?

She spoke again. "Do you suppose these Butterfly Weeds became confused? Really, they're supposed to be fond of fields."

Who cared! He took a cautious step forward. Danger was close. She should take care. Move. You are incredibly vulnerable to threat. Come to me. You are not safe. He sniffed. Putrid, flesh decayed. Too close.

"Can't say I blame them," she continued, soft voice mesmerizing. "I think I might grow here too. It's one of the most beautiful spots."

Not nearly as beautiful as she was—sounded. He needed to see her face. At last.

Head tilted back, she whispered, "Look. I just knew that I'd see them tonight. A rare thing in Maine, but it happens."

Tentative, he moved forward a few more steps and gazed up. A deep blue-green array of lights slithered across the sky. The Aurora lights.

"Like I said," she continued, "rare. But I had a feeling. You, them…magic?"

Devin took a few more steps, wanted so much to talk to her but could not.

"I'm glad you came."

Did you lure me? Are you a ghost? Voiceless, he closed the distance and sat beside her. Head bent now, hair hid her profile. Why did she hide?

"Things are different now," she murmured. Her slender hand cupped the pedal of a Butterfly Weed, its ivory texture delicate against the vibrant orange.

How so? Tell me! Devin edged closer.

"No, no, no," she said sadly. "I wanted more time."

Another scent filled the clearing. Branches snapped. Devin stood, walked around her and stopped. Every nerve ending vibrated. Danger edged closer. The same low growl he'd heard before rumbled again.

Closer.

Another growl. Had that come from him?

Bring it on, he thought. I'll tear you to shreds! So strong was his feeling to protect her, Devin felt the absolute need to kill. Annihilate whatever threatened. He licked his lips and eyed the tree line. Blood. He wanted blood.

The notion made him shiver. Here came the warlock in him, that which he wanted no part of…evil. But the rustling grew closer, the stench of death compelling. To run, flee from this, would be impossible. Leaving her unprotected was not an option.

Another low growl rumbled from the night.

Closer.

"Go now," she whispered urgently. "I am not worth it."

Not worth it? How could she think such a thing. He paced, waited. Whatever came was nearly here, perhaps had always been. Watching. Waiting. That pissed him off further. What sort of monster baited like this? Drove an innocent woman to fear so?

Come out and face me, he wanted to roar. Instead he glared, locked his muscles, ready to fight. Kill. Wanting battle so badly he almost strayed from her side to seek out whatever lurked so cowardly within the darkness.

Crash. What the hell?

A split second before he reacted she whimpered and crouched down further. Black and mighty, the darkness had limbs, jumping at them with a ferociousness he could never have anticipated. Devin crouched and sprung, met the beast in the air moments before it landed on her.

They rolled and rolled until water engulfed. Caring nothing for site, Devin punched, kicked and clawed. Sonofobitch. Blasphemous rage filled him and made thought impossible. Blood, death, hellish afterlife fire, he wanted it all for his adversary. The cool water barely touched his skin as they thrashed and fought.

Where is your strength and might fool? You dare challenge me.

Ignoring the beast's words within his mind he sank his teeth into the pelt on its shoulder. Laughter rang. Yellow fangs crossed his vision. Still they rolled.

"Stop, no, please!" she pleaded.

Splash. She pursued them.

Go back, he thought. I will protect you.

But as he battled the beast, Devin started to panic. Could he protect her? This monster was strong, powerful, relentless. He should use his gift. But he didn't. Mere minutes into the war he knew himself defeated.

"Let him go! You must!" she screamed.

Devin twisted to the right and tried to shake the monster off. It clung to him, paws a vice grip, claws digging into his vulnerable flesh. Pain ripped and tore through his body, a cruel unseen knife of destruction across his midriff. With a yelp he struggled to regain footing. The sharp tang of blood filled his nostrils, the absolution of defeat a mere breathe away.

"Get off him!"

Did it rip me in half? Why does the night blur? Devin saw her pounce on the creature determined to end him. "No," he pleaded. Nothing came out.

His head slammed against grass. Pebbles cut into his back. The edge of the stream cornered him. He scrambled. A fist size rock provided leverage. He pushed and flung forward. This gained him two feet of grass. Such pain. The creature bit and tore. Movement, coherent thought, became more and more difficult. Her screams sounded far off. A Butterfly Weed crushed beneath his nose, smeared into the ground.

There existed no more scent.

You dared challenge. You lost.

And he had. Even fury and vengeance held no appeal. Death however, lulled and pacified. No! How could he think such? Again furious, he lurched forward. Only to be dragged down once more. The beast's body pinned him, its growl close to his ear.

Its bite to his jugular—fatal.

Through the slim veil of night he watched his crimson blood drain and stain the grass. Why had it not occurred to him to call for his cousins? He knew well why. Avoidance. To be a warlock, something so sinister, had become his worst nightmare. Devin had all but tried to change his personality to avoid accepting what he'd become. Had he not done so he might've been able to protect Isabel. If only he could rewind time.

But what good were regrets now?

Pain fled.

His eyes slid shut.

***

"The Mr. ain't gonna be too happy with this."

"Naw. But he ain't happy with much."

Chomp. Chomp. "Suppose we outta just throw him into the river, then?"

"Gimme some of that chew. The river? Naw, right now it's his hide. We do that, it's ours."

Devin groaned and opened his eyes. Bright daylight burned his vision. So bright, he shut them and tried to manage the throbbing pain in his head. Label this a hangover from hell. Did he drink?

"One less body, more pay for us. Nobody'd ever know."

A kick to his side. Splicing pain. "You awake?"

Covering his eyes with a hand he said, "Kick me again and I'll screw your bloody arse to a wall."

"Fuckin' wastrel. Wanna say that again?"

Huh? His eyes snapped open. It all came rushing back, the battle with a massive wolf, death…defeat. He sat up quickly, patted his body, felt his neck. All intact. No blood. No pain. Devin blinked and took in his surroundings. It appeared to be early morning. Had he fallen asleep out here? Damp forest filled his nostrils. Two fairly grungy men filled his vision.

"Well?" One of them asked.

"Well what?" he croaked.

"Lad's not right in the head don't think," the man said to the other.

"Don't look like."

Damn. Devin tried to stand but fell back. What the heck had happened to him?

"We best get back. Mr.'ll be expectin' us soon."

"Yep."

Devin watched as the two men lopped away into the trees, apparently no longer concerned with him. Screw them. Head braced in his hands, he breathed deeply. What a nightmare. Even behind the darkness of his closed eyes he saw Isabel. Beautiful. Kind. Different.

He studied his surroundings again. They were much as he remembered them. A steady roar filled his eardrums and he glanced over his shoulder. The trickling stream was now a raging river. Had it rained that heavily? Devin frowned and stumbled to his feet. The world tilted. He braced his legs. Everything evened out. Wiping a hand over his face, he stared at the rushing water.

"You betta get movin' wastrel."

He spun. One of the vagrants vanished once more into the forest. What was he talking about? Devin kneeled and splashed cold water over his face. Time to get back to the house. This mystery needed to be figured out.

As he walked, Devin experienced a strange sort

of déjà vu. Obviously, he'd come this way before but somehow it didn't feel the same. Had it appeared this stagnant before? For some reason, colors had been sharper, smells far richer. Old colorless leaves crunched beneath his feet, the woodland in daylight, rather grim with its muted greens and dusty browns.

"Come on then."

Believe it or not, the two vagrants had waited for him. Devin shrugged and followed. If anything, Andrea would be able to point them in the right direction. How bloody desolate was this area? When the forest ended, he paid little attention. A fresh cup of coffee and maybe a few hours more sleep would do him wonders.

"Where have you been?" a feminine voice whispered.

Devin froze. Isabel? Aye! Dawn broke over the pines and caught her full in the face. Long glorious blond hair framed a face he could've only fantasized existed.

Absolutely beautiful.

Her brows, a shade darker than her pale blond hair, drew down over deep, dark sapphire eyes. So deep a shade of sapphire they appeared violet. Cherub-like, her soft easy cheeks combined with a defined jaw and full, heart-shaped lips. His eyes fell easily to her curvy, touchable figure.

"And you might be?" Isabel asked.

Who might who be? Her pristine skin nearly glowed. Her slender frame built to be protected.

"Are you daft then?" she said.

Devin snapped to attention. "Isabel?" he whispered.

When their eyes met she paused, confusion

evident. "Yes, of course. Do I know you?"

"Don't think he knows himself," one of the vagrants provided.

"No worries, missus," the other vagrant muttered. "He's slow but no harm I don't think." He shrugged and nodded his head, saying each word slowly and with great care, "bein' Irish and all ya see."

"Oh yes." She nodded solemnly and patted vagrant number two on the shoulder as she winked at Devin. "The Irish are, indeed, a difficult breed to understand."

"Yes, missus." The vagrant smiled.

"Go on," she urged both vagrants. "Building starts soon."

They nodded and left.

Not once did Devin remove his gaze from Isabel. When her attention became his, the entire world could fade away and he wouldn't notice.

Isabel held out a hand. "I'm Isabel, nice to meet you."

He took her small and vulnerable hand. Instead of shaking or kissing it, he squeezed lightly. "I'm Devin."

A wide, genuine smile split her face. "Devin. Welcome."

Pull her close. Feel her against your body. Devin closed his eyes then opened them. Still he held her hand. "It's so nice to finally see you…like this."

"Thank you." She continued to smile. "Again, do I know you?"

"Yes." He shook his head. "No." Keep on blubbering fool. "Nice dress."

His brows drew together. Nice dress for sure. But why was she wearing it?

"Again, thank you." Isabel cocked her head. "What job do you do?"

"Job?"

Tinkling laughter erupted. "Yes, job."

Her delicate, white throat caught his attention. Lord, she was pristine. "Paranormal investigator."

Isabel's fresh laughter poured over him. "Do you study the materials before they're laid then? Never heard it phrased quite like that."

Devin took a step forward and breathed in her scent. "Butterfly Weed clings to you. Is part of you," he murmured.

Isabel's hand came to her chest, a light, fluttery movement. "Butterfly Weed? Sounds most unfavorable...what do you speak of?"

A strange heaviness settled in his chest. Devin stared into her eyes. "Butterfly Weed, your favorite flower."

She blinked rapidly and gasped before pulling away. "I am sorry, I do not know what you speak of. My favorite scent is that of the rose."

What? "But you just told me last night how you loved the scent of Butterfly Weed."

Pulling up to full height, easily eight inches below his, Isabel shook her head. "I can assure you I did not."

"But—"

"I do not stray from my mistress at night. How dare you, sir!"

Snap. That's all it took. Reality blindsided him. Devin staggered back a few steps. Gone was the sole sight of Isabel's face. In its place, new comprehension. He didn't know what to focus on first. Isabel's long skirts, the smaller field leading up to Andrea's new home or the fact that...Andrea's house wasn't there!

Not an entire truth. Half the foundation was laid. Devin took a few steps forward and blinked. Nope, he was seeing things correctly. Andrea's house was all but gone. He fell to his knees and shook his head.

"Devin, are you all right?" Isabel peered down, concerned. "You look rather ill."

Rather ill? Bloody understatement. Devin closed his eyes, focused his mind and screamed internally, "Seth! Leathan! I need help!"

He waited. They had to hear him.

"Sir, please. Should I send for a doctor?"

Leathan! Seth! Hear me you arses.

"Perhaps a priest?" Isabel continued.

No one responded, at least not who he needed to. Devin tried again and again.

"I will send for a doctor."

Devin opened his eyes and sat back on his heels. Isabel paced in front of him.

Finally she stopped, fists on hips and stared down. Her bright eyes were afire, cheeks crimson with distress. "You must communicate with me or I cannot help you."

Devin shook his head. "Give me a second, okay?"

The back of her slender, cool wrist fell against his forehead. "Have you the Pox then?"

The pox? "No offense but if you thought I did, would you actually touch me?"

She flipped her hand from the back of her wrist to her palm. "I don't believe the Pox is spread that way." Isabel leaned over and studied his face, searching for sickness. "Do you?"

He brushed away her hand and stood. "I know it isn't."

"I thought not." She nodded and tossed a curious glance his way. "But what makes you think so?"

Enough with this. "What happened to Andrea's house? Why are you dressed like you are?"

"I should ask the same." Isabel's eyes scanned him. "Is that how the Irish dress nowadays?"

Eying his blue jeans and black T-shirt he responded, "Um, this is how everyone dresses, lass."

"Everyone indeed!" Isabel started toward the half foundation. "You have no fever. Come on now. Work starts soon."

Devin didn't move an inch. This had to be a joke.

Isabel kept walking, her slim hips swaying. Many others waited. Some looked like the vagrants he'd followed here. Others appeared cleaner, studying the surroundings with a steadfast eye. This wasn't a dream. He wasn't imagining things.

"Isabel."

She stopped and turned slightly. "Yes?"

"What year is it?"

With a heavy sigh, she shook her head and walked back. "You really are ill."

Devin stayed her hand before she could touch his forehead again. "No, I'm not. Just answer the question."

She frowned. "It's seventeen twenty-two. But you knew that already."

This is all part of the haunting, he thought. No doubt about it. "So I'm trapped within the house somehow, even though I'm outside?"

Isabel shook her head. "Then you are not ill but mad?"

She had no idea. Then again, she was trapped as well. Without doubt, she had no clue she was merely a ghost, no matter how solid she seemed.

"Come." Isabel held out her hand. "Stay with us until we can find you help."

Of course, that made sense. Confused, trapped wherever she was, to reach out—offer solace—would come naturally for her.

Best to play along. "I'm not mad. It's just been a long night."

"You're quite sure?"

"Absolutely." Devin inclined his head. "Please, lead the way."

Isabel eyed him for a few more seconds then nodded. "Fine then, this way."

About twenty men were milling about the foundation, all in period clothing. Some nodded at him. Others were too distracted. The sun sat steadily above the tree line when a carriage rolled up the rocky, haphazard drive. Everyone lined up in strict formation.

Vagrant One urged Devin to fall in beside him. Whatever worked. He waited patiently as the carriage rambled slowly up the drive. Had all these men been trapped by the house as well? Leaning forward, he squinted and looked over everyone. Where was Andrea's husband?

Isabel greeted the carriage as it rolled to a halt in front of them. An older man with graying brown hair stepped out. Sharp eyes surveyed the men from behind precarious spectacles. Isabel—obviously their spokeswoman—started to talk. The man gave a sharp shake of his head and held up one long fingered,

delicate hand, cutting her off effectively. "The

master will not be here today as he has other obligations. See that the foundation is completed and supplies made ready for the framework."

"But—"

"The wood will arrive later today," the man provided, nostrils flaring in distress. "I would suggest you make sure everyone is bathed by tomorrow."

Devin did his best not to laugh. The petrified look on Isabel's face made it a tad bit easier.

"Yes, sir."

That irritated him. They were all stuck in some sort of time warp. Why didn't she tell him where to shove it? Then again this had to be a massive residual haunting. None of these people knew they were living the same moments over and over again. In her defense, in the year she claimed it to be, women didn't stand up to men. Then again, they weren't put in positions of authority as she so obviously was, were they?

The master's right-hand-man nodded briskly, not before Devin saw his lustful gaze slide quickly down Isabel's slender form. "Very well then. We will see what is accomplished by tomorrow morn."

"Indeed." Isabel bowed her head as the man turned away, crawled back into his carriage and disappeared back down the drive.

Devin didn't miss the compassion that filled Isabel's eyes as she scanned the row of men. As quickly as it came, the sentiment fled and she barked, "You heard him, let's get to work!"

For all they appeared bedraggled, Devin was surprised by everyone's response. Like a well-oiled machine they fell to task with swift efficiency. Nobody seemed to mind that a woman had given them an order. He couldn't help but contemplate how long and hard she must've had to work to achieve such respect. Or did it have more to do with the absent, "master?" Maybe they were romantically involved. Did they respond so promptly because to treat the master's woman with disrespect would mean a lack of employment?

"You may sit aside if you are confused. There is a basket of fruit over yonder."

Hands on hips, still amazed by his surroundings, Devin looked at Isabel. "You're too kind."

Her bluish purple eyes roamed over the workers. "No, just practical. I sense you do not belong here, lost somehow. Right now you are simply in the way."

Devin grinned at her. "Ah then, a good manager." He nodded. "I'll take you up on that. A wee bit of fruit might just clear my head."

"Without doubt," she agreed, her eyes lingering a moment too long on his face.

For a split second, he wanted to flirt, entice, and be his old self. But what was the point? She didn't exist. This didn't exist.

CHAPTER THREE

The day had gone well.

Isabel sat back against a waist high rock as twilight descended and the cool night blew through. Some men were gathered around their tents. The locals had gone home for the night. They had done a good job. The entire foundation was laid. All equipment was set neatly aside, ready for tomorrow. She stared at the half moon. What she wouldn't do to be up there, to be anywhere but here right now.

But life wasn't about wishes and wants. It was barely about needs. Truth told, most of this didn't bother her. It was reality. Accept it or fail in life wondering why you did. Still, what was it like to go home to a cooked meal, made with care? What was it like to go home to anyone at all?

"Come join us missus. Food's tasty, be it as it is."

Isabel smiled at one of the workers. "Of course."

Off duty, she didn't have to be so tough. Isabel counted her blessings the men respected her at all. Then again, she'd been thrown in with a good lot. Better than most. She sat down around the main fire and welcomed a cup of beans. Spoon in hand; she shoveled a scoop into her mouth, relishing the bitter taste.

"You can stomach that stuff?"

Frowning, she focused on the source of critique. Devin, the Irishman, sat nearby, his surreal gaze unnerving. The firelight highlighted the dark auburn tints in his oddly cut short hair and chiseled his strong chin to noticeable definition. Her pulse skittered as it had when she first saw him. Quite unaccustomed to such handsome men, Isabel tried her best not to show an untoward amount of attention his way.

"Frankly, it tastes like heaven," she declared and scooped more into her mouth.

"Aye, so you say." He snorted. "Quite the trooper, aren't you?"

"Grateful and far more polite than you, to be sure."

A capricious smile crawled onto his face. "You might be right there."

"Without doubt."

Legs bent, leanly muscled arms casually resting on them, his strange eyes did not leave her. "Must admit, you're one strong woman."

Not sure what to make of that statement she continued to eat. Men didn't like strong women. Typically, she didn't care. As the mushy beans slid over her tongue, Isabel wondered why she did now. Regardless. "If you have a problem with me being in charge, you can leave at any time."

"And I intend to."

The gall! "Then I suggest you do so on the morn."

"I intend to tonight."

So be it. "The closest town is miles away. I suggest you providence well and travel safe."

When he said nothing more she decided she wouldn't either. Good riddance to him. Men like him did not and never would get on with a woman like her. Food consumed, she made her way to her tent where her 'mistress' already slept. Her mistress was fictional of course, regardless what she told Devin earlier. Usually she read for an hour or so. Tonight she felt no desire. Snuffing her candle, Isabel lay on her beddings and tried to focus on her future. Would it be everything she hoped? Was she being made to run a fool's errand now? Could he really save her as promised?

Well past what she knew to be the midnight hour, Isabel continued to stare at the canvas roof of her small tent wondering…pondering. I need to get out of this tent. Get some fresh air. She rose and threw on her day dress. The late Maine night was silent. Not even a slight wind blew against the trees. Everything was drenched in complete darkness beyond her candle.

Tempted by the night despite its dark threats, she drifted toward the foundation of the house they were building. Would it be as grand as they hoped? She could only imagine. Halfway there, she stopped. A soft light glowed beyond. As she drifted forward, Isabel narrowed her eyes and held her breath. Someone was in the foundation framework. Who would be up at this hour? What could they be doing?

Clank. Clank.

Though faint, Isabel definitely heard something. Was that a chisel on stone?

Clank. Clank.

She blew out her candle and crept closer, her feet soft and soundless on the summer grass. Falling to her knees, Isabel crawled then fell to her belly, until she could peer down into the 'would be' basement.

"I know you're there. Cute that you tried to hide though."

Isabel frowned when she spied Devin, pick in hand, chiseling away at the foundation. How dare he!

Scurrying to the stairs, she descended and approached. "I must say though I determined you were ill of the mind, you go too far, sir!"

"You'd be amazed how far I can go."

"You are decidedly insane."

"Bank the fake English accent," he commented. "You're no good at it."

Isabel snapped her jaw shut the moment it fell open. "I've no idea what you mean."

Devin continued to chisel in the strange reddish-maroon light. "Trust me. If any nationality truly sucks at mimicking another's accent, it's an American."

"Well, I'll be."

"What?" He didn't pause from chiseling. "An American?"

"You are ill sir. For this I will forgive you."

"I'm sure."

"Rude!"

He pulled back the chisel and cocked his head at her. "Not rude. Truthful."

How did he know when no one else did? She could be equally shrewd. "You are a spy, sent by the master's competitor."

One brow slowly rose over his strikingly pale smoky green eyes. "And you call me mad. Is there not a fine line between paranoia and craziness?"

"And is a paranoid nature not essential when working for someone so well renown?"

"Tell me, how renowned is your master, lassie?"

Despite herself, Isabel couldn't help but be enchanted by the lilt in his voice. Nor the lips in which they came from. "First, tell me what you're doing here. Why are you chiseling away at freshly laid work?"

"Why aren't you trying harder to stop me?"

Because you make me nervous. Because I find you intriguing. "Do you answer every question with a question?"

"Only when flirting typically." He grinned. "But don't worry. In this case, I'm not."

"I see." She didn't see at all but there was something different about him. He didn't fit in here.

"So, why is an eighteenth century American woman with a fake British accent, in command of such a project?" he asked.

"Why are you chiseling away at my foundation?" she countered.

"Stalemate," he muttered.

"No." She grabbed his forearm.

He froze.

Isabel yanked back her hand and rubbed her arm, frowning.

"You felt that too, like electricity," he murmured. His eyes appeared wild for a minute before he shook his head and continued to chisel.

She had felt that. But what was that? "Please, I'd rather not wake up the others to stop you. They have put in a hard day's work. Tell me what you're looking for. Did you see a stone laid wrong? Are you trying to fix it?"

"Lady, you wouldn't believe me if I told you."

Oh no? "You might be surprised, sir."

"Doubtful."

Long muscles bulged beneath tanned skin as he continued to chisel. A trickle of sweat slowly rolled down his strong neck. Dear Lord. She had to handle this. Isabel shut her eyes, counted to five and reopened them. She flung herself, back to the wall, next to the chisel and put a hand on his hard chest. It felt steaming hot. "No more! Do you want to get me dismissed from employment?"

Devin paused. His gaze flickered down to her hand then rose to her eyes. "Doesn't matter. None of this is real."

He resumed chiseling. Hand still on his hard chest, fingers following the movement of his pectoral muscles as they worked, she'd beg to differ. He couldn't be any more real. *I'm a decent lady. I should pull my hand away.*

But she didn't.

He stopped.

Devin's eyes again slowly dropped to her hand. "It feels so real. You feel so real."

Her fingers curled in slightly. She really should pull away. "Of course I am. As are you."

Something flashed in his eyes. Pity? Whatever for? "I need you to stop doing this," she pleaded.

He sighed and his arms fell to his side. "You do realize you're merely a prisoner to this house, aye?"

"What house?" She remained still. "This is but a foundation."

Devin stared at her for a time before turning away. "For now."

Isabel clenched her fist, holding onto the warmth of his chest. She pushed away from the wall. "Yes, of course, for now."

"If it were only that easy." Devin paced the dirt between the foundation walls and muttered, "There's got to be some way I can reach them."

The man was going beyond insane. "Reach who?"

His brows drew together. He continued to talk to

himself.

"Who?" she repeated

Finally, he slid down against the far wall. A deep frown etched his face. Knees bent, he held his head in his hands.

Having dealt with a lot of defeated souls in her time, Isabel knew one when she saw it. Seeing Devin so utterly overcome, Isabel couldn't help but make her way across the foundation floor where she sank down next to him. She smoothed her skirts and folded her hands together on her lap. "Tell me your story."

He grunted and shook his head. "You wouldn't believe me if I told you."

"Maybe not," she agreed. "But it seems to me you have an awful lot bothering you. Perhaps getting it out will help."

He sat back, then shook his head again. "I'm not sure I should even mess with your reality. I'm in way over my head right now."

"I see." Isabel focused on his hands, now casually perched on his knees. Good, strong hands. "So you are running from the law then?" She leaned over and whispered, "Or perhaps somehow involved in the war?"

Devin's exasperated gaze slid her way. "Huh?"

"Well, I agree, it seems unlikely an Irishmen part of a war betwixt the English and French but—"

"Silence, lass," Devin interrupted. "I'm not part of any war. Not running from the law. Whatever that happens to be in this day and age."

"Then tell me your story."

"No."

"How does an Irishman end up sprawled out on the side of a river in Maine, then?"

Now she had his full attention.

"So you saw me there? And here I thought you knew nothing about any of this." Devin's shrewd gaze locked with hers. "You remember last night!"

Isabel rolled her eyes and shook her head. "So we're back to that. I remember nothing. There is nothing to remember. Did I see you wake at the side of the river? Yes."

"Why didn't you admit it earlier?"

How had she ended up on this end of the discussion? She'd never meant to tell him anything. Devin had a way about him. Time to be more careful. "I saw no point."

"No point. Mmm hmm." Stretching out his long legs, he crossed one ankle over the other. "And tell me again why you're faking an English accent?"

"I never admitted I was." Isabel jutted out her chin. "In fact, naught but the British and French roam these parts."

"And the native Indians…and those of you whom descend from Europeans who previously settled here."

So he knew what he was talking about. Regardless. Isabel wasn't about to give him any answers. "I do not know of what you speak. I was born in England and came over here when young. Enough about me. What about you, Devin. What are you running from? Please, I urge you to share your story with me. Perhaps I can help."

"I'll get answers out of you eventually, Isabel."

Lord, he was persistent. Give him some hope then continue to whittle away. "I am quite sure you will but not this eve." She gracefully smoothed her skirts, lowered her voice—hid behind her lashes. "I'll not ask again. Share with me, Devin. I would really like to know what disturbs you so."

Devin's low chuckle warmed her insides. "You think to get answers from me by flirting? Good luck, lass. I invented that method."

Isabel's eyes flew to his. Insolence! She almost faltered at the devilish twinkle in his gaze, the languid way his come-hither eyes roamed her face. Indeed, he did flirt well. She squelched the lop-sided grin she felt beginning to erupt. "I see no reason for your secrecy." Isabel again leaned close and whispered in her best co-conspirator tone, "Then you really are a spy."

His thick-lashed eyes fell to her lips and he leaned closer as well. "In my own way, that is exactly what I am."

Now she was getting somewhere. "Ah, I knew it."

"Did you?" His gaze slowly slid down her neck and she'd swear his finger grazed the soft skin. Goose pimples rose on her flesh.

"Yes, I did." She continued to follow his gaze, could almost feel how he saw her…feminine…enticing. "It makes perfect sense."

"Aye." Devin's gaze fell to the swells of her breasts peeking out from the top of her dress. "You found me out."

A deep inhale, then he exhaled slowly, his hot breath flaming across her chest. Nipples tightened. Searing warmth flooded between her thighs. Isabel inhaled sharply. His eyes met hers, knowing. How did he do that? What exactly had he done without moving an inch?

"What did I find out?" she murmured, her mind swimming in pleasure, relaxed, not nearly as sharp as it had been moments before.

A ravishing grin crinkled the corners of his eyes, made enticing sweeps of his dark eyelashes. "That I'm not quite who I seem to be."

"No," she whispered, body suddenly afire. When his hand rose to cup her cheek, she leaned into it, cherished, worshiped. Blazing heat burned her flesh, the calloused touch of his palm an enticing contradiction to her soft cheek. Isabel closed her eyes, lost in a strange and incredibly arousing lull. When his smooth lips gently touched hers, she moaned. Isabel tingled with awareness. When his lips covered hers more thoroughly, carefully guided, she followed his lead.

Though she'd been kissed before, it had never been like this. Devin took her down the unfamiliar path with the ease and talent of a well-traveled sea captain. Waves of emotion rolled through her as his lips pried hers apart. When his tongue slid slowly over the lower cushion of her upper lip, Isabel moaned again. Tentatively, she met his tongue with hers.

This time he groaned.

Taking her other check in his hand, his mouth slanted and his tongue ensnared hers. Isabel had never experienced anything so sweet, anything so engaging, consuming. If she were the decent lady she prided herself on being, she'd pull away. Maybe even slap his face. But no, she felt little desire to fill the shoes of her 'proper' self. The tall, exhausting pillar she'd built and perched on for so very long. No, she dove headfirst, met his tongue with vigor, swirled, let him explore, deepen the exchange.

Her limbs burned with a heavy, needy weight. The warmth between her thighs became a raging inferno. Isabel wanted his hands there, his mouth, something, anything.

"Who goes there?"

Isabel pulled back sharply and stared wide-eyed at Devin. He gazed back, a lazy grin and twinkling eyes made obvious he wasn't the least bit embarrassed by their immoral engagement. Swine! She made to slap his face. He caught her wrist before her hand made contact. He shook his head and put a finger to his lips.

A small orb of candlelight from above trailed slowly alongside the walls of the foundation. When had the reddish light down here vanished? Now they were completely enveloped in darkness. Devin leaned over close to her ear and whispered, "I'd suggest you keep quiet lest you lose the respect of your employees."

Eyes narrowed, she weighed her options. Stand and make a scene. Chastise him for treating her so…loosely. Or keep quiet and ensure her dignity remained intact. In this day and age, being down here alone with a man was more than enough to crucify her as loose.

Damn Devin.

Then again, what was she really damning him for? She'd done nothing to stop him. However, he should have been gentleman enough to never have kissed her to begin with. And touch her! Wait, had he touched her? She couldn't be entirely sure. There stood a very good chance she'd imagined that…or wanted it so much, it'd become real within her mind.

The small orb of candlelight continued to make its way around the foundation. Would whoever it was come down the stairs? Isabel remained still. Tried to ignore the haphazard trail Devin's finger made up her vulnerable and over sensitized inner arm. Relentless swindler! A wicked shiver rolled through her body. Fair to say, he was an extremely talented, relentless swindler.

The light stopped directly over them. Its thin stream of illumination fell inches above their head. Isabel didn't breathe. Devin's finger continued its casual stroll, playing idly over the rapid pulse thrumming away like mad in her wrist. His warm, masculine scent washed over her, an interesting mixture of forest and musk and something sweet.

Isabel licked her lips.

The light traveled further away.

Devin whispered, "I can hear your heart pounding for me. Do I arouse you that much?"

Biting her lip, Isabel scowled.

He nibbled her earlobe. "I know you do me."

The light faded. Whoever had been exploring vanished.

Isabel shoved him away. "You go too far."

"Do I?" Devin smiled and stood, held a hand down to her. "Regardless, what say you and I return to your tent and go further."

The unmistakable bulge in the front of his pants made Isabel blush. She ignored his offered hand, stood and shook out the bottom of her skirts. Anything to keep her eyes from wandering to his erection. Part of her was mortified she'd behaved the way she had, given him the idea that she was his for the taking. Part of her was furious he'd treated her with so little respect, to the point of thinking she'd willingly bed him tonight. Did he do this with all women? Degrade them in such a way? Or just those like her, who behaved the way she had.

Isabel swallowed the sudden lump in her throat.

Never in her life had she acted this way with a man. Not even her former fiancé. Then again, he'd never come close to inciting the sort of feelings in her Devin just had. However, feminine notions aside, Isabel didn't particularly like Devin at the moment. Nor the way she'd acted with him. He was, by far, too crude for her taste.

"It is obvious I will not be getting any further truths from you aside from the fact that you are a spy. I am going to bed. Without you."

Thankfully, Devin said nothing as she climbed the stairs.

At last, she lay once more in her tent, staring up at nothing.

A tear rolled down her cheek. She swiped it away and closed her eyes. Now was the time for strength, not weakness. Despite how he had stormed into her life Isabel knew that Devin was the very least of her problems.

Time was running out.

CHAPTER FOUR

Devin wiped a salty bead of sweat from his eye and sighed. The sun hung hazy and surprisingly hot overhead. He hadn't slept a wink last night. Isabel had consumed his every thought. When his mind wasn't obsessing on the crappy way he'd treated her it was busy obsessing about her hot little responsive body and his ever raging erection.

Every damn time he tried to pleasure himself an uncomfortable rush of shame would wash over him. Ample sized breasts, teeny tiny waist—raging hardon. Treating her like a piece of meat, disrespecting her—instant withered cock. What was the matter with him? Most of the way he'd behaved the previous evening wasn't him at all. Oh no, it'd been the warlock. That ever-denied newfound evil beastie within.

Some men would love being able to sway a woman like he had. Have her feeling his hands where they'd never been placed. Have her mind swim in the languid pools of desire he himself had helped implant.

For all Devin had tried to stay away from her, one look into those wide innocent eyes followed by her small, tentative hand on his chest had unraveled a recipe for disaster...had thoroughly unleashed the dark magic in him.

And the hot-blooded man.

"The Mr.'s comin,'" Vagrant Two said, spooning a ladle of water from a large wooden barrel.

Devin looked down the drive. Nothing. "How do you know?"

Vagrant Two poured a ladleful over his head and shook it. "Missus always gets extra edgy."

"Ah." Without doubt, Isabel was pacing back and forth, hands on hips, eyeing the progress. The wood had been delivered and men trekked around, some lost in thought as they planned, many busy laboring.

Isabel hadn't looked at him once. Devin didn't blame her. He wouldn't look at him either if he were she. Damn it. He'd handled last night poorly. But he'd been under duress, out of his mind really. It'd been on the tip of his tongue to tell her everything, come clean. But what if it messed up whatever crappy haunted cycle they were in? Would Devin telling her everything put her at danger if this was all really one big residual haunting?

He thought about how sweet and soft her lips had tasted. How exceptionally gorgeous she'd appeared when she'd waited for his lips to fall on hers. How her hips had jutted up when she wanted more between her thighs.

When she'd wanted him between her thighs.

Hell and damnation.

"Here he comes," Vagrant One said, having approached to get some water as well.

Devin's eyes flew down the drive. A sleek black coach rolled their way, its wheels passing smoothly over the pit holed dirt beneath. Had the 'Master' figured out a way to create modern day shocks?

A shrill whistle resounded. He glanced at Isabel. Hell, she'd created that ear-splitting noise with her mouth. Everyone started to line up. Wow. While he'd given her ample credit for leading these guys yesterday, he was again astounded by her knack for management. It definitely made him feel more the arse for having put her in a position last night that could've cost her this level of respect.

No need to further incite her. Devin got in line. Ever the dutiful worker lined up behind his warrior woman, he watched as the carriage halted in front of Isabel. The driver hopped out, pulled down steps and opened the door. He stepped back and stood silently.

Nothing happened.

Devin couldn't help but watch Isabel. She was the perfect example of a leader. Today, her hair was pulled back tight and wrapped into a small chignon. Clean and incredibly presentable, considering their current living conditions, she stood, back ramrod straight, head held high, hands folded neatly in front of her. Almost like an eighteenth century nanny presenting children to their father. Where'd that thought come from? Still, she did seem to suddenly carry a haughty, I'm-better-than-most scholarly air.

Hands shoved in his pockets, it took everything Devin had not to run up to her, rip loose her hair, rumple it and lightened her eyes. Make her look as carefree and sensual as she had the previous night. Bank that thought, lad. She'd probably try to slap you again. And there is the 'respect thing.' Damn, but she did have his mind going in circles already. He wanted to kiss the back of her hand then toss her over his lap and slap her cute little arse. Again, that whole good-versus-bad thing he experienced whenever he thought about her.

A pair of shiny black shoes descended the first step outside the carriage. Isabel's back straightened more. The shoes quickly gave way to long legs, a strong upper half well-dressed, a top-hat...a handsome face.

Devin's jaw dropped.

Calum?

Isabel issued a curtsy. The man tipped his hat, his dark gaze briefly sweeping over everything before returning to her. When he spoke, Devin did his best not to hit the ground.

"It goes well." The 'master's' attention turned to the line of men. He made a flick with his hand. "Back to work."

The line of men fell away, leaving only Devin. There's no way he was seeing correctly. Taking a few steps forward, he squinted, looked closer at the man bending his head talking quietly with Isabel. That face, that voice...it had to be.

Devin, can you hear me? Where the hell are you?

Devin continued to stare at the man who was surely Calum. But the sound of Leathan's voice in his mind was far more important. He spoke back within the mind, Leathan?

Calum turned his way. Isabel stopped talking. "Who are you, young man?"

Devin didn't like the unusual gleam in Calum's eyes when asked that.

Leathan, you there still?

No answer.

Calum strode his way. "Again, who are you?"

Oh yeah, it was definitely him. "You know bloody well who I am, ghost."

Stopping short, Calum looked truly affronted. Then, in a split second, his face dropped all expression. Just like the 'Calum' he'd met at the

Victorian. Devin didn't hesitate, kept on talking.

"What, you don't recognize me?"

Isabel kicked in, flying up alongside Calum. "Forgive this, he is new. Irish." She faltered, unsure what to say next. "You know how odd the Irish can be."

An unexpected plethora of rage suddenly poured through Devin. Here stood the man who had been the reason behind him becoming a warlock. Here stood his ancestor, a mar upon Devin's very existence. The very one who had turned his world inside out. Enraged, he met Calum halfway, stopped when nose to nose. "Don't tell me you don't know who the hell I am."

Devin was so furious he hardly noticed the dark clouds rolling in too fast. The driving rain that started to pour, creating a convenient barrier between him, Calum, Isabel and curious ears.

Calum's eyes started to glow. A black crackling aura appeared around him. Devin brushed his wet hair aside, so furious he couldn't see straight. Isabel whimpered beside them.

Where the hell are you, lad?

Leathan's voice was stronger now.

Come back, cuz. Now. This from Seth.

He didn't care where the hell they were coming from. He wanted blood.

He wanted Calum.

Screw this. Devin lunged and wrapped his hands around Calum's throat. They fell to the ground. Enraged, bloodlust driven, Devin rolled, gripped, didn't go.

"Shit man."

Somehow it wasn't Calum but Seth.

"You asshole! Get a hold of yourself cuz or we'll

go down now, both of us," Seth said.

Hands around Seth's neck, Seth's around his, they finally stopped rolling. What the hell? Panting rapidly, Devin stared at his cousin. Not Calum at all. Just Seth, face red, eyes wild. Trying to get his rage under control, Devin willed his hands to loosen. No luck.

Seth flipped him, put more pressure on his windpipe. That did it. With no air left in him, his hands fell away from Seth's throat. His arms fell listlessly to his side. Clenching the warm grass, the red slowly receded from his vision until nothing but Seth straddling him and Leathan standing over, remained.

"Shit," he muttered and closed his eyes.

Seth panted and tried to catch his breath. "Shit's right." He rolled away, landed on his back next to Devin and stared at the same bright blue sky overhead.

Leathan plunked down in the grass on his other side. "Thought we'd lost you there, lad."

Devin stared at the sky, the pleasant, ignorant puffs of clouds billowing overhead. Anger still bubbled near the surface. "I had him. I almost had him."

"Who?" Seth said, still trying to catch his breath. "Fucking Satan?"

"Fucking something," Leathan agreed.

"Fucking, Calum is who," Devin muttered.

"Enough!" Andrea stood over them, shaking with fury. "All three of you shut your mouths. Listen to you. You never swore like this before the Victorian. You sound terrible. Not the guys I knew." She swung around and headed for the house. "And she doesn't deserve this. You guys are completely nuts…and….nasty!"

All three remained lying in the grass looking up at the sky.

"You saw Calum?" Seth asked.

"Yep," Devin responded.

"No kidding."

"Oh yeah, and you're never gonna believe where."

Leathan asked, "What's up? Where'd you go?"

"Pretty sure, back to when this house was built," Devin said. "Hell of a thing."

Now that he'd calmed down, it felt bloody good to be back in the twenty-first century with his cousins.

"Back to when this house was built?" Leathan asked.

"Yep."

"Holy hell," Seth said. "What year?"

"1722."

"Damn!"

"Yeah, you've no idea."

"So what's this about Calum?" Seth asked.

Devin shook his head and watched one cloud swallow another. "Think I met him when he was mortal. Or should I say, alive."

"No!" Leathan said.

"Yep."

"Shit," Seth said.

"Hell," Leathan added.

Devin, rage dissipated, crossed his arms behind his head and truly relished being home, such as it was. "Andrea's pissed, eh? Are we really cursing more than before?"

He could hear the frown in Seth's voice. "Don't

think so."

"Question," Leathan said.

"Yeah?" Devin and Seth asked simultaneously.

"Who's 'she'?"

"Who's who?" Devin asked.

"She," Leathan said. "Before she called us nuts, Andrea said—" He held his hands up in the air and made quotation marks, "She doesn't deserve this."

Seth shrugged.

Devin continued to look at the clouds overhead. She. She? No! Sitting upright, he watched as Andrea led a woman into the distant house. Watched the woman's long, blond hair blow in the breeze. It couldn't be. Seth and Leathan sat up as well.

Seth cleared his throat, eyes on the blond vanishing into the house. "You were gone one night. There something beyond your reunion with Calum you're not telling us about?"

Devin stumbled to his feet. Was it really her?

"I'd say yes," Leathan said.

There's no way on Ireland's green Earth, Isabel was here. In person. No, he had to be seeing a ghost. With long strides, he headed for the Georgian. Had she traveled with him to the future? Had he really fought then chatted with his cousins when she had just been thrust into true hell? A place totally foreign to her? Bursting through the front door, Devin looked around frantically. Where was she?

"She's in here," Andrea said.

Devin walked into the living room slowly. His hand instinctively fell to his hip to make sure her picture was still there. Now, away from complete terror, on his own territory, it was hard for him to breathe when the woman curled up on her sofa matched the woman in the picture.

"Isabel," he said gently.

She didn't respond, distant eyes focused on the fire. He wondered if she'd even heard him.

Andrea shook her head. "Why don't you…go fix something to eat, Devin."

Go fix something to eat? He stared intently at Isabel. His ghost turned human. His fantasy turned reality. Biting his lip, he shook his head at Andrea.

Andrea shot him a look that made walking on red hot nails with sun-burned feet seem more preferable than her appraisal. He frowned and backed away. No one messed with Andrea when she was determined to protect.

Leathan and Seth stood behind him. He turned, shook his head and pointed toward the kitchen. Both followed. Devin sat on an island stool and braced his head in his hands on the countertop. This couldn't be happening.

"Who is she?"

Devin pulled out the picture and set it on the countertop without looking at them.

"Wow," Seth said softly. "You serious?"

He ran his hand through his hair and stared at the picture now in Seth's hands. "Aye."

Leathan took the picture, narrowing his eyes at it. "Unbelievable. You brought the ghost back with you?"

"I think we all know she's no ghost," Devin returned. "At least…not right now."

"You have no idea whether she's real or not," Leathan countered. "If nothing else, the Victorian taught us that."

"Damn straight." Seth issued a wide grin and rubbed his hands together in anticipation. "Here we go again."

Leathan batted him upside the head.

Seth frowned. "What?"

"Have a little compassion, eh?"

"Why?"

Devin ground his teeth. "Because that woman in the other room is definitely on the rough end of things." He stood and grabbed the picture from Leathan. "Because, whether all of this excites you or not, Andrea's husband is still trapped somewhere in this house and things are only bound to get worse."

Bloody Americans. Why was he sitting here listening to Seth when Isabel was in the other room no doubt having a much deserved break-down on Andrea? He should be in there helping her through this. Devin headed down the hallway and stopped at the doorway to the living room.

Fully expecting Isabel to be sobbing in Andrea's arms, surprise froze him at the door jam. The eighteenth century lass stopped pacing and narrowed her eyes at him. "You!"

Lord she was gorgeous and apparently furious with him. So much for the delicate, hysterical damsel in distress. He took a step into the room. "You all right?"

"Do I look all right?" She stalked his way. "What the hell am I doing in the twenty-first century? Walking in this house?" She patted her front, sides. "And not a ghost!"

Devin glanced at Andrea. She shrugged and offered a small grin. "Just told her what century she was in and she freaked."

"You seem a lot better with all of this than you did a few minutes ago," he responded carefully to Isabel.

Her violet blue eyes flared with disgust. "That's because I'm not supposed to be here. At least not in this form." She poked him in the chest. "You're not supposed to have brought me here. My ghost would've got through to you enough eventually."

He wrapped his hand around her obtrusive hand and squeezed gently. "What the bloody hell are you talking about?"

Isabel yanked away her hand, accent changing slightly, taking on a slightly southern and very American drawl. "Simple. I, like this house, exist in multiple dimensions." She shook her head and turned away. "All of which are of Calum's making."

CHAPTER FIVE

Isabel continued to pace the room restlessly and cursed to herself. How could this be happening? Damn Calum to hell. This had never been mentioned. How odd it was to not be a…ghost anymore! Even though she still technically was. At least herself in the twenty-first century. She glanced in the mirror. Nope, no scar. Isabel was definitely in her seventeen twenty-two body with her twenty-first century self's ghostly knowledge. What a disaster.

But perhaps a good thing. After all, if her twenty-first century ghostly self was still trapped in the house, so wasn't the beast.

Devin remained standing at the doorway, face wary. "Care to elaborate?"

She'd really rather not. But as she gazed around at Andrea, Devin and the other two men whom had entered the room, she realized she had little choice. How to make them believe though? It was never supposed to happen like this. But then again, nothing really surprised her anymore and frankly, she had nothing to lose by coming somewhat clean.

Her heart swelled when she looked at Devin. He didn't know anything yet. Oh, but to see him again. To see him knowing all she did. Unlike her 1722 self who knew nothing of him. She and Devin were only starting out there. Isabel plunked down on the settee.

She decided to start at the beginning. At least the one she was willing to talk about right now. If they found it too much unbelievable information…who cared? So she started talking, half convinced they wouldn't believe her anyway. "I was born in 1698 in the colony of what would a few short years later be founded as Jamestown, Virginia. My mother died in childbirth leaving my father to raise me and my four siblings." Sharp memories threatened to resurface but she shoved them down and continued. "As you can imagine, it was a busy time in Jamestown then. Immigrants kept filtering into town. It was quite hectic."

Isabel stopped for a moment. She could almost smell the pungent rotting fish, the sour sweat of men passing on the street. The groping hands on her young flesh.

Devin sat next to her. "Go on."

She glanced at him and tried to gather her thoughts. "I'm assuming you know Calum."

"Yeah, we know him," one of the men offered. "Names's Seth," he continued when she stared absently at him.

Yes, she knew Seth. Devin had spoken of them all already, though he didn't know it yet. Seth was handsome with black hair and piercing blue eyes. American like Andrea. Good. Funny, she felt slightly detached. Was she in some sort of shock? Wouldn't surprise her.

"Go on," Devin urged gently.

His nearness suddenly swamped her senses and she shifted away, put some space between them. If she didn't Isabel was likely to fling her arms around him. Plead with him to remember all they'd shared. "By the time I turned seventeen, I'd had enough. I cut my hair, dressed in men's clothing and boarded a ship heading up the coast."

"Had enough of what?" Andrea asked.

If they only knew. "Enough of Southern life. Women were far beneath men. It didn't suit me at all."

"The north wasn't much better," the third man said, his accent different.

"I'm Leathan, by the way. Sorry we didn't greet you properly before, Isabel."

Isabel conjured up a weak smile for the good-looking man with blond-streaked brown hair and a stern countenance. She vaguely recalled meeting him…and Andrea and Seth for the matter. But how? When? Isabel shook off the feeling and continued. "Nice to meet you." She fiddled with her skirts. "You're right, Leathan, the north wasn't much better but little did I know that at the time."

"Where did you end up?" Devin asked.

"Boston." Isabel closed her eyes briefly, remembering. "Another busy town. Lots of commerce."

"Still ruled by the British. Damn, the Boston massacre didn't happen until sixty or so years later. I can't imagine what the city was like back then," Leathan said.

Andrea frowned and shook her head.

Seth walked into the room and plunked down into another chair. Andrea looked at Isabel. "Ignore him, Leathan loves all history. Even American. I know, odd for a Scotsman."

Ah, that's right, Scottish. That was the accent. Isabel let her eyes wonder over the group briefly. A Scotsman, two Americans and one Irishman. Odd bunch. Then again, like the colonies and history in this country, the perfect melting pot.

Leathan's dark brown eyes caught hers and he smiled warmly. "Sorry, we can be distracting. Ignore us and continue. Please."

Leader. He was typically in charge of this group. Or so Devin had said. Not to mention, her ghostly self had heard everything these four had said when they entered this house. "It's all right." Isabel tried to ignore the fact Devin seemed to spread out, legs casually wide, one knee dangerously close to hers.

"I got lucky in Boston. After working for some time as a 'boy' I was able to save enough to purchase forged papers saying I was a British nanny." She glanced at Devin. It was odd telling him all of this again. But for him, it was the first time hearing it. Ooooh, Calum ought to be shot for putting her through such a time-twisting mess. He ought to be shot for a lot of reasons! "Hence the beginning of my new visage. That of a proper English lass."

"You actually convinced people you were a boy?" Devin's eyes, though incredulous, ignited with that same devilish twinkle she so adored.

She ignored him and continued. "Believe it or not, I had a special skill that was most welcome in some parts of the higher Bostonian society. Those which wanted to remain as discreet as possible."

"And that was?" Devin asked.

"I could school the deaf."

No one said a word. Devin stared at her so intensely she felt a slow burn start to cover her cheeks. So strange, his reaction was nearly the same as when she'd told him in 1722. Isabel responded appropriately, as she had then. "What, do you not think the deaf deserve a higher education, even in my day and age?"

"I'm sure they did," Devin murmured, his hand on the settee, so close to the edge of her skirt Isabel almost swore she could feel him rubbing his hand against her thigh. It would be a gesture of reassurance. She kept her smile hidden. Knew he worked his dark magic on her, a dark magic that could do some incredibly wondrous things. Isabel worked hard to ignore the tingling between her thighs, the sizzling hot memories provoked by being near him.

"Devin works with the deaf as well," Andrea volunteered. "In fact he's raised a great deal of money to fund education for the deaf in Ireland."

She did well to pretend this caught her off guard and met his eyes. "Really?"

He nodded but said nothing. Always so humble, her Devin. She continued. "I stayed with one family for quite a while and all but raised one of their children before moving on."

"Your actions strike me very modern for a woman of your day and age," Devin said.

"They were," she conceded. "But I had trouble…staying in one spot too long."

Seth's eyes lit up and he grinned. "I get that."

Devin shifted beside her. Closer almost.

"Funny thing though," she murmured. "All I really wanted to do was settle down. Live a normal life."

"Why didn't you then?" Devin asked.

Had you lived my life you would've kept moving too, she almost voiced but held her tongue. Isabel only shrugged. "Settling down in my time meant marrying and definitely not showing any sort of affiliation to helping the disabled. Women simply did not do that. Most men didn't either for that matter. In its own way, aiding the deaf was almost considered witchcraft."

Dear God, it almost felt like Devin's arms came around her, comforted. She shot a quick glance his way. He hadn't moved.

"Ah, witchcraft. Tricky thing that," Seth agreed, his gaze lingered on Devin before returning to her. "So you moved on, where did you go?"

"Portsmouth, New Hampshire." Isabel bit the corner of her lip. "It was the nicest place of all of them."

And cleanest, she thought. "Though nearly as busy as Boston, the people there seemed to work together more smoothly. The commerce was less rushed. The immigrants less frantic."

"Fascinating," Leathan said.

"Mmm. I had no trouble finding work there. After all, my credentials were very good. But mind you, the Puritans had established this community and remnants of their beliefs still overshadowed. I had to be careful to a degree. But in little time, I was nanny to a wonderful deaf girl there."

"How old were you at this point?" Andrea asked.

"Twenty three. It was here, well, when walking along the shoreline, that I met a man."

She hated to tell him this...once again. Devin's hand clenched slightly on the settee beside her. "Calum?"

"No," she said softly. "If only it had been that simple."

A song filled the room. The laidback lyrics sang, "One love, let's get together and feel all right."

"Sorry, be right back." Leathan pulled a black device from his pocket and left the room.

Seth chuckled. "Ignore him, Isabel. Newly married. Changed him something fierce." He looked at Andrea and cocked a brow. "Reggae love...Leathan?"

"It's a ring tone, Bob Marley's popular," she returned, rolling her eyes before looking at Isabel. "Go on."

She'd do just about anything to cease this line of conversation, no matter how necessary. "Reggae love?"

Devin sniggered. "In case you haven't figured it out, Leathan's the most uptight of us all. For him to have a Reggae ring tone when his wife, Dakota calls is...amusing."

"Oh." She tried to ignore Devin's scent. That same masculine, sweet smell. "What's Reggae?"

"You don't know what Raggae is?" Seth asked, a wide grin smothering his face.

Andrea raised her hand and shook her head. "Did you not get the memo, Seth? She was born in 1698. Time of slavery. Raggae wasn't exactly topping the charts back then."

"Memo?" Isabel repeated.

"Disregard," Devin said, shooting her a completely charming grin. "Catch you up later."

Catch her up later? Isabel couldn't have felt more misplaced had she tried. Yes, she'd haunted this house for many generations but...still. For all she thought she'd kept up, she really hadn't. Her entire world had consisted of bits and pieces of this Georgian for far too long. And blips in time at that. In fact, being here now felt off. Best to remain calm. Go with the flow. Never say too much.

"In Portsmouth, I met a man. Very handsome," Isabel continued.

"Oh yeah?" Devin asked, his striking eyes staring at her a little too intensely. As if he had some stake in her opinion of other men. As if he had a stake on her. Isabel almost smiled.

"Yes," she responded, not shying away from his gaze. She'd kissed him already. Many times. To his mind, once. So, to her mind now, he shouldn't act as though he had any sort of claim on her. But Devin was Devin and he'd long held her heart. Her eyes drifted down. "Exceptionally handsome and quite taken with me."

Devin frowned but said nothing.

"It was with this man that I left New Hampshire and traveled into Maine." She sniffed delicately and said softly, "It was also with this man that I first became engaged."

A strange sound came from Devin. She glanced at him. His face remained impassive. He lifted an eyebrow. "And, did you marry?"

Leathan returned and sat.

"No," she murmured. She had to tell them everything, stop playing this game. But honestly, handling it this way seemed the best way to…ease into the situation. She knew they knew Calum, ghost that he was in this day and age—and knew they had a very unusual story. Still, best to take this slowly, let them lead the way. Say next what would seem most logical to them. "But before I tell you the rest, tell me how you know of Calum. I need to know I can trust you."

She didn't miss the brief glance they all shot

Leathan's way before Devin spoke. He told her the tale she already knew. That they were warlocks, part of Calum's curse.

Devin cleared his throat and continued the story. "It was a year ago that the curse started to unravel. A Victorian house in New Hampshire. It trapped the first creature, a vampire."

This she knew too.

Devin stopped talking, obviously uncomfortable.

Leathan continued. "Apparently Calum had used talismans to lock each creature. You see, when he did so, he ensured if the curse ever started to unravel, three future male descendants would become warlocks to fight these creatures. Each talisman would be connected to a warlock. Each would match the color of their aura when they implemented magic."

This was her opening. Isabel clenched her fists and closed her eyes. Confirmed what she already knew. "You three are the warlocks."

Leathan and Seth nodded. Devin stared at floor, frowning.

"And the Victorian." Eyes opened and locked with Leathan, she said, "Was where your creature was imprisoned. The vampire entrapped by the talisman that matched your aura?"

Leathan nodded gravely.

Isabel placed her hand on her chest. Knew she had to share this with them. Carefully, she reached down and pulled the delicate chain around her neck up until what was on the end of it appeared from beneath her dress.

Everyone gasped.

"It's a dark red stone," Andrea said. "Another

talisman."

Isabel wrapped a protective fist around it, her gaze sliding to Devin. His smoky green eyes had turned turbulent. His lips thinned. A throbbing dark red light pulsed around his frame for a split second then vanished. Long enough for her to know that which she'd known all along…which warlock was connected to this house.

Long enough to know—and painfully remember—which warlock would be battling a Lycan. More commonly known as a werewolf.

CHAPTER SIX

"Me," Devin whispered and stared at the damning stone hanging around Isabel's neck.

Her fist enclosed it. Stole it from his sight. Somehow kept it from his magic. A magic he'd not practiced much since the Victorian. Their gazes entangled. She knew what he'd tried to do.

"Give it to me," he repeated.

She shook her head and started to roam the room aimlessly. "I cannot give this to you nor anyone else here. If I take it off for a second, he...it will find me." Stopping abruptly, she again met his eyes. "And you."

He shouldn't really be shocked. Of course it was his turn. The second talisman had shown up. The one that matched his magical aura. "At least tell me where you found it."

"That's the tricky thing." She screwed her delicate mouth into a tiny little ball and said, "I didn't exactly find it."

"I don't understand."

Isabel cleared her throat, her skirts swooshing as she restlessly paced. "More like I stole it."

"No shit!" Seth grinned.

"Cursing," Andrea muttered. "Too much."

"You stole it," Leathan said incredulously. A wry grin tugged at his lips. "From Calum?"

A blush stole over Isabel's cheeks and she nodded. "But there was more to it. It wasn't as if I spied a pretty bauble and had to have it." When she fingered the stone this time Devin swore a dreamy expression flickered in her eyes. When they met his, the blush deepened and she looked away. "It had sentimental value." She tucked it back beneath her dress. "Or should I say it developed sentimental value."

"Why?" Devin asked.

Isabel put a hand over her mouth and shook her head, still flittering around the room like a butterfly trapped in a box. Finally, she stopped and stared at him. "Mayhap I've gone about this all wrong. I just wanted to ease you all into this as easily as possible."

Devin shook his head not comprehending. He was shocked when she crossed the room, plunked down beside him and grabbed his hands in a vice grip, her violet eyes brimming with tears. "You don't remember me at all, do you?"

The room fell so silent one could have heard the lilt of a pipe all the way from Ireland. He responded carefully. "I don't follow your meaning, lassie. Do you mean our time in the foundation in 1722?"

Seth snorted.

Andrea shook her head at Seth.

Isabel shook her head at Devin. A tear slipped free from her eye and rolled down her cheek. For a split second he felt such a strong sense of familiarity toward her, much like he had when he looked at the picture of her when she'd been a ghost. As quickly as it came, it vanished.

Apparently pulling herself together mentally, Isabel released his hands and brushed the tear from her cheek. "We spent a lot of time together in 1722, Devin. Not just the evening in the foundation. Though that was our first night…" Her voice dropped very low. "It was not, by any means, our last."

Devin's jaw dropped. He didn't know which fact to process first, that he'd be traveling back in time again...or that he'd obviously not only developed a relationship with Isabel but that he'd slept with her. His cock instantly responded to the thought. Hell. Shifting positions, he did his best to think clearly and ask the right questions. "How do you know that?"

"Because I've already lived it," she responded.

"I don't get it. You just traveled forward in time with me. Doesn't that mean that you technically haven't lived after the time we left together yet?"

There you go. That was rather sharp of him considering.

She nodded and straightened her back. "It would make sense you would think that but no. Interestingly enough, while I look like the 1722 version of me, I've all the memories of the ghostly version of me trapped in this house. This building seems to cross not just time but dimensions."

Isabel said it in such a matter-of-fact tone that they all nodded their understanding.

Silence descended again.

Seth scratched his head. "Wait a sec...so you're the 1722 version of you with the memories of your ghostly self. So that means your ghost is still haunting this place though you're sitting right there?"

Isabel stood abruptly and started her impatient stroll around the room once more. "Exactly!"

Leathan spoke low. "But how do you know you're neither your ghostly self or your 1722 self? And if you're neither...which of...yourselves outside of those two could you be?"

Devin couldn't help it, he chuckled. The chuckle

turned into a full burst of laughter. They all glanced his way, expressions equally askance. He shook his head, smiling, feeling more and more like his old self. "Sorry. But listen to us." He tried hard to not chuckle again and quirked a brow at Isabel. "So my dear, where will we find the real Isabel, behind door number one, two or three?"

"Devin!" Andrea chided.

Isabel's serious expression began to melt as she looked at him. A small smile hovered just out of range. "You know, 1722 Isabel watched you vanish that morning, when you leapt at Calum. When you returned, your personality had changed some." The hint of a smile vanished but her eyes remained warm. "Now I know why. You'd traveled here. I can't help but wonder why you didn't tell 1722 Isabel when you returned."

Devin shrugged. "Who knows. Must have had my reasons. Maybe this particular version of yourself doesn't truly remember everything though you think you do." He winked. "Or perhaps you'll know before we leave this time period."

Her eyes rounded. "Devin, you do understand when you travel back to 1722, that Isabel will know none of this. After all, she hasn't lived it yet." Again, she plunked down on the settee next to him and grabbed his hands. "You'll have to be very careful. You'll have to go through all the motions with her. Tell her everything I already know, woo her, be gentle."

Isabel's pupils flared and she pulled away, obviously embarrassed. "I'm sorry. This is a little confusing for me."

Aye, he and his cousin's had been through a ton

of crap. For the last year he'd turned bitter, resentful, denied his curse. Now, hearing everything Isabel said, everything she was going through, had been through, he realized how self-centered he'd become. He wasn't the only one suffering under the burden of Calum's curse.

No, this curse had touched many.

He looked around at Andrea, Seth, Leathan, then Isabel. Oh yeah, Calum had screwed them all equally. Bastard. All aside, it was time to focus on how he could help Isabel. How he could remove that tortured expression from her face. Had she said 'woo her?' He could do that, no matter the time period because if he'd ever met a woman who he wanted more than a casual fling with, it was Isabel.

Suddenly he felt lighter, as if a weight had been lifted off his shoulders. Calum's curse could very well work to his advantage. Why not? He'd been given magic, albeit dark. While he detested it before, he could now accept it; perhaps embrace it if it meant protecting her…which led to his next question.

"What beast is trapped in this house, Isabel? What creature am I doomed to fight?"

Her hand fell to the stone nestled beneath her dress. Her eyes skirted the walls more with anger than fear. When Isabel's eyes locked on his, he once more saw the 'warrior woman' who led Maine laborers while they built a house, who faced Calum head on. "Lycan. You go up against a werewolf, Calum." Her back straightened. "You go up against the beast who was my former fiancé."

***

Very little shocked Seth but when Isabel said that, for the first time ever, his jaw fell open. Man, what he wouldn't do to be in Devin's shoes right now! For more reasons than one. Damn Irishman had all the luck.

His gaze—not for the first time—ran over Isabel's thirty-six-twenty-four-thirty-six inch figure with unabashed appreciation. Hot as hell, this one. Even if she was clothed in such a long, conservative dress, Seth had no problem visualizing her wearing a tight little red dress, six inch black heels, with her long legs all tucked into his Mercedes. He'd take her for a drive along the drop-off cliffs of Maine she'd never forget. A hundred miles per hour plus every second of the way!

Even though Devin had just been dished some heavy shit he still managed to shoot Seth a death glare. One that made his eyes take on an otherworldly flare. Oh yeah, Devin wanted Isabel for keeps. Seth put his hands behind his head and shot him an until-you-claim-her-she's-up-for-grabs look. Devin's eyes narrowed. Seth shrugged.

"You did hear what I said, right?" Isabel asked.

"Oh, he heard you," Seth said, leaning forward. "But I've got a quick question of my own before we continue talking about the Lycan."

Isabel's gorgeous violet eyes landed on him. Holy hell, he'd like to pluck her right off that couch and strip her down bare. Couldn't help himself, he had a thing for blonds.

"Yes," she answered politely.

He also had a thing for uptight polite blonds. Go figure.

"How do you know you're not your ghostly self right now?"

"Because I wouldn't be so easily released from this house I don't think." she responded a little too quickly.

"You're lying."

"Seth!" Andrea interjected.

Leaning forward, he narrowed his eyes at Isabel and repeated, "You're lying."

Interestingly enough, neither Devin nor Leathan said anything. They knew too. It was part of their gift.

When Isabel figured out she wouldn't be getting any help from Devin she squared off with Seth. Ah, there it was in her eyes, that stubborn fiery something extra she tried so hard to conceal. "Fine. I lied." Her eyes still locked with his she seemed to debate something internally before her shoulders pulled back and she said, "I know because my ghostly self is scarred."

Damn obtrusive answer. "I don't get it."

Isabel started to wring her hands. Her shoulders quivered slightly. "I mean I was scarred. My face. Badly."

Well, that put a damper on things. Still, hot blond, scarred face, meant she had a bit of dare devil in her. He could work with that. "Sorry to hear that. You okay?"

Isabel seemed surprised by his response but her gaze kept flickering to Devin. It was pretty obvious she was more concerned with his response.

That's okay, Seth thought. He wanted Isabel too. And he usually got what he wanted.

***

"So what?" Devin said, far less concerned with Seth's gawking than he was Isabel's declaration. He hadn't missed the shift of her shoulders nor the turn of her head. In fact it reminded him much of what she'd done that first eve when he'd traveled through the woods and found her sitting beside a stream beneath the Aurora lights. That first night when a beast attacked him.

Lycan.

Another strange feeling of familiarity washed over him. This time it had nothing to do with Isabel. No, he was thinking about how he'd been unable to speak words to her that night. How his sight and hearing had been sharpened. How he'd fought the large wolf as though he, himself was...

"You should know. It's past time I stop worrying about this," Isabel murmured, breaking him from his reverie.

"Know what?" he asked.

"That I was disfigured. I'm not the girl you remembered." She shook her head, frustrated. "I'm not that same girl you just met in 1722."

"So?" he said, not following her distress at all, his mind still totally wrapped up in that night by the river.

Thunk. What? She'd just hit him upside the head with one of the couch pillows! Frowning, he grabbed the offensive bit of fluff from her.

Cheeks rosy, eyes wild, Isabel said, "For nearly three hundred years I've worried what you'd think of me becoming scarred and all you have to say is, "so!" She rolled her eyes and stood, hands on hips, staring down at him.

He sat back and stared up, incredulous but humored at the same time. "Why the hell would I care if you're scarred?"

"Cursing," Andrea muttered again.

Isabel touched her cheek. "Does this visage not please you?" Her eyes boldly wandered to his crotch. "Don't I arouse you as I am now?"

Seth made an indiscernible sound from behind her.

Devin didn't bother glaring at his cousin again. Problematic Yankee. Gazing up at Isabel from beneath his brows, hands casually perched over his raging erection, he replied, "I can assure you, scarred or not, you would always arouse me."

Ah, there was the telling stain on her upper cheeks. He enjoyed bringing that blood to the surface. Enjoyed watching her go from pale to pink in response to his words. Truth told, it was more of a turn on than anything else.

"Easy to say now," she whispered. "After all, you haven't really seen me yet, have you?"

To his mind, they had much bigger things to worry about at the moment than her insecurities. "Another question."

"Yes?"

"Where do you suppose this you—the you I'm speaking with now—goes when I once again travel back?"

Isabel rubbed her lips together and breathed in deeply through her nostrils. "I have no idea."

"Isabel, can I get you some tea? Anything?" Andrea asked, concern in her eyes.

Isabel sank down slowly onto the settee next to Devin, her skin chalky white, as though everything was suddenly catching up with her. "Yes, please. That would be lovely."

Andrea left the room.

Devin again felt a flood of protective compassion

toward her. What would it be like to know you existed in three places at the same time? He couldn't imagine. He took her hand. It was ice cold. "Listen, why don't we simplify. Not worry about your other selves. Right now you're you. This you. That's it. Okay?"

Isabel nodded weakly. He wrapped his hand around hers. Tried to give her all the warmth he could.

When she said nothing he continued. "Why don't you share some happy memories. Those before all of this began for you."

Blinking rapidly, she tried to pull away but he pulled her hand onto his lap and covered it with his other hand. "Please, a little something." He squeezed softly, smiled. "We won't tell. Promise."

Swallowing, she nodded then said softly, "My best memories are of the time I spent with you. I'm sorry."

Again he was struck by the bond she felt they shared. By the bond he'd sensed all along. "Don't be sorry. I'm glad I was there for you."

Had he sounded clinical? Like a therapist consoling their patient?

Staring at her hand in his she said almost sadly, "I know you are."

Don't be sad. Don't show your heart in your eyes like that. We only just met! Devin almost said such but caught his tongue. They had memories with one another. At least within her mind.

"Tea," Andrea said, entering the room. She handed a cup to Isabel. Devin instantly felt the loss of her hand in his. As though he'd held it many times. But of course he hadn't.

Yet.

Isabel closed her eyes and took a sip. He stared. How could he not? So perfect.

"Why don't we let them be alone for a few minutes?" Andrea said to Seth and Leathan. "I'd say it's obvious this time they have now is short lived. I think we have all the answers we need for now."

Seth and Lethan nodded and stood.

"No." Isabel set her tea aside. "You don't."

"Go on," Leathan said, slowly sinking back into his chair.

Isabel smiled thinly at Andrea. "You could have asked me earlier you know. I suppose I should have just told you."

Andrea's face dropped in immediate understanding. "Tim?"

Nodding, Isabel looked toward the wall that had taken Tim. "I saw him when he was pulled into this house."

A small whimper came from Andrea.

"He's not dead," Isabel assured. "Just trapped like I was."

"Is he hurt? Scared?" Andrea looked around frantically. "Can he hear me if I talk to him?"

"Sometimes. Bits and pieces. Much like how it is for my ghostly self. He's simply stuck between dimensions right now." She glanced at the wall again. "There's always the chance he can hear us."

"Wow!" Seth said.

"Can he communicate with us then?" Devin asked.

Isabel shook her head. "Highly unlikely. It took me years to learn how to make my presence known. I think it was years. Not sure. Such a strange and misplaced reality. Anyhow, it was sporadically at that. You have to sort of draw energy from things around you."

"Ha!" Seth said. "That's what many paranormal investigators have always believed was the case."

Fists balled by her side, Andrea said, "Isabel, has your ghostly self interacted with him? Is he scared? Can the beast trapped in this house hurt him?"

Devin watched the way Isabel's shoulders shifted slightly. The way her slender hands remained perfectly still.

"I have not interacted with him yet. Mind you, it's only ever been me and the Lycan in this house. Will the Lycan hurt him? No, it only wants me. Better yet, what's around my neck. Then…" Her words trailed off, eyes slid to Devin.

"Do you think Tim will be released when the beast is?" Leathan asked.

"I can't imagine why not. After all, wasn't his imprisonment the lure to get you here, Devin? Which makes him part of the curse now. When the curse is lifted I've little doubt he will be released from the house," Isabel replied.

Andrea swallowed hard. Devin had to give her credit for keeping her composure.

"What about the werewolf…your fiance." Andrea looked from Isabel to Devin then back, worried. "You say Devin will travel back in time again. The wolf's there, isn't it? And it's not trapped in the house."

Isabel nodded carefully. "And that's the bigger problem."

Devin got a chill down his spine at the look in her eyes. A near feeling of panic when she said, "He's hunting us both."

CHAPTER SEVEN

"What do you mean he's hunting us both?" Devin asked. "The curse hasn't even been cast on him yet!"

Isabel's face wavered.

He frowned and blinked. Her visage sharpened.

"Yes, but you see…"

Though she kept talking he suddenly couldn't hear her. Glancing at his cousins he found them wavering too. As though he were looking at them through a foggy window. He entered Seth's mind. Can you hear me?

Seth sounded far away. "Yep, but barely. You're starting to fade! Damn."

When Devin turned to Isabel she was gone. For that matter, so was all the furniture and the house itself. In fact, he was sitting on the dirt in a houseless foundation once more. Heck, time traveling went smoother than he ever would've anticipated.

"Not always. Time travel can be quite jarring for some."

Startled, Seth looked to his right. Adlin! He hadn't seen the ghostly wizard since the Victorian. Dressed in white robes with long trailing white hair and piercing light blue eyes, Adlin sat, legs crossed, against the far wall.

"Didn't think I'd see you again," Devin muttered.

"Hoped, you mean."

"Blame me?"

"Not in the least."

"What brings you here?"

"You, naturally." Adlin stood and dusted off his robes. "Haven't found the journal yet, have you?"

"Hadn't really thought much about it since that first night." Devin stood, eyeing the wizard with little trust. "Can you blame me?"

Adlin's Scottish accent thickened. "You do know why you haven't found it, aye?"

The wizard didn't know how to talk directly, did he? "Again, haven't given it too much thought."

Adlin strolled casually his way. "Not much common sense to you, is there boy?"

"Listen—"

Adlin cut him off. "You haven't embraced your new gift at all." A thin white eyebrow shot up. "Do you think that makes you less…evil?"

Both uncomfortable and irritated, Devin responded, "I don't think I'm evil in the least."

"Ah." Adlin eyed the stone wall as if it interested him. "Then what gives you the ability to use dark magic?"

"Calum and well you know it!" He cursed his sudden anger.

Adlin strolled along the foundation, studying it. "Only because it was imprinted in your blood, laddie." His eyes cut to Devin. "And make no mistake, your blood is very much part of you."

Shaking his head Devin said, "Why are you here this time? To rub in my face what an evil son of a bitch I am?" He waved him away and turned. "Get the hell out of here."

"How could you say such things? You're lucky Calum is in a good mood today!"

Devin swung around. Isabel had just stepped

down into the foundation. Blue eyes furious, she pointed a finger at him and kept her evident fury at a surprisingly quiet octave. "I don't know why I defended you!"

A warm feeling flooded his chest. This was the 1722 Isabel. Devin remembered what the future Isabel had said. Be careful with her, gentle. She knew nothing of what they'd share. But, she did know about her fiancé. The werewolf. However, there still remained so many gaps. How had she learned her fiancé was Lycan? How had she met Calum? Bloody amazing how they'd all managed to not cover the most important details before he got whisked back in time again. He supposed he'd have to learn things the good ol' fashioned way...by getting to know her better. Devin glanced around only to realize that Adlin had vanished.

"Well? What was that all about?" Isabel prompted.

Where exactly had they left off? It looked to still be morning based on where the sun was in the sky. But how had he gone from confronting Calum to sitting down here in the foundation crossing swords with Adlin?

"Um..."

"Um?" she repeated.

The sun hit her hair at such an angle that it seemed to ignite white gold from within. It took all his willpower not to bury his hands in its rich length. However, her blazing and thoroughly aggravated eyes told him she awaited a solid explanation. Wasn't going to happen! Think fast. Let's see if she'd buy this...

"My head." Putting one palm over his skull he

leaned back against the wall and squinted. "Been killing me all morn. Honestly, I don't know why I acted that way. The pain is searing. Guess it's affected my mood."

Her long lashes fluttered, eyes widened, completely stunned. "You expect me to believe that?"

"Of course!" With his best incredulous expression he worked on whittling details out of her. "Didn't you kind of get that when I confronted Calum?"

"Honestly, I believe you confirmed what I thought of you when first we met. You're mad! Really, you confront him as though you know him then you stop mid speech, turn and walk down here. As if you didn't have a care in the world!"

If she only knew. Interesting though. So he'd never throttled Calum while they traveled forward in time, or crossed dimensions, whatever they'd done. His physical form had remained? And functioned? Bloody damn strange! "Where's Calum now?"

"They're getting ready to build. He's looking over the supplies." She frowned. "Strangely, he doesn't seem overly disturbed by the things you said. Then again, no one did. It was odd really." Isabel's eyes narrowed. "What did you mean when you said what you did? You called him a ghost. You said you knew him. Have you met before? If so, what happened?"

Devin started to talk and stopped. What a thing to deal with 1722 Isabel. What the hell was he supposed to tell her at this point? Best to stick with the 'hurting head' ruse—not that she seemed all that concerned. He gripped his skull again, shook his head and dished out more lies. "I guess I thought I knew him. Some people come and go so fast in your life, we Irish called them ghosts." Shrugging he worked at what he hoped appeared a pained smile. "Please forgive me?"

For a moment he thought she'd soften but whatever caring feeling she may have had fled. "You mock me, sir! I don't believe you for a second." Worry entered her eyes. "But I do believe you've the madness about you." Nodding, Isabel took his free hand. "You need help and it can't be found here. At least not the sort of treatment you require. I'll see if Calum's—"

"No." He cut off her words as smoothly as her path to the basement stairs. Holding her upper arms gently but firmly he leaned down until they were nearly nose to nose. Flecks of light purple sparked to life around her iris'.

"No." He repeated. Time to be persuasive. "My place is here. I desperately need the money. Please." Squeezing her arms ever so slightly he leaned forward another scant inch. "I have family to take care of."

Surprise tempered the purple flecks of unwelcome desire on her part. "You have a wife? Children?"

Devin shook his head. Instinct and an incredible need to rekindle that desire she worked so hard to hide kept him from taking the lie that far. "My ma and da are being overtaxed by the landlords. They're about to lose their home."

He might not know much history but when it came to Ireland's slippery and tragic past, Devin knew more than most. Enough to make up a plausible story that suited the moment.

Compassion warmed her eyes, turned them a soft, silvery purple. "Did they know you were mad when you came over?"

Don't roll your eyes! Instead he closed them and counted to five. The woman wouldn't let this idea of hers go. When he opened them he caught her staring at his lips. He started to lean forward but stopped. Present day Isabel's words echoed in his mind. Be gentle with her.

"For the last time, I am not mad." Pulling back, he released her. "But perhaps I seem that way because of the distress I'm under." He shot her his best pathetic look and slumped his shoulders a fraction. "You understand?"

Though her eyes narrowed slightly, if she thought he still lied to her she didn't voice it. A few moments passed before she finally spoke. "I will give you one more chance, mainly because Calum seems to have no issue with you. From this point forth however, I expect you to be on your best behavior." Back ramrod straight, shoulders back, warrior woman returned with full force. "If you do one more thing to disrupt things or to in any way undermine my authority, I will declare you insane and have you shipped right off. Are we clear?"

Ah, but he did like this version of her. Practicing at period etiquette he bent slightly from the waist and lowered his head briefly. "You have my word. I will be on my very best behavior."

"Very good then." Breezing past him she said, "I suggest you get started helping with the framework."

Glancing up he realized men were milling about and the first lay of woodwork had begun. "Yes mam."

As he followed her up the stairs his attention hesitantly turned from the gentle sway of her backside to all the activity swarming around them. Calum was easy to find in the crowd. This time Devin didn't confront him but appraised his relative from a leisurely distance. While he knew Calum had been raised in the early nineteenth century he'd adapted well to the early eighteenth century. Tall with black hair and piercing blue eyes, Calum showed a stronger resemblance to Seth than Devin had previously realized.

"Bit mighty with the mister back there."

Devin took a piece of wood from Vagrant One, glad to see a familiar face, one who helped him get right to work at that. Nodding he said, "We Irish can be strange at times. Thought I knew him is all."

Grunting, Vagrant One nodded. "John's the name."

Devin stacked his wood alongside John's, for the first time really taking in his appearance. Young beneath all the dirt, his co-worker looked to be in his early twenties with brown hair and eyes. He might have thought him altogether unspectacular had he not suddenly caught the intelligence hidden in his evasive eyes.

"Devin," he replied with a nod of his own.

Vagrant Two fell in on Devin's other side, wood in hand and nodded his head as well. "Andy's the name."

Nodding in return and stating his name, Devin reevaluated this new friend as well. Shorter than himself but several inches taller than John, Andy was fine boned and too thin with a narrow face, broad forehead and blond hair. Surprisingly enough, he spied the same sharp intelligence in Andy's near black eyes.

"That was a bit o' business with the boss back

there." Andy all but repeated John's sentiment.

"Irish is all," John said under his breath.

Andy hefted a long board onto his shoulder. "Thought as much."

John lifted his own board beneath an arm. "Thing for the missus then?"

"I'd say," Andy responded.

Devin swung up a board as well. "Just met her boys. Too soon to tell."

As the three men carried their boards toward the foundation, all eyes found their way to Isabel who talked adamantly to Calum's secretary across the way.

"She's a beauty," Andy said.

"Good woman," John added.

Mine! Devin thought. Awe, what the hell was he thinking? She wasn't his quite yet. "So I take it she arrived here with Cal…um, the mister?"

Neither responded but Devin couldn't help but notice their grim expressions. Did they really dislike Calum that much? If so, why? As they plodded on he knew he needed to take advantage of this situation while he still had it. Had to keep grilling the boys.

"C'mon, did she really arrive in that grand carriage with Calum and left to lead all of you?" Shaking his head, Devin said, "Seems a lot to throw on one's lassie if you ask me."

"She's not his," Andy said softly.

A shiver of warning shot down his spine. Was it his imagination or did their way of speaking seem to switch from really bad American English to neat and clean?

"Who the hell's is she then?"

Neither responded but kept walking when Isabel

called out his name. En route to grab another piece of wood, Devin switched directions and headed her way. Stern, hair swept back in the same dependable bun from before, Isabel met him halfway. "Calum would like to see you. Please follow me."

Shit. Well, this was bound to happen. Swiping one hand across his sweaty forehead, the other through his too-greasy-for-his-taste hair, Devin followed Isabel into a tall tent set up closer to the line of pines. He was fairly surprised to find it simply furnished.

Calum sat in front of a small wooden desk. A cot lay off to the side. The only thing that bespoke wealth was an oval oriental carpet richly woven in black, crimson and gold. Honestly, opulent carpeting aside, if felt more like a 21st century USA military commander's personal tent during wartime.

Calum didn't stand. In fact, he kept scribbling away in the book in front of him. Devin's eyes narrowed. The journal! Sudden understanding dawned and what Adlin had said previously made perfect sense. What he'd actually said of it that is. The journal couldn't be found yet because Calum was still writing in it! He'd only just begun building this house. While he'd already stowed away the Victorian's journal his Georgian was still under construction…as was the journal that belonged with it.

Unreal! So how the hell was he supposed to refer to the journal then when dealing with all this crap?

"I would think it's obvious."

Devin's eyes shot to Calum's. A fission of dark energy ran between the men. Connected them. Had Calum sensed it?

Calum continued, "That you overstepped your bounds out there earlier." Setting the writing quill aside, he sat back. "Explain yourself."

Was this a test? He studied Calum's eyes. Saw nothing but stern curiosity. Perhaps a touch of wariness. Ha! No doubt. Devin knew he was under a ton of stress right now. After all, the bloody werewolf was roaming around out there somewhere. Humph! Little did he know the future decedent he sought to protect stood before him.

And he didn't know, hadn't felt that connection of energy.

How? Why? When this man was, in all reality, the head warlock.

Devin knew he was right. A tiny thrill traveled over his skin. He had 'one up' on his enemy Calum right now.

Clearing his throat, Devin thought it best to stick with the story he'd told Isabel. "I thought I knew you. Was mistaken. The worry about my family back in Ireland has given me too many sleepless nights. I'm not myself." Now to drive home the fact, pull the family card, one which Calum was bound to affiliate with. "Just trying to take care of and protect my own." He ducked his head. "So sorry, sir. It won't happen again."

Keeping his head bent in what he hoped appeared a sign of both respect and personal defeat, Devin awaited a response.

Calum didn't make him wait long. "I understand watching out for your own." A pause. "What's your job here, son?"

Devin almost snorted at this compassionate response. He knew all too well how evil Calum was.

Regardless, things were working in his favor. Raising his head, he once again locked eyes with Calum. "Simple laborer, sir."

Calum gave him one more glance over and nodded. "Very good. You're dismissed."

Nodding, Devin turned to leave.

"One more thing," Calum said and he stopped.

Here it comes. Busted.

Devin turned back.

With a wink Calum said, "Thank you for your help and keep in mind...there's nothing simple about a laborer. You're as important as the man whom designs the house."

Devin smiled slightly, nodded and exited as quickly as possible. Though he had a funny way of going about it, Calum had him pegged because there was no way the man inside that tent had been genuine. An uncomfortable feeling settled in his chest. Why had Calum acted that way? What game was he playing?

Isabel didn't come out of the tent after him. Had he really expected such? Despite what John and Andy had said, she and Calum must have some sort of physical arrangement. Only thing that made sense.

Halfway between the tent and thriving metropolitan of working men, Devin stopped. A strange spike of warning shot up his spine. Every sense went on alert. Though it'd been a year since he'd last done such a thing, he gently pulled forth his dark magic. Instantly, the stream of voices building the house vanished. His hearing focused primarily on the forest off to his right.

The sound of lazy mid-summer crickets. The distant pour of the river. But there was something else. Better yet, someone. Come on, move. Breathe. Anything. Let me detect you. Because I already know your scent.

A low growl rumbled in his throat when a chuckle rode the wind. Saliva pooled on his tongue. Devin once more felt a familiar bloodlust. Part of his dark magic…but not. Rolling his shoulders back he felt a new power flow through him. Not all that new, the same from the Victorian, but unused, needing release. How could he not embrace this? Do what he had to do to protect Isabel?

Oh, but it felt good.

Free.

A small smile—eyes locked on a far off distance—Devin, much as he had with Calum, simply nodded and continued on to help the others build a Georgian.

Sooner or later, the warlock would face the werewolf.

CHAPTER EIGHT

Isabel needed more.

"Are ye sure then?" John asked.

Nodding, grim faced, she flung out her hand. "It needs to be bigger."

Devin snorted.

Glaring at him, she paced along the floorboards of the first floor. Though she hated to admit it, he looked good leaning casually against a newly erected support beam. At some point he'd bathed in the nearby river and his dark auburn hair gleamed in the sunlight. Due to the heat and his complete lack of shame, he'd ripped the sleeves off the white worker's shirt he'd been given and muscles flexed all the way from his shoulders to his forearms. Instead of turning him red as the sun should any decent Irishman, it seemed to favor him with a deep golden glow, irritating really when combined with those ethereal smoky green eyes that seemed a little too bold by half when they swung her way.

"I take it you disagree?"

"It's not what I think that matters," he returned.

It had been three days since she'd brought him into Calum's tent and the man's attitude had progressively...changed. What really stung her backside was that for the most part, the change had been incredibly favorable. The madman had vanished. It's his place, a gracious and oftentimes flirtatious Irishman with a way of tugging smiles from her when she least expected it. Why did this irk her? Simple.

There was no room for romance in her life. That and the fact any romance would surely be snuffed out by...

Her gaze wandered once more to the tree line.

"Isabel?"

Blinking, her attention returned to the matter at hand and she turned away from Devin. Not before saying, "Mam to you."

John still stood nearby, appearing far more respectful than Devin. Again he said, "Are ye sure then?"

While it would mean quite a bit more labor she felt strongly the house needed more, at least another thirty feet in either direction. Right now it was way too small. In fact, the current dimensions nearly made her feel claustrophobic. A wave of dizziness overcame her and she swayed.

Suddenly, strong hands were on her arms from behind. Devin whispered close to her left ear. "You all right, lass?"

Nausea overwhelmed, Isabel shook her head.

Leading her off the first floor onto the dirt, he kept a sturdy arm around her waist. Thankfully, the moment she left the house the feeling passed. Breathing in deep gulps of air, Isabel gently dislodged from his hold. "I'm sorry. I don't know what came over me."

"The heat is getting to us all," Devin replied.

If only he knew. "I'm just overtired. This project has kept me very busy."

Nodding, he said, "I know. It has us all. When do you expect Calum back?"

Isabel hadn't expected her boss to leave so soon but had no intention of letting Devin know that.

"Within days."

"Bet you wish he hadn't left, eh?"

She frowned.

Holding his hands up, he shook his head. "You misunderstand. I was just curious if you'd hope he'd stay to oversee more of the project at such a crucial time especially in that you want the structure larger."

Few men made her feel so unstable. This one did. But he was not the first of his kind to come into her life. Memories of Lucas tried to resurface but she pushed them away. "I will make no requests of my men until Calum returns." Isabel shook invisible dust off her skirt. "But I'm sure he will agree. The house needs to be larger. As it is, the size will suffocate whoever lives here."

Devin's eyes slid to the already massive proportions of the house but he made no comment. "I was hoping I might be able to talk to you about something in private."

Private plus Devin equaled no. "I'm sorry, it would look inappropriate if I walked off alone with you."

An arched eyebrow rose over one of his magnificent eyes. "I see."

Fire scorched her cheeks. Surely, he understood. Why such a look?

"Well, what if we have either John or Andy walk with us?" Devin shrugged a shoulder. "They've become…friends of mine and wouldn't it seem less than out of the ordinary if one were to walk with us?"

Naturally, that made perfect sense. Wetting her lips, Isabel gave a brief nod. "Yes. John then."

Devin gave a small wave John's way and he trotted over. After being told why they wished him to walk with them, she and Devin walked together, his friend, her employee, more than a few paces behind.

Late day sun spliced across the pathway leading through the trees. While she treaded this path to bathe only, Isabel made a habit of avoiding the woods lately. But with Devin by her side, she felt that old familiar calm infuse her. It felt wonderful walking within the heart of nature. Perhaps it was his tall, strong stature but she didn't think so. It was more the way he carried himself, as though he inherently challenged anything that may try to accost them from within the shadows. As though in some odd way, he welcomed it.

It felt as though he were her protector.

But of course that was not the case. God was her protector. Devin was a mortal man. And to her mind, a mortal man needed idle conversation.

"It's beautiful here," she said.

Green eyes scanning the forest he replied, "In its own way, aye." A twinkle lit his eyes when they glanced her way. "But there are far more beautiful things to admire."

Although the comment was horribly cliché she appreciated the easy decency of it and replied such. "You flatter me."

"Do I?"

Isabel could not help herself. "No, not really. Is that what you meant to say or are you just saying what I want to hear?"

Chuckling, he made a gesture with his head toward the man distantly trailing them. "What you want to hear can't be said with him so close." He winked. "Does that offend you?"

Often times, she did not know what to make of

him. Devin had a way of giving her the impression of being a perfect gentleman while simultaneously hinting that a much more forthcoming nature lay beneath the surface. Either way, he'd not approached her the same way he had the first night. Had not tested her dignity nor morals. So did he offend her?

Not really.

After all, she had not led the life she portrayed to him that she had. She was no proper English lady. No, she was a Southern girl with far too many secrets.

But he did not know that. Best to keep it that way.

"What did you need to speak with me about, Devin?"

"Your relationship with Calum."

Isabel did well not to trip or choke on her next breath of air. Instead, she nodded and kept on walking. "He is my employer, as you know."

"Is that all?"

So much for him being the perfect gentleman. Scowling, head still high she responded, "Of course."

The trees broke and the very spot she'd first found him sprawled on the ground appeared. Calmer today, the river glistened dark blue with pockets of shade speckling the shoreline.

"So there is no romantic involvement?"

Eyes rounded, she stared up at him in astonishment. "No! And if there were, it would be none of your concern."

"Well it might be."

"No," she continued, becoming more aggravated by the minute. "And for you to even imply that there is would make me a common…" She could not spit out the words so vile was the implication.

Devin's brow slowly rose. He cocked his head. "A common what, Isabel?"

Crossing her arms over her chest she said, "You know what."

"No, I don't. Enlighten me."

"And here I thought you'd changed. Or that I'd met the wrong you to begin with."

"The wrong me?"

Lips tight together she nodded.

As if he suddenly sensed he had overplayed his hand, Devin's almost harsh expression softened. Oddly enough, in that singular moment, with the sun glittering off the water and the grass warm and green beneath her feet, it felt as though...magic surrounded her. A heartwarming, cuddle-in-for-life sort of magic.

"Irish," she murmured without meaning to.

"Last I checked," he murmured as well. "So if there's nothing between you and Calum, perhaps..."

Had his eyes ever looked so strikingly emerald? His lips so perfectly matched to hers? A warm feeling of rightness poured over her.

"I'd say that's a yes," John volunteered from the edge of the forest.

Isabel blinked. It felt almost like she had been daydreaming. "What is a yes?"

"Based on that warm, dreamy look you just had, I'd say you're willing to allow me to...court you, lassie."

"Court me?" Isabel blinked again. The warm fuzzy feeling had faded. In its place a blazing fire of need burned where her heart should be. "You?"

Devin winked. "Why not?"

"Why not indeed, Missus!" John piped up.

Shaking her head, Isabel said the very opposite of

what she wanted to say. "Absolutely not! What are you thinking?"

"Indeed," muttered John. "She's too good for the likes of us, Devin."

"Aye lad," Devin replied in kind.

Jaw dropped, she looked between Devin and John. "No, that's not it at all."

"No?" Devin asked.

"Well, course not. We caught her all mixed up is all," John provided.

"You did?" she asked.

Devin nodded, expression grave, "We must've."

"No ways around it. The missus is a good and kind woman. Not to judge a person's station in life."

"Nay, indeed," Devin concurred.

"No, you both know I would not," she added.

"And a tall, strappin' lad likes our Irishman, now a turn or two on the dance floor, now that'd be just fine," John said.

"Of course it would!" Isabel said. "But what dance floor?"

"This one." Devin bowed and held out one hand.

Dumbfounded, she stared at him.

"Don't ye see it, missus," John provided.

Shaking her head, she again glanced between Devin and John.

"Just there." John nodded in Devin's direction. "The Irishman holding out his hand. The grass beneath your feet. Looks like a dancin' floor to me!"

Isabel once more looked at Devin, seemingly frozen in time, hand held out, a slight wind blowing his hair. Looking back she was about to tell John how wrong he was when she realized he'd vanished. Devious that one!

"Well?" Devin asked.

"Well wh—"

Isabel abruptly stopped talking when he leapt forward and put one arm around the small of her back. One of his hands held one of hers. While he did not pull her too close, the gesture, the contact, felt exceedingly erotic. Gasping, she shook her head.

Devin nodded, winked and spun her before Isabel had a chance to voice how entirely inappropriate the whole situation was.

"Please don't," Devin said, spinning her slowly.

"Do not what?"

"Tell me how inappropriate this is. Because it's really not." He smiled warmly. "Plain daylight after all, with full permission from our chaperone I might add."

"Was that what that was? Permission?"

But she allowed him to lead her a step or two before saying, "There's no music."

"Oh, don't make me break out the Irish on you. C'mon! Can't you hear the river flow, the trees blowing in the wind?"

A giggle erupted. "So that's the Irish in you? Well thank the Lord for small favors!"

Devin's smile blossomed further. "Was a rather corny, poetic thing to say, aye?"

Pursing her lips, she allowed another spin. Truth told, there was a certain sound to the air. A way nature clicked together to provide a little jig. One in which completely suited the man she danced with. Isabel did not even complain when she felt him pull her a bit closer.

It felt good to be out in the middle of nowhere dancing with a handsome man, carefree for the first time in her entire life. Feeling protected for the first time in her entire life.

"Yes," she whispered then shook her head immediately. Why had she said that?

A wide grin broke over his face and he dipped her back, apparently finishing the dance. Staring up at the blue sky, puffy white clouds billowing overhead, a bit too much happiness trying to wheedle its way into her heart, Isabel had the distinct feeling she had just given Devin all he needed.

When he pulled her up slowly and stepped away she shook her head again. "No!"

"Aye!" Devin laughed.

"I simply cannot, I'm sorry."

"You can and you will." Continuing to laugh he pulled her back down the path, away from the river. "But there's no rush, lassie. We'll play by your rules."

"My rules?" She couldn't help but smile a little as they hurried back toward the house, toward reality. Though it had only been at best half an hour, Isabel felt she had embarked on a new journey with Devin. One which she already knew they'd both regret. But how wonderful to feel this way for a minute or two.

"No!" She repeated as they entered the field before the house.

Devin never disputed her but squeezed then released her hand and wandered back toward the other builders. Not even a backward glance. But she knew he grinned.

Just like her.

Hours later when Calum, finally returned, asked her into his tent, Isabel had no idea she was still glowing.

As always, her employer and friend sat at his desk, head bent to work. When she entered he scribbled for another minute before sitting back.

"Dine with me, Isabel. I grow lonely."

"And worried," she provided.

"Very."

As if the afternoon had never happened, reality once more dawned. They cleared away the paperwork on his desk, filled a few dishes with beans from the side table and sat. Her on one side of the desk, he the other.

Neither ate straight away but sat back, eyed one another.

At last Calum spoke, "I heard rumor you want the house larger. Why?"

Isabel knew this was coming. "It is too small. I just know it."

"It is but a cage, love. And cages need not be that large."

Doubt that! A shiver of apprehension crawled over her skin. "But they need to be efficient."

"It will be. We don't need to add the extra space."

Sighing, Isabel scooped some beans into her mouth. When finished chewing she said, "Twenty feet, on either side. Would it really set the project back much?"

"By months and well you know it."

"But you've time. The ground is months from freezing."

Calum took a bite as well, his keen blue eyes watching her face the whole time. At last he said, "You'd risk its wrath for this infatuation you have with an Irish laborer?"

Isabel should have known. That's just how men think.

"No, Calum. I have a feeling more space is needed in the house. I don't know why. Furthermore, no such infatuation exists for any man and I certainly would not further a project at such expense over any romance, however non-existent it is."

"Mm hmm." Calum shook his head. "You're glowing, Isabel. Do you think me blind? I've seen the way you two look at one another."

This line of conversation needed to end, even if it meant starting one far less savory. "Do you think he...I mean, it's close? Do you think it's already found me?"

"Closer than before."

Calum's simple admission made Isabel's blood go cold. Please, no. "How can you be sure?"

"Just a hunch." Taking another bite, he chewed slowly. When finished he said, "But it doesn't know exactly where you are."

"I still don't understand why we didn't travel further. Really, we stayed in the same state!"

"Do you honestly think distance makes any difference when dealing with this sort of monster?"

Appetite gone, she set the beans aside. "One would hope."

"We both know it doesn't work that way. And we both know it is more me it wants than you. But, regrettably, we are both in mortal danger."

Grimacing, she replied, "And we both know that the whole point of building this house is to bring the beast set to kill us to our very door."

CHAPTER NINE

"Just step through the door."

Isabel smiled and said, "This will officially be the first time."

Devin returned her smile, hand held out. While much of the house's framework was still being built, the door frame now existed. He stood on the inside, she on the outside. That she appeared hesitant didn't surprise him in the least.

"Remind me again why it is I once more stand out here in the middle of the night with you?"

Pulling back his hand, Devin leaned against a support beam and shrugged. "Well, I've noticed over the past week you purposely have not walked through that door. Thought it's high time you did."

"I see."

But there she remained, the moonlight gleaming off her long blond hair. Her posture set to go to war. Again, he didn't blame her. After all, he understood her hesitancy even if she didn't. Day by day, as this house was constructed, every board hammered into place, she seemed more and more put off by the very project she oversaw.

So many times he'd wanted to tell her everything. About what he knew of her and this house. Then again, there remained so many puzzle pieces still missing. Tonight he was determined to unravel a wee bit more about this mystery.

"What are you so afraid of, Isabel?"

Her body tensed further, if that was possible. "I'm not afraid of anything. I simply don't understand your need to see me walk through this door."

For the past few days, Devin had been trying very hard to be patient with her. 'Woo' her. Tiresome really. While he couldn't fault the very slow process in which it took to show a woman interest in this day and age, he sorely missed the more up front approach remnant of the Twenty-first century. Maybe a movie, a drink, romantic dinner. Hell, even a little foreplay wouldn't hurt at this point.

And by foreplay he didn't mean hammering nails in the blistering sun as she overlooked or eating stale beans by the firelight with a bunch of sweaty men as she shot him shy smiles here and there. Nope, he'd determined this eighteenth century 'wooing' officially sucked.

But if there was one thing Devin was good at when it came to women it was patience. They deserved that at the very least.

"Well, if you can't walk through the door, walk through the framework wall and join me, eh?"

Her eyes slid left then right. "But why? Especially at this hour."

"Why not? It's the perfect hour. The moon's three quarters full overhead and the entire framework is built. You really should see it from the inside."

Isabel frowned.

Be more convincing Devin.

Looking properly depressed he said, "And I'd like the chance to really talk with you. Get your impressions of this project."

"Oh, this is silliness."

Holding back a grin, he watched her walk down

the steps and go to the side. "I will need a hand up from here."

So no door yet. Not a problem. Leaning over he put a hand down and neatly pulled her up. While every bone in his body told him to let the momentum bring her body against his, he didn't. Twenty-first century Isabel's words kept resonating in his head. Be gentle with her. So far he had and it'd worked. That he'd managed to have her somewhat agree to him courting her at the river was a Godsend in itself. And an opportunity he had no intention of screwing up.

"Thank you," she said.

"You're welcome." Grinning, he took her hand and walked them into the foyer. Interesting to have seen it the way it would someday look and now only see a starlit sky where there would be ceiling. To see stairs leading up to vacant hallways and more stairs leading to more emptiness. "A home really does develop a soul as it's built," he murmured.

"Excuse me?" she said, not pulling her hand away.

"Well, just think of it." He pointed at the stairs. "Someday those stairs that weren't there a week ago will eventually be lined by walls full of pictures. Of family, loved ones." He walked her into what would someday be the living room. "This room I see with a huge fireplace, full of comfortable furniture. A family sharing everyday life with one another. Memories being created."

Much like the life you shared in this very room with my cousins and me almost three hundred years from now.

"That sounds lovely," Isabel said softly.

"And this room." Leading her into what would

one day be the dining room. "Someday this will see a family sitting around a table, eating a delicious meal."

"Oh really, and who will cook this meal?"

Grinning, he replied, "Most likely the husband."

Laughing, she responded, "That's the most absurd thing I've ever heard."

Devin figured she'd say as much. In this day and age, the woman cooked the meal, not the man. So much fun to play with her though. "Why? Men can cook too."

"Can they?" Though she shook her head he couldn't help but notice her gaze lingered on the center of the room where a table would be.

"I can cook," he said.

Again she laughed, her eyes a silvery gray beneath the moon. "Why is it that I believe you think you could indeed."

"Because I do and I can." Pulling her along he lead her from the dining room into what would be the kitchen. "And this is where I'd work my magic."

"Ah ha." Nodding, she released his hand and sauntered around the wall free room. "I suppose you would cook something scrumptious. Fill this whole house with a wonderful smell."

"You better believe it." He slowly trailed after Isabel, suddenly infatuated with the way she gazed around the barren room. As though she visualized everything that would someday be there. Her dreamy, wanting expression made him wonder just how deprived she'd been in her life. "The first thing I'd make for you, blueberry pancakes with warm maple syrup. All from scratch of course."

"From scratch?" She said absently. "And what are blueberry pancakes?"

Ah yes, early eighteenth century. Pancakes must've been around, just called something different. Where was Leathan when you needed him? Time to make some sort of sense. "Yeah, scratch, a way we Irish say using every ingredient in its truest form. Blueberry pancakes? Um, comfort food. At least for me."

Luckily, Isabel's dreamy expression kept her from becoming overly inquisitive. "Comfort food. Sounds good." A wide grin released her from deep thoughts. "Anything would be better than beans at this point."

Devin laughed. "Couldn't agree more."

Merry eyes slid his way. "I think I might like to have you cook for me."

"Would you?" Stopping within a foot, Devin practiced great restraint in not touching her. Seriously, if this wasn't the perfect environment for having a little fun, he didn't know what was. "Well, I'll tell you what, the minute this house is complete we'll go somewhere else and I'll find a way to cook for you. That is if you've no other plans."

Isabel's eyes lowered but she didn't move away. "We'll see."

"Ahh. Okay." He moved a fraction closer. "When do you expect this house to be complete?"

With a slight shrug she replied, "Hopefully before winter. At least the walls and roof."

"Good goal. A lot of hard work ahead."

Nodding, she moved away. "Yes." Continuing her stroll around the 'would be' kitchen Isabel said, "And do you intend to stay through the whole process?"

"You know I do." Devin held out his hand.

"Come, let's explore more."

A suddenly nervous burst of laughter erupted. "What more is there?"

Taking Isabel's hand, he pulled her along. "Up!"

"What? No! There's barely enough flooring between each level!"

Walking backward, he continued pulling her. "So?"

"So?"

Stopping one stair up, he said, "What, are you afraid of heights?"

A silly look crossed her face. He liked that. Perhaps a glimpse beneath the fake personae she displayed in this time period? "No, I'm not afraid of heights. But I haven't done anything so spontaneous since…"

"Since what?" he prompted.

"It makes no matter." Isabel's eyes took on a determined look, as though she sought to recapture a bit of who she really was. As though she suddenly needed to remember that there was more than just the lie she lived. "Up, let's go."

Pulling her to his stair, he paused a moment, keeping her trapped next to him if only to smell her. Still spicy…still Butterfly weed. Leaning close he sniffed. Isabel pulled back, not quite frowning. Their gazes held. Her lips drew his attention. Full, stern, but soft at this exact moment.

"Up, let's go," she whispered.

"Ladies first."

Nodding she headed up the stairs. While Devin knew he had the magical ability to stave off any structural collapses if the staircase didn't hold it somehow felt better having her in front of him. Best to be on the downward side of gravity if she tripped. And, for the first time since meeting her, it wasn't about checking out her overly clothed ass. Well, mostly wasn't.

"Look at this." Isabel stopped on the second landing.

Only pathways of floor had been built on this level making it rather dangerous. Stopping behind her, Devin said, "Nice."

And it was. To look down and see the floor, then up and see another floor, then the sky. Impressive. Yet. "Come." Turning her he urged Isabel to keep climbing the stairs.

At the top she stopped short which conveniently put his face in her...

"Look," she whispered.

Coming up, Devin looked around. Yes, he'd been up here plenty during the daylight hours building this house but she was right, at night it looked spectacular.

"The moonlight turns the wood to pure silver up here," she murmured and walked forward. "It's like a waking dream."

Isabel was right. Diamond shards made it look like something he'd only ever seen when he and his cousins had been experimenting with dark magic. Even dark magic appeared beautiful...in the right light. Following her Devin said, "Good workmanship."

"Most certainly." Nodding, Isabel laughed and started to walk across a particularly thin plank to the next landing.

"Careful, lass." Devin followed. "The reason it glistens like this is because there's a light layer of dew on the wood already."

Poising on a single beam she turned and winked. "Oh, I know!"

Trying to ignore sudden panic for her well-being he pursued. "You like to take risks."

"Every once in a while, yes." Another soft round of laughter erupted and she turned away, walking further. "Refreshing."

Now this aspect of her personality well suited Seth. As far as he was concerned, it sucked. Not the reason he brought her up here. Catching up quickly, he pulled her off onto a solid six feet of floor.

"What Devin?" She asked, blue eyes suddenly smoky and challenging. "Does the way I'm acting not suit you?"

Suit him? Hell no. Urging her to stand in front of a window frame he replied, "That depends. Is this the real you? Or the just the you wanting to rebel?"

The word 'rebel' seemed to offend her and she stood straighter. "Forgive me if I'm wrong, but have I not detected from you all along the desire for a woman with a bit of rebellion in her?"

She had him there. Yet, wouldn't that seem an obvious observation from a woman who lived in the eighteenth century dealing with a man from the twenty-first century or was she sensing the warlock part of him he was slowly starting to embrace? Damn, in the past year he'd buried himself so thoroughly, Devin was starting to feel out of touch with the man he'd once been.

Devin almost said, "What do you want me to be?" but caught his tongue. Never in his life had he asked that of a woman and didn't intend to do so now.

Instead he replied, "Yeah, you're right on some

counts. But I didn't mean for you to ever think I'd want you to risk your life." Nodding toward the floor far below, he said, "And falling over forty feet will kill you, lass."

If he didn't miss his mark, Devin would swear he caught a 'so what!' in her glimpse when she peeked at the floor far below, which efficiently brought him back to his original intentions. "Tell me more about you, Isabel."

Glancing out the window she replied absently, "There isn't much to tell."

"I don't believe that for a second."

"Well you should."

"Where were you born?"

Blinking, she looked at him then back out the window. "England."

Bullshit. "Where in England?"

"Devonshire."

Of course she'd have a quick response. "Right. And you came to America in what year?"

"1715."

"Was it a pleasurable voyage?"

"Enough so."

"Did you find Boston's harbor a nice port?"

"Not really." Isabel stopped short. An uncomfortable pause. "Had I landed in Boston."

Little liar. Play dumb Devin. "Oh, I'm sorry, I naturally assumed. Where did you make port?"

"Portsmouth."

"Ah. How was that then?"

"Very nice."

Isabel kept a steady thrum of believable words streaming from her mouth. Had to give her credit for that. "And was Calum waiting for you when you came ashore?"

"Perhaps."

"I see."

"You question as though you don't believe me."

"Yep."

"Why?"

Devin purposefully didn't move closer to her though he wanted to. "Because I'd hoped you would tell me the truth."

Without missing a beat she said, "But I have!"

"No you haven't. Again, was Calum there waiting for you when you came ashore?"

Obviously debating a moment she replied, "Perhaps he was."

"I see." With a wry grin he looked out the window, purposely not looking at her. "Why?"

"Why not?" she replied too hastily.

All the answer he'd needed.

Sighing, Isabel shifted position, obviously uncomfortable. "You're obviously looking for answers, Devin." He didn't look at her. "Look at me."

That he liked, so he did. Her eyes were fiery blue-purple now, defiant, curious. "Why, Isabel? I don't think you're being truthful. You're telling me what I want to hear."

Moving slowly toward her, a subliminal step, he continued, "Can't you offer me a small part of your truth?"

Spine straightened, lips drew together. She didn't like that question. "I am telling you the truth."

"Are you?"

Eyes narrowed, she responded, "Yes."

Gotta give her an A for effort however much she lied her cute little ass off. "So you got off the boat and met…no one. How'd that go?"

"It went fine." Chin up, she said, "I'm an independent woman after all."

"Of course you are." Devin moved a bit closer. "But I still find it unlikely that you traveled alone all the way from England or at the very least had someone to greet you once you arrived."

"Why is that so hard to believe?"

Reaching out, he ran one long loose curl through his fingers. "Have you looked at yourself lately? You're rather beautiful."

Sounding slightly winded she replied, "Thank you."

How polite of her. Devin wanted to rip this façade away. Figure out how she ended up with a man turned werewolf. How she ended up with Calum, a man on a mission to trap the beasts haunting him. Isabel had deep, dark secrets and he desperately wanted her to reveal them. Here. Now. Not in the future.

"I want to kiss you again, Isabel." Carefully, he twirled her hair strand up his finger. Bit by bit, reeled her in. Isabel didn't try to shift away. In fact, she moved closer. Her scent, skin, the way moonlight cast shadows on her face suddenly sharpened. Before she had a chance to deny him, Devin leaned in and brushed his lips across hers.

No response.

Just about every part of him wanted to implement magic right now, make her melt like she did before but she'd asked him to be gentle with 'this' her. He feathered his lips over hers again. Come on, want me!

Nothing. Isabel simply stood there, her fingertips curling but her lips unresponsive. Cupping a hand behind her head, Devin deepened the kiss. This time she responded, barely. What? Would only magic make her respond? Screw that! Pushing her back against the wall, Devin cupped her face and kissed her with all he had.

Nothing. No response.

What the hell?

Running a hand up her side, he cupped the side of her breast. While he could have sworn he heard a purr Devin knew he also heard board cracking. Regardless, the feel of her skin, the way she tilted her head, allowed the kiss to deepen, kept him enthralled. Isabel kissed him now, her tender lips opening, welcoming. Devin wanted to bite, eat her alive, be inside her. The feeling came so fast he barely recognized it as his own.

Crack.

Deeper. More. Devin couldn't get enough of her.

Crack.

His hands found the top of her dress, started to unbutton. Quickly and efficiently, he had her cleavage exposed. Isabel groaned.

Crack.

Lips down her neck. Sweet. Hot. Perfect.

"Devin?"

Running his lips over the top of her breast, he reveled at the pure softness. God, she tasted good.

"Devin?"

Pulling down her dress, he nearly clamped his lips over her nipple before...

"Devin?"

Ignoring the plea he closed in, sucking deeply on

the tender nub. She didn't taste like he thought she would. No, she was rather tasteless.

"Damn it, Devin, snap out of it!"

Crude. Foreign. Very un-Isabel.

Suddenly, everything started shaking. Isabel vanished from his grasp, melting into the wall. Her visage was quickly replaced by Seth.

"Are you with me, man?"

Blinking, Devin tried to adjust to the site of Isabel turning into Seth. Shutting his mouth abruptly, he prayed he hadn't been sucking on thin air…or Seth for that matter!

Crack. The same sound he'd been hearing. Devin glanced around. Though he was still in the same part of the attic, the house was now whole. The cracking sound, a branch whipping against the window pane. "No, no, not yet." Spinning, he saw all his cousins were with him. He'd returned to the future. "Where is Isabel? Downstairs?"

Andrea shook her head. "No. You both vanished a few hours ago. You're the only one to return."

CHAPTER 10

"A few hours? I've been gone weeks," Devin replied. Grumbling, he headed downstairs. Had he gained any ground with the Isabel from the past? He definitely needed more time.

"Hello to you too," Leathan said.

They followed him down to the kitchen, every eager face curious.

"Did you see Tim this time?" Andrea asked.

That snapped him out of his own misery for a second. "No, hun. I'm sorry."

Blinking back a tear she nodded and said, "That's okay. I really didn't think you would after what Isabel said about him being trapped in the house."

Seth squeezed her shoulder. "Don't worry, sis. We'll get him back."

"So you were gone weeks, eh?" Leathan shook his head. "That's amazing."

"How went the 'wooing' of Isabel?" Seth winked. "Bet that drove you crazy."

Ignoring Seth, Devin reached into the fridge and grabbed a beer. Twisting off the cap he took a long swig. The last thing he wanted to do right now was chat with his cousins about his time with Isabel in the past. Better yet, how little he'd actually found out about where her former fiancé/lycan was.

"So what did you learn?" Leathan asked.

Sitting on one of the island stools, he shrugged. "Not nearly as much as I'd hoped to."

"How'd it go with Calum?" Seth asked.

"Better than I would've expected," Devin replied. "He's actually a pretty decent guy. Treats his workers well."

"Now that surprises me," Leathan said.

Seth grabbed a beer as well. "And the journal, did you find it?"

"Yeah, actually." Devin said. "In fact, as of a few days ago, he'd only completed about one quarter of it."

Andrea raised her brows. "He's still writing it? Well, I suppose that makes perfect sense. So that means it's definitely here somewhere if you saw him writing it."

"Not necessarily," Seth shook his head. "Devin could've seen him writing it in the 1700's but he never finished it."

"True," Andrea concurred.

"But it's best for now to assume he did," Leathan added. "And keep looking."

"So I take it you didn't confront Calum again when you went back. How'd that go anyway? Did he recognize you at all? Show off any of his dark magic?" Seth asked.

Devin drained the beer. He really didn't want to talk about any of this. Instead, he'd rather focus on trying to contact Isabel's spirit. Damn, he missed her already. "Listen guys, I'm wiped. Gonna—"

"No you're not," Leathan interrupted. "Tired or not you're still a paranormal investigator and Andrea's husband is still trapped in this house. Not to mention, you've got a monster after you...or did you forget that?"

Well, at least Leathan had his mind where it should be. That didn't make less the fact Devin wanted to crawl into the nearest bed. But maybe he could kill two birds with one stone. "Alright, why don't we run an EVP session, see if we can make contact with Isabel."

The way Andrea eyed Devin he knew she knew exactly what he was all about.

"EVP session? Count me in!"

Everyone turned to see the source of the voice. Dakota! Leathan's face split into a wide grin and he scooped up his new wife, neatly plunking her on his lap when he sat. "Glad you made it," he murmured.

Devin grabbed another beer while they kissed hello. He couldn't blame Leathan for kissing her so soundly. Only a year ago, Devin wanted to do the same. Dakota had this certain eroticism that tended to drive guys crazy. Her blue black hair cut in a stylish bob, tall willowy figure and striking features didn't hurt any. Funny though, for the first time ever, Devin was amazed how blunt her features appeared compared to Isabel's. How much louder and brazen than Isabel she seemed.

Then again, Dakota was a modern day woman who owned a paranormal social networking sight and hunted ghosts for fun. Isabel was a woman from a different era who'd had to learn how to survive in a very transitional age.

Dakota's gaze finally fell on Devin, Emerald eyes sharp. "For the most part I've been kept up to date on things." She wiggled her cell in the air. "But last I heard you'd vanished back in time. What gives? Isabel didn't return with you this time I take it?"

"No, afraid not." Devin nodded when Seth plunked some paranormal detection equipment down on the counter. "Gonna try to make contact now."

Dakota exchanged a look with Leathan. Was it that apparent he was smitten with Isabel? Devin couldn't really deny it. While it hadn't been that long, he really liked what he knew of her…both from the past and the present.

The sun was setting and an orange glow covered the island countertop. As Devin organized the equipment his mind wandered to just a few hours past. Walking through this very room with her. Teasing, talking, pancakes. Now it'd all vanished. And even though the room he'd stood in before had literally been the shell, the current room with all of its appliances felt more the shell for her not being present.

Not yet anyways.

Eying the EMF (Elecro Magnetic Field) detector and EVP (Electro Voice Phenomena) recorder and a twist top flashlight she could turn on if possible, Devin wondered if it'd be enough.

"Camera's rolling too," Leathan provided.

Devin nodded. He really hoped they'd be able to make contact with Isabel. No matter what people might think, it typically took a great deal of time and patience to catch evidence of an entity. Then again, this house was part of Calum's curse so there stood a very good chance they wouldn't have to wait long.

Nobody said a word. This was his gig.

With both the EMF and EVP going and flashlight ready, Devin said, "Isabel, it's Devin. Please, if you can, try to communicate with us…with me. If you step close to this box—" He touched the EMF detector. "It should blink. If you speak—" He touched the EVP recorder. "We should be able to hear your voice in this."

The flashlight turned on.

"Niiiice," Seth murmured. "Good girl."

A ripple of pleasure went through Devin's body. "That's right, you've got it."

The flashlight turned off. All five green lights on EMF detector lit and stayed solid.

"That's great," Dakota whispered.

The flashlight lit again and slowly started to spin. The EMF flickered to one light then back to a solid five. The temperature started to drop.

Leathan pulled out a digital thermometer and winked. Carefully, he placed it on the countertop. Seventy degrees. Sixty-six degrees. Sixty-two degrees. Fifty-eight degrees. A low rumble started, as though thunder rolled in the distance. Then it vanished.

"Touch my arm," Devin said softly, holding out his arm. "You know who I am, Isabel."

Sniffing deeply, he prayed to smell her scent. Instead, the fine hairs on his arm started to lift. Closing his eyes, he smiled. When he opened them, the outline of a human form slowly wavered beside him.

"Let me see more of you, Isabel," he whispered. "Please. I miss you."

Devin didn't care if the others heard him. She needed to hear. Gradually, bit by bit, the form wavered, becoming more solid. Her long blond hair, shimmering golden curls, the shape of her face. Isabel was right there, materializing before his eyes. And she smiled, he could see it already.

Before he knew what was happening a black light slithered out from Seth. Instead of fear, Devin saw only interest when she looked in his direction.

His reaction, however, was far different. What the hell was Seth doing? Thump. Thump. Devin's heart started racing.

Between Seth and Leathan stood Calum's ghost.

Leathan had started chanting something. Where Seth's black aura had sparked to life, a deep pulsing blue surrounded Leathan.

Sonofabitch! Dark magic.

There hovered Calum, a look of approval on his otherworldly smug face. When his eyes narrowed on Devin he could all but hear the ghost ask, "And why aren't you using your gift, lad?"

Truth told, even if he did use his dark magic right now…he had no clue what his cousins were up to.

Leathan's chanting increased. Latin. A language that apparently came built in when one became a warlock. With the chanting, his aura expanded and surrounded Seth's aura and Isabel's ghostly figure. The temperature dropped until Devin could see his heavy breaths puff on the air. Isabel still didn't appear frightened. No, at this point, all her attention was focused on Calum. Calum, who apparently was not part of whatever was happening save as an observer.

Interestingly, as his cousins used their dark gifts, Devin began to feel something akin to strength fill his body, a distinct feeling of power and anger and determination. In some ways, it was similar to the feeling he'd had in the basement of this house with the Isabel from the past. Except then, he'd channeled all of these feelings into lust and getting what he desired.

The low rumble started once more. This time it grew louder, a steady drum roll that soon started to vibrate the floors and walls. Pans clanked against the walls. Dishes clattered. The more the rumble increased, the calmer Devin felt.

"Grrrrrrrrrr."

Devin didn't have to turn around to know what was coming. A smooth well-honed rage filled his body. His hearing became acute. Mangy mutt filled his nostrils. Turning—not hesitating for a second—he flung out a hand. Blood red surrounded him then spiked out and muzzled the wide gaping ethereal fangs of the wolf before it clamped onto Isabel. Glaring, he directed all his anger at the huge Lycan head coming out of the wall. Their eyes met and Devin knew his eyes blazed forth the same deep ruby red as the beasts. He also knew that their rage and hatred of one another was equally matched.

The ghostly werewolf flung its head back and forth and tried to slam against Isabel. Between Seth, Leathan and Devin's magical protection, it wasn't getting anywhere near her. Leathan started chanting something different.

The beast grew more furious.

When Devin once more met its eyes, he keenly remembered the forest by the river. The need for blood. Death. Destruction. The overwhelming urge to conquer and defeat. Yet the strongest emotion then as it was now remained the need to protect.

Devin used his free hand to wrap Isabel in his aura as well. Through that link, he gained the added strength of his cousins. With a furious roar he pushed all his hatred at the wolf. The muzzle snapped off and the head went whipping back into the wall as though it'd been shot at with a warhead. A loud whine echoed off the wall and the wolfish visage vanished. Bits of plaster fell to the floor.

Isabel remained, caught in all three auras. Nobody could question that her expression was one of triumph and pride. Leathan said a few more words and he and Seth pulled their auras away.

Only his remained around her. Isabel smiled. She knew exactly who he was. This ghostly self of hers knew everything they'd been through together.

"Isabel," he whispered again. "I miss you, need you. How do I release you from this house? Please tell me."

As his rage vanished, so did the power he'd used on the Lycan. When the last of his red aura washed from her form and left only the dying rays of sunlight to splinter through her, Isabel once more looked Calum's way then vanished.

"Bravo! Bravo!" Calum's ghost clapped. "Well done, chaps!"

Devin sat slowly, still staring at the place from which Isabel had vanished. Where a year ago—even a few weeks ago—he would've spit in Calum's face, now Devin didn't quite hold the same anger he did before. How could he when he'd seen a different side of his ancestor in the eighteenth century?

"Wow, that was extremely intense," Andrea said. "What exactly did you guys just do?"

"They helped my girl," Calum provided. "Used their magic and protected her from the creature in a fashion far better than I've ever been able to do. Now she can manifest at will without that beastie being right on top of her." Calum nearly cackled. "And, they managed to desensitize her better than I ever could. It'll be a lot harder for that damn dog to track her down within these walls now. Really, very well done my boys!"

Devin turned his head slowly and narrowed his eyes. "Do you mean to tell me she's been trying to evade this werewolf ghost for three hundred years within these walls?"

"That's precisely what he means," Adlin said appearing out of thin air. This was the first they'd seen of his ghost since the Victorian. It seemed he was determined to keep a close eye on Calum. More importantly, he was determined to keep an eye on those descended from him...of course, only because Adlin adored Calum's parents so much.

"Oh, hell," Calum muttered. "Guess the whole crew's here."

"When I can come I do," Adlin replied. "I wish I could be here more often. Someone needs to protect everyone from you."

"Always the same tale, old man." Calum adjusted his top hat. "I still don't understand why you feel the need to tag along during every haunting."

"Aye, but you do, laddie." Adlin's white robes dusted the floor. "Only solid bit of good magic in your life."

"I don't need good magic!"

"Humph. So says you."

While Devin was near furious with Calum for trapping Isabel in this house for three centuries trying to get a word in edgewise between this warlock and wizard would take a miracle.

"So it's a love match between Devin and Isabel this time, eh?" Calum asked.

"Well, why not?" Adlin said. "The very least they deserve."

Both kept rambling on but as their words grew more distant, so too did their forms.

The Georgian Embrace

"No!" Devin said. "I need more answers!"

Too late. Calum and Adlin were gone. Zapped from this plane of existence as quickly and efficiently as they had been in the Victorian.

"Mmm, that blows." Leathan trailed a finger up Dakota's arm.

Dakota offered a small grin. "There's nothing quite like the after effects of you boys using your powers."

Seth yawned and rested his chin in his hand, propped up by his elbow. Devin's stomach issued a loud growl. Awe hell. He'd forgotten this part. Then again, it'd been a year since he'd used his gift to such a degree. Things were just as they'd always been…Lethan became aroused, Seth tired and him? Starved!

Andrea shooed Leathan and Dakota out of the kitchen saying, "Girl, pick any room upstairs and let him…do whatever he needs to but I better not hear anything. Ick!"

Next, Andrea opened the fridge and pulled out a bowl of cut up assorted fruits and plunked it front of Devin with a wink. "See, I prepared. No need for you to get fat because of your gift."

Popping a piece of cantaloupe into his mouth he watched her wake up an already sleeping Seth and drag him out of the room, most likely to the couch.

Damn the hunger. It overwhelmed. He could barely think of anything save the next bite of food. Why'd he get the gluttonous aftershocks and Leathan the erotic? Must be nice. Even sleeping like Seth would beat this extreme need for food.

Andrea came back into the kitchen and sat across from him. "Taste good?"

"Where's a homemade bagel when you really need it?" he mumbled around a mouthful of strawberries.

Crossing her arms over her chest Andrea smiled. "You'll thank me later that I kept it healthy." For a few minutes, she merely watched him eat. When she spoke he knew she'd debated whether or not to say anything. "Are you going to be okay, Devin?"

He finished chewing and sat back. "Honestly? Had you asked me that when I first arrived here I would've said, "Probably not." Grabbing his beer he took a sip. "Now, yes. I'm going to be just fine."

Andrea's brows lowered. "What I mean is...will you be able to get back to your old self a little bit?"

"You mean the happy-go-lucky Devin you knew? Doubt it." He plopped a blueberry in his mouth, chewed and swallowed. "But I can tell you one thing, if anyone inspires me to, it's Isabel. No offense."

"None taken." Andrea sighed. "So what you're essentially telling me is that a woman who you may never know beyond your experience with this house is our only hope to have somewhat of the 'old' Devin back?"

Devin noticed the dark rings beneath Andrea's eyes, her slight weight loss and chose his next words carefully. "Despite what happens in this house, I've decided to embrace my new gift so one way or another I'll be somewhat as you remember. Want me to cook one of my famous breakfasts now?"

Eyes narrowed, a little grin broke free and Andrea shook her head. "Oh, no. Nice try!"

Smiling he replied, "C'mon, can't you hear the bacon sizzling already? Smell the bread toasting?"

His stomach growled again and they laughed. Standing, she put the bowl of fruit in his hands and pointed upstairs. "To your room with the fruit. Like Leathan, soon enough you'll need sleep too. Why Seth skips everything and crashes immediately beats me!"

Devin looked at her. "You gonna be alright, cuz? I know this is rougher on you than any of us."

"Yes," she said softly. "After what I just witnessed, I know you guys will get him back for me. Now go." She pushed him toward the door. "Eat and sleep."

"Okay, okay."

Even as he walked down the hall and trudged up the stairs he could hear her sniffling in the kitchen. Devin tried not to think about the fact that this house had already changed him and if it had done so to a man not trapped inside its walls…what would it do to a man that was?

CHAPTER 11

Lightning flashed. A rumble of thunder bubbled overhead. Heavy raindrops hit the window. The curtains blew in on a warm gust of wind and swept across Devin's shoulder.

Cracking open an eye, he realized he'd fallen asleep with the near empty bowl of fruit on his stomach and a half eaten strawberry in his hand. Another flash of lightening revealed that he'd stripped down to nothing. Unreal. What sorta guy ate a bowl of fruit alone with no clothes on?

After he peeled the half dried, sticky strawberry from his hand he put it in the bowl and placed it on the table next to him. About to sit up, Devin froze when something brushed over his palm. Another gust of wind blew through the open window and the sheer curtains floated in. With a heavy blink, he stared closer. Was that Isabel standing beside them?

When he blinked again, she was gone. Had she even been there? Lord knows, he wanted her to appear. "Isabel," he whispered. "Are you here?"

Something brushed over his palm again. This time it felt warm...almost like a tongue. Suddenly, he got the impression she was there, licking the juice. Though he stared at his palm, there was nothing there. His cock didn't believe him and began to stir to life.

Taking a deep breath, Devin repeated, "Isabel, are you here?"

Thunder clapped again overhead but he swore he heard her whisper, "Yes."

Devin's mouth fell open when he felt a hand graze the side of his face, neck, then collarbone. The air chilled. His skin heated. Hands placed by his side, he didn't move a muscle. He'd heard of ethereal sex but...seriously? Could it really exist? The thought of Isabel's ghost taking advantage of him just about made him release then and there.

Lips. Warm. Trailing across his chest. Devin closed his eyes. Holy crap! His member was beyond ready. But for what exactly? Sex with residual energy? He almost laughed but didn't when a tongue flicked his nipple. He arched. Hell that felt good. Open your eyes. See if she's there. But he didn't want to. Why risk her vanishing? The tongue swirled away from his nipple, down the center of his midriff. It didn't matter if his eyes were open—they were rolling back in his head.

"Yes," he whispered. "Yes."

Soft hands on his hips. Thighs. Climbing. Tongue going lower. "Yes!"

Then nothing. Devin opened his eyes slowly and saw only his rigid piece standing to attention. "Isabel?"

Another flash of lightning. Another clap of thunder. Rain poured harder. Where had she gone? Was she trying to manifest energy to do this to him? He knew damned well an electrical storm could aide in manifestations. But how could he help? Yeah, he could turn on the lights, give her more energy to draw off of or...

Devin closed his eyes again and focused on his gift. It was most likely too soon for such a thing, but he didn't intend to use nearly as much. Inhaling, he drew it in, pulled forth the feeling of power, sexual need, lust, desire. Culminating it in his own little light bulb of raw energy he slowly, carefully exhaled and released. The whole time he visualized Isabel. Her beautiful smiling face.

When he opened his eyes it was not her smiling face he saw.

But one of lust and equal need.

She kept repeating, "Can you see me? Can you feel me?"

Within the dim red light he'd provided, her form slowly started to appear. The warmth of her thighs as she straddled him became obvious, the delicate touch of her small hands upon his chest. First, he saw her slender legs, then the tiny cinch of her toned belly. Inch by inch, her breasts appeared, full and luscious, with perfectly aroused nipples. Next, the gracefully curve of her neck, the lovely planes of her face… then the hair appeared. A living thing, it drifted in long, floating wisps.

Damn!

"Can you see me? Feel me?" Isabel continued.

Instead of answering, he reached up and put his hand to her heart. As Devin suspected, he couldn't feel any skin but the air around her almost had a soft density about it…like the feeling one might have if they lightly brushed their palm over the cool, clear surface of water.

Isabel smiled and said, "I feel your energy." She closed her eyes, sighed, and then reopened them. "I miss you too."

When she leaned down so close their lips were inches apart, Devin could see the violet-blue swimming inside, the red of magic highlighted the red of her lips, the blush of her cheeks.

"I feel your heat against me," he said even as the hot breath of his words met the cold air of her ghostly presence. But warmth spread over the one place he needed it to most.

Isabel's lips came close but didn't touch. Her thighs tightened. Her breasts grazed him. Devin felt the smooth, tight cheeks of her backside brush him. "So many times you and I. Now this first time we touch in bits," Her tongue flicked out and brushed his lower lip, "and pieces."

Running his hands along her ethereal form he replied, "Good bits. Good pieces."

Letting the energy channel through him, Devin pushed gently at her hips, nudged her back, down. Let this work. Let me feel her. Give us this at least.

"Devin." Isabel's voice seemed to float on air. "Yes."

When her straddling form drifted lower breathing became more difficult. She lifted, then slowly lowered. Head flung back, a low moan erupted. He'd never seen anything so hot in his life. Somewhere in the midst of all that beautiful otherworldly energy was his cock. It had, to the best of his sight, vanished inside her.

"Feel me," she murmured. Sight alone was doing a good job. When her head fell forward and their eyes locked a pure jolt of lust hit him.

Then he felt. And felt. And felt.

Like nothing else he'd ever experienced. While not the tight heat of a woman, Isabel's spirit caressed, surrounded. Slickness and pressure stroked while she rode.

"Isabel." Groaning, he grasped the sheets by his

sides when he couldn't find purchase on her hips. The way she moved. Up, down, around, fluid energy, drawing him up and up, harder and harder. He wanted to wrap his hands around her small waist, force her down until she wailed. He wanted her beneath him, crying out in tortured pleasure. But no, this time was hers. His time to cry out in tortured pleasure.

"Always so good," she moaned, her body moved faster, her pleasure obvious in every thrust of her hips, grind of her body.

Panting, he twisted the sheets tighter, thrust his body up sharply. When a strangled gasp of pleasure came from Isabel and her body arched, Devin cried out in the perfect mix of pain and pleasure, his body shaking with release.

He was so lost in pleasure that it took several minutes for him to realize she'd grown quiet. Though his red light had faded, between its dull glow and the lightning flashes he saw the large ethereal wolf stalking around the bed. It's now yellow eyes glowed as it watched them. It paced with hackles raised. Devin knew it couldn't get near her now. Still, it was here. Hovering. Making its presence known.

Her former fiancé had watched them make love.

A low growl filled the room. Surprised, Devin realized it had come from him. Isabel's form slowly faded but not that of the wolf. No, it watched, waited, invited. It had, somehow, made what they'd just done feel dirty. Because it could. Thump. It sat and watched him from the corner of the room, yellow eyes glowing in the dark.

Devin didn't move but stared back. In some ways, he wanted the otherworldly animal to approach. He wanted to battle, fight, and taste its blood.

So he waited.

"Don't wait. Throw the water on him!"

The wolf vanished when icy cold water covered his face and blurred his vision. He sat up and yelled, "What the bloody hell!"

"Is he awake then, missus?"

"Certainly looks it."

Wiping a hand across his face, Devin blinked against the blinding sun. "What the?"

Andy and John peered down. Behind them he spied the roofless Georgian. He was back in the eighteenth century.

Just like that.

"Sorry to wake you like this boys. I didn't know what else to do." Isabel sounded as good and pure as the Virgin Mary. He'd just had her. She wasn't nearly as sweet as she led everyone to believe. Yet there she stood, as fresh and innocent as could be, staring down at him. And, in her defense, this Isabel was probably still a virgin.

Still.

Best to focus. The last thing he remembered in this time they had been starting to kiss the night before after a bit of late night house frolicking. He sat up and rubbed the back of his head. It hurt like hell. "What happened?"

"Very good question." Isabel crouched beside him. "I came out early this morn to look over what had been done to the house and here I found you. Imagine my surprise!"

"Yeah, yeah." When Devin narrowed his eyes, Isabel promptly stood and dusted off her skirts. "Best you boys get him down and fed before Calum finds out he spent the night up here."

John and Andy tried to help him up but he brushed them away. "Just make sure the 'missus' gets down safely. After all, a woman shouldn't be up this high in a house not all built."

Devin winked when Isabel's eyes met his. A tight little frown twisted her lips as she accepted John's assistance down the stairs. He and Andy followed. Once out of the house, Devin excused himself, grabbed a change of makeshift clothes and headed for the river. Why the hell couldn't he have awakened in modern day Maine? A warm shower and a hot cup of coffee would've done him good. As he walked down the path, Devin couldn't help but admit that no matter where he awoke his thoughts were still all about Isabel and to be here with her mortal self wasn't really such a bad thing.

The woman had really gotten to him.

At the river's edge he stripped off what he'd been wearing—grateful he had been wearing something to begin with—and waded in. The cold water soothed his overheated skin and he sighed in contentment. He liked that it was deep in this time period. Devin dove beneath the water and watched the current sweep by him in little bits of plant life and fish. When he resurfaced, the sun warmed his face.

"You've some nerve!"

Ah, there she was. So stunning it blew his mind. He swam over and found a spot that remained deep near the water's edge. "How do you figure?"

Hands on hips, blond hair pulled back, Isabel replied, "You know how I figure."

Devin grabbed a tree root that'd snaked its way into the water and shook his head. "I guess I need reminding."

"First to touch me as you did then...then..."

"Then what, Isabel?"

Not moving, she stood near the shore. Close enough that he could reach out and touch her. She looked down her nose at him. "You shouldn't have touched me that way again."

Tired of the coy game, he thought it time to be direct. Devin slicked back his wet hair and shrugged. "You knew I would. Why are you acting as though I created some sort of affront on your person? Seriously, are you that naïve?"

Isabel breathed deeply and shook her head but didn't step away. "You passed out."

Enough. Time to dive in head first. "I traveled to the future or should I say another dimension. To a reality that exists when the house is completely built."

Isabel stared down, expression blank.

"What do you make of that?" he said.

Her mouth fell open. She blinked rapidly. If nothing else, she appeared lost. Wits suddenly gathered, she said, "You fell. Hit your head. Now you make no sense."

Walking slowly, he climbed the shore bank. "I make sense and I think that you know it."

Isabel started walking backwards, shaking her head. "I have no idea what you mean. Of that you can rest assured."

"So you know nothing of why Calum is building this house?"

Her eyes flickered down, took in his nudity. Though a blush stole over her face, Isabel met his eyes directly. "No, I don't."

"Oh really?" Devin pulled on his clothes and laid it on the line. "Listen, I've met you in the future. You told me everything about your upbringing in Virginia, traveling up here, meeting your fiancé, then Calum."

Eyes round as saucers she began shaking her head. "That's impossible. You speak nonsense."

Before she could turn away, he grabbed her arm. "Do I? Am I wrong about any of it?"

Startled, scared, her eyes turned a dark shade of violet. "Of course you are. You've no idea what you speak of!"

He pulled her closer and shook his head. "Then why are you responding like this? Why do I see the truth plain as day in your eyes?"

Eyes narrowed she tried to yank away her arm but he kept a solid hold. "You see only a truth you've made up. I act as I do because your insanity is most obvious. You're quite mad!"

"Lose the English accent, Isabel. You were born in Jamestown, Virginia. Your ma died in childbirth. Your da raised you and your four siblings."

Isabel shook her head and spoke. Nothing came out.

Devin continued. "Eventually, you'd had enough of Jamestown so disguised as a lad you traveled to Boston where you transformed yourself into a proper English lass and nanny to boot."

"How could you..." Her words trailed off. She kept shaking her head.

"You have a gift with the deaf. Ended up in Portsmouth."

"No. No. This is absurd." Isabel yanked free her arm, spun and stormed away. "You're wrong. Clearly addled."

Devin didn't chase after her but continued. "In Portsmouth you met your fiancé. Turns out he had a bit of a bite."

Isabel stopped short, not moving for several moments. Slowly, she turned. The confusion in her eyes turned to steely resolve. "I refuse to run. Trust me, I've thought long and hard about such. As much as I planned to stand tall and brave, honestly, I thought when you finally found me, I'd run screaming in the opposite direction." Breathing deeply, she continued. "Granted, it may help that it's daylight but truth told I've no desire to run. I hate you and will stand and fight."

Hmmm. She did know how to surprise him! But...huh?

"Okay," he replied slowly. "I suppose the first thing I should ask is why you hate me and thought you'd run?"

Feet pounding across the grass, she came at him so fast he almost stepped back. Within a foot, she stopped, glared up and said with a one hundred percent southern drawl. "You're a blasted wolf! A man monster!"

Didn't see that one coming. Carefully, making no sudden movements, he replied, "I can assure you I'm no wolf. As to the man monster part, that's debatable."

Isabel's eyes narrowed. "I've seen you transform and we both know it."

A flash of fear overtook. "You did? Where? When?"

"You know precisely when." Looking him up and down with contempt she continued. "And you know well when."

"I thought that was a dream," he murmured. By the river that night. It had to be. "Was I really a wolf?

You saw me turn into one?"

"Of course I did!"

Isabel spat in his face.

Devin froze. Had she really just done that? Incredulous, he reached up and wiped the wet fluid from his cheek. Sudden rage welled and he grabbed her shoulders. "What the hell is your problem? As far as I can remember I didn't harm you. All I could think about was protecting you!"

"Protecting me!" Isabel struggled within his grasp. "You tried to kill me!"

Shocked, he released her and shook his head. "No." He backed up a step and kept shaking his head. "I would never do that."

Would I have? How did he really know?

Tears streamed down her face. "But you did! So I ran. I've been running ever since."

"I don't understand. This makes no sense," he muttered.

"How could you even say that, Lucas?"

His head snapped up. "What?"

"You heard me."

"Aye, I did. You called me Lucas."

Swallowing hard, she wiped away a tear. "What else would I call you?"

"Um...Devin?"

"That I will never do again," she said, eyes accusing. "This deviousness is terrible. Even more horrible than what you've become."

Okay, now this was getting really confusing. "I seriously don't understand where you're coming from, Isabel."

"An Irishman? Why the disguise? I didn't realize your sort could so completely transform its appearance." She sniffed in derision. "I thought you were so proud to be southern?"

It couldn't be. But that's exactly what it was. Isabel thought he was Lucas and Devin would bet just about anything that Lucas was her fiancé turned Lycan.

So the story unravels. Good.

"And here you told us you hadn't met your fiancé until you'd stepped off the boat in Portsmouth," Devin murmured. "I wonder why you said that."

Frowning, Isabel seemed perched in suspension. Perhaps deciding how to kill him here and now?

"Isabel, my name is Devin. I am not Lucas. I am however, one of Calum's ancestors. The reason I'm here is because Calum managed to trap your fiancé in the house currently being built."

As if she didn't hear him Isabel said, "What I'd like to know is how you can disguise yourself in another body altogether. Such deceitfulness. Cunning!"

Devin tried to grab her hand but Isabel backed up three steps and cast a nervous eye to the sky. Was she just now worrying when the sun would be going down? When night might swallow them and reintroduce her to her fiancé's darker nature?

"Look at me, Isabel," he said calmly. "Look into my eyes. Hear my voice. I am Devin. Nobody else."

She bit her lip and for a split second she appeared defeated, confused, before all question vanished from her eyes. "You are Lucas. A coward who hides in many forms."

"Then take me to Calum now."

A flash of interest entered her eyes. "I will not!"

"Ah, so you know that the beast that hunts him is

the same man that is your fiancé."

"As do you, Lucas." She backed up more, edging toward the forest. "Calum has been good to me. You used me!"

This was obviously a no win situation.

Only one thing to do.

Centering himself, Devin called on his dark magic and used it much more forcibly than he had before in this time period.

CHAPTER TWELVE

Isabel heard the wind blow through the forest. Saw the strange crimson light glowing in Lucas's eyes. How could he have fooled her so entirely? Not for a split second since she'd met Devin had she even suspected. *I cared for him! How many times will I be played for the fool?*

Now he would kill her.

Clouds rolled in overhead, dark and boiling. Leaves rattled restlessly. A pulsing red aura appeared to glow around Devin…Lucas. The man beast she'd been running from for so long.

"Enough!"

Isabel whipped around. "Calum. Thank goodness."

But he wasn't focused on her. "Enough!" he bellowed again and Isabel swore the ground trembled. Eyes on Lucas once more, she watched as the light dwindled and his eyes returned to smoky green.

Nodding, he said, "Forgive, Calum. I needed to get you here fa—"

Isabel stumbled back as an arch of lightning shot from Calum and flung Lucas far into the air. He landed with a splash and sunk into the stream. Kicking and flailing, he tried to surface. Calum walked to the edge of the river, eyes black as night, aura even darker.

Isabel looked frantically between the two.

Lucas was going nowhere.

Calum was drowning the werewolf here and

now.

Flashes of memory started to bombard Isabel. Devin kissing her in the basement. Devin by this very river dancing with her. Devin in the house last night talking of the families that might live there.

No. No. No. Something wasn't right here. "Stop!"

But Calum—despite her stepping in front of him—was ruthless for another minute or so. Then, when she thought all lost, Lucas was suddenly ripped up out of the water and tossed alongside of them, his sodden body thumping to the ground.

As he sputtered and gasped for air, a gush of water rushed from his mouth. Lying on his back, he stared up at them silently. The wind ceased. Clouds dispersed.

"If you ever implement magic like that to summon me again, you won't live to see another day." Calum straightened his jacket, eyes sharp and direct. "You're no wolf. Or particularly good at embracing the dark side for that matter. Who are you? Speak quickly."

"Warlock," Devin croaked and closed his eyes. "Relative."

A flood of relief washed over Isabel. Devin wasn't Lucas. Calum would know. But...

Calum's eyes narrowed and he continued to study Devin closely. When Devin slowly sat and looked up, Isabel was shocked to see from Calum a flicker of recognition and...emotion? "You are from the future." He stepped closer and whispered, "And you have her eyes. How did I not see it before?"

"Whose eyes?" Devin said.

"My Anna's. Just like my Anna's."

Isabel's mouth fell open. She had heard Calum speak of his Scottish bride. How he had left she and their son behind in Scotland to live with her family when he fled the three creatures of the night hunting him. All part of the curse lain upon him by his former coven. Now through the use of time-travel, he lured each to a different era and trapped them in a house.

Regrettably, with this particular creature, a Lycan…she had become involved. To Calum's credit he had taken her under his care and kept her safe. After all, the creature who had claimed to fall in love with her also desired not only to destroy Calum himself but his very lineage.

No! It couldn't be! When she looked between Calum and Devin however, Isabel saw the truth plain as day. How had she not seen the similarities in their build? The defined set of their jaw? Quite honestly, how often did six-foot-three, broad shouldered, exceedingly handsome men come along? Never mind two in one year!

"Devin's one of your ancestors," she whispered. Swallowing hard she stared at the bedraggled man sitting on the ground. "And Lucas is set to destroy him."

"Ya think, lass?" Devin concurred sarcastically. "About damn time everyone saw the whole picture." He continued to mutter. "Been spit at in the face, nearly drowned, bunch of bullshit."

Calum merely crossed his arms over his chest as Devin ranted on and stood, still dripping wet. "Nevermind being flung back and forth in time. Damn house. Dunno if I'm coming or going. Have had enough of this crap."

"Enough."

Devin stopped talking at Calum's firm word.

"Come." Calum started walking. "We'll continue this conversation in my tent where I know it's safe."

Isabel didn't look at Devin but swiftly followed Calum. She wasn't sure why she suddenly felt so shy or awkward. Well, some of it was because she'd accused him of being a liar, a wolf and there was that spit in his face to contend with. Perhaps he'd simply let that one go. Why not? She'd been in her right...sort of.

"This isn't over, lassie," he said softly from behind.

Ignoring his overwhelming presence Isabel tried to catch up with Calum but he stayed at least ten feet ahead. Devin, however, had no such issues keeping pace and walked up alongside her. Figuring he'd launch into more swears and negative words she jutted forth her chin and kept up a steady stride.

But he never said another word. His silence accomplished far more than words ever could. Isabel tried not to think about the fact that a warlock from the future walked beside her. That he'd so valiantly been trying to woo her. That he'd kissed her in the basement of the house. *He's not Lucas. Everything I've come to feel for him hasn't been erased. He's really Devin!* She tried to ignore those last thoughts. Tried to ignore how elated she really was about the news.

When at last they arrived at the tent, Calum invited her in as well. Why that surprised her, Isabel couldn't say. She sat in a chair beside Devin and watched Calum dig in his trunk. He pulled out a bottle of wine, three tin cups and set them on the desk. After sitting behind the desk, he removed the cap, poured the smooth red liquid into each cup and pushed two across.

Calum looked at Devin and went straight to the point. "Tell me your story."

Devin downed the wine in one long gulp, set the cup on the desk, and pushed it Calum's way. "What, you don't already know?"

Calum refilled the cup and pushed it back. "Tell me."

Devin sipped this time and set the cup down. When his gaze met Calum's a little shiver went down Isabel's spine. These two did indeed possess the same ruthlessness.

"Well," Devin said. "There are three of us. All from the twenty-first century. My cousin has already gone up against the vampire." Arching a brow, he took another sip. "Now apparently it's my turn with the lycan. I can only imagine what my other cousin will face. Mind giving me a head's up? Then again, I might never see my cousin again to tell him his fate, eh?"

Calum took a small sip, sat back and contemplated Devin. His deep, dark eyes searched and prodded. Devin, in return, did the same.

Should I speak? Do I really want to? While Isabel appreciated the pure power she knew surrounded her, a cut-throat up front southern upbringing and real life experience got the better. "Enough boys. What I'd like to know from you, Calum...how did you not know right away Devin was one of yours? And Devin...why not confront Calum right away with what you knew?"

"I can answer both," Calum replied, eyes still glued to Devin's. "I didn't know Devin was one of mine because I wasn't looking. Foolish that. I'll not make the same mistake again. And Devin did confront me right away but it was misunderstood. Don't you remember? Why did he not confront me yet again? Simple. Because of you, Isabel."

Me? Though she glanced at Devin his gaze remained on Calum. "Is that true?"

"Aye," Devin replied, his gaze slowly settling on her. "Do you truly want to know why? It might totally shock you."

"Yes, of course I do."

"Because, according to you, we fall in love. Telling Calum the truth of things in this time could disrupt that."

The clinical way he said it, his eyes still steely cold from dealing with Calum's magic, made her reply come easily. "I highly doubt we fall in love."

"Don't." As if he realized how hard he sounded Devin said in a softer tone, "You told me we do and I believe you. Truly, it's not such a far-fetched notion."

"I told you we do?" Isabel shook her head then sipped the wine. "Rest assured, I've told you no such thing."

"But you did. Three hundred years from now."

She and Calum stared incredulously at Devin. "You can't be serious!"

"I am." Devin shrugged. "Through your ghost. Well, sort of. Through you traveling forward in time with me. Then you vanish. But your ghost is still here."

Calum started mumbling to himself and whipped out his journal. Frowning, Isabel said, "Why are you writing in that now? You can't possibly believe what he says!"

"Why not?" Devin asked. "Is it really such an extreme idea considering you were engaged to a werewolf?"

Oh, he had her there. Regardless. She becomes a ghost! That was about the last thing she wanted to hear after all she'd been through in life. Surely God would welcome her into Heaven and her time on earth would be through.

"So Isabel ends up haunting this house," Calum muttered, scribbling away. "Unbelievable."

But wait a minute. Wasn't the purpose of building this house to trap the very beast that hunted her and Calum? Why would she end up haunting it? It seemed Calum was coming to the same conclusion as he'd stopped writing and once more stared at Devin. Another sharp chill ran down her spine.

Devin swigged the rest of his second cup of wine. The set of his shoulders was more relaxed as was his tongue. "So you're starting to put the pieces together. Good."

Lord, she disliked men when they were in their cups. Was Devin a drinker by nature? Tempering a look of disgust she ignored her trepidation and asked, "Why not save us the time and come straight to the point?"

"I couldn't agree more," Calum said dryly.

"Fine." Devin sat back and crossed his ankles. "You." He nodded at Calum. "Trap Isabel in the house alongside your monster." Now it was Devin's turn to look disgusted. "I don't know how yet but sure as hell, somehow she's a ghost in this house alongside the wolf and you're to blame for it."

"Impossible. I'd never!" Calum said.

"Oh, but you did." Devin nodded.

Isabel tried her best to keep a level head. "Why?"

"I don't know yet," Devin replied. "I'm still hoping your 'future you' will tell me."

"My future me?" Isabel laughed nervously. "I won't even ask what you mean by that."

"You should." Devin's green eyes met hers. "Seems to me we're all at a point that communicating is the only thing that'll see us survive this."

"He's correct," Calum said, a faint glimmer of admiration in his eyes. "He's my blood. My blood would not lie at this point. My blood would most likely be concerned with saving his own life."

"Damn straight!" Devin nodded at his cup. "More wine please."

Calum's eyes narrowed but Isabel didn't miss the flicker of pride in his eyes. What a complete disaster. Because if she didn't miss her mark…she herself was in the greatest danger if what Devin said was true. "How could I end up trapped in this house, Calum?"

"You wouldn't. I'd never allow it."

"How?" Devin repeated softly.

"There is no way," Calum stated. "The curse is only to trap the beast, no other."

"What if she had the stone?" Devin asked.

This time Calum took a deep swig of his drink. "That would be impossible."

"Well." Devin leaned forward and poured himself more wine. "In the future, she's got it."

"Impossible," Calum admonished.

"What stone?" She asked.

"It matters naught," Calum said.

Devin shook his head. "It matters much and damned if you don't know it."

"What stone?" She repeated, trying not to get

irritated. It served no purpose.

When Calum fumed but said nothing Devin continued, "There are three stones, each to trap the beast hunting Calum's descendant's. Each matches the magical aura of the future warlock. Mine is a red stone. This stone will be hidden somewhere in the world. Without it, the monster can never escape Calum's prison." Devin took another deep swig of his wine and wiped his mouth. "The first blue stone was found by a woman in the future. That unlocked the beast doomed to kill my cousin. As you might have guessed, his aura was blue."

Isabel contemplated this. She remembered well the color that'd surrounded Devin at the river. A strange shiver of apprehension sizzled over her skin when she addressed Calum. "Is the stone that is meant to trap Lucas, red?"

The slight tensing of Calum's shoulders and set of his chin told her what she needed to know. "It is," she whispered.

"It is," she repeated, gulping down her wine.

"Aye, lassie, it is," Devin said. "Where is it, Calum?"

"Not here."

"Where then?"

"Far away." He looked at her. "There is no way you will get your hands on it. Even if you did, I would never trap you in that house. Surely you must know that."

"Tell ya what buddy, you become capable of a whole hellava lot as time goes by." Devin said.

"Please, enough." Isabel sighed. Her whole life it'd been one thing after another. Survive, survive, survive. Could it really be that up until the very end for all she'd learn to toughen it out she'd become trapped by the very man she'd put all her trust in? God please, no. Looking at Calum, she saw only genuine emotion. Doing so with Devin, she saw the same.

They both believed what they said. So where did that leave her?

She needed space, needed to think about all of this. "Excuse me."

Isabel set down the drink and left the tent. Twilight had descended, casting a deep purple over the men at work. Walking down a path that led away from the house and river, Isabel tried to make sense of everything she'd just learned. Perhaps when Devin said she haunted the house that meant her soul had still managed to pass on. Isabel crossed her arms over her chest as she walked. No. He had meant she was still here three hundred years from now. And obviously still trying to avoid Lucas. Her biggest mistake.

While she knew it was only a matter of time before he found her, Isabel didn't think twice about walking down the darkening path. She needed to get as far away as she could from everything she'd just learned. Away from the bizarre reality unfolding before her. Escape from it all.

As if to mock her, a dark figure walked onto the path ahead.

Isabel stopped short…and once more looked her fiancé in the eyes.

***

"Look at how you shine. So very beautiful."

Devin had just stepped foot on the path to follow Isabel when he first heard the words. Slowing, he allowed the wind to carry the conversation his way.

"You found me," she stated flatly.

"I would say that is obvious," he replied.

Slowly, carefully, Devin moved forward and summoned his magic to aide in stealth. The twigs beneath his feet didn't snap. His scent on the air remained non-existent. He all but blended with the trees. Isabel stood nearly face to face with a tall, dark haired man.

"You come for Calum."

"No sweetheart, I come for you."

Devin tensed but moved closer. Branches bent in the breeze. The day had passed within what seemed a blink of the eye. Odd how magic worked that way. But it had gone by in a flash and the sun had nearly set. He searched out the moon. It was not yet full. Did that mean they were safe from Lucas changing?

Something is not right about Lucas. He poses no real threat right now.

Devin wasn't surprised to hear Calum speak within his mind nor see him standing alongside. No matter how innocent Calum seemed about the events that would happen with Isabel and this house, he was still pissed by how the warlock had nearly drowned him at the river. Not bothering to respond, Devin watched the strange reunion unfold between Isabel and her former fiancé.

She backed up a few steps. "I want nothing to do with you."

"Of course you do."

"No." Isabel shook her head, a look of both fear and something else in her eyes.

A rush of jealousy passed through Devin. Isabel hadn't completely got over her feelings for this guy.

He should've known that by the way she'd responded by the river when she'd thought he was Lucas. Damn it.

"Have you forgotten our long walks? The nights we shared?" Lucas asked.

"Oh, I remember the nights. Of that you can rest assured." Isabel glanced up at the sky as Devin had. "And I remember exactly what you become."

Lucas stalked closer. "Do you?"

Frowning, Isabel backed up more. "How could I forget?"

"Why don't you turn and run then, Isabel. Why do you still face me... speak with me? Could it be your heart is divided?"

Devin held his breath.

"My heart is no more divided that yours." Isabel stood her ground. "You are half man, half beast. What does it feel like to be a monster? To use people as you have."

Lucas stopped stalking her, his expression softened for a moment. "I have feelings for you, Isabel. I am still a man."

Isabel said nothing but Devin saw the way her posture relaxed. He could only imagine what she was thinking right now. Did she believe the lies coming out of his mouth? Screw this. Devin discontinued spying and headed their way. Calum grabbed his arm but he pulled away. Twigs snapped beneath his feet, leaves crunched. Interestingly enough, while Isabel looked his way, Lucas didn't seem concerned.

As Devin strode up to them he said, "You've got balls showing up here. Do you have any idea what you're up against?"

"Devin, don't—"

"Don't what?" He interrupted never taking his eyes off of Lucas.

Funny thing, Lucas kept looking at Isabel as though Devin hadn't approached. He might've thought this normal for an overly arrogant lycan. Too late he realized his error as Lucas smiled at Isabel then vanished.

Incredulous, he stared at the spot in which Lucas had stood. "You've got to be kidding me. He was a ghost?"

Coming up behind, Calum muttered, "You think I tried to stop you because you were about to interrupt a lover's spat? Ignorant fool."

"You didn't try that hard to stop me," Devin countered.

Frowning and obviously distressed Isabel said, "I think the more pressing matter is why did Lucas appear as a ghost?"

Calum walked to where Lucas had stood and closed his eyes. "Because somehow he's locked onto you, Isabel. It is only a matter of time before he makes his way here."

Devin tried not to roll his eyes. Why did he have to be the cousin to travel back in time and deal with Calum? "Locked onto her? How? And why give us forewarning by appearing as a ghost? Why not just show up fangs bared?"

"Games," Isabel whispered. "Lucas is never forthright about anything."

"Mm Hmm," Calum said. "And he wasn't a ghost but an astral projection."

"Oh no, not that," Devin said sarcastically. "Sure, whatever. Anyone want to answer my questions more directly?"

"He wasn't real," Isabel said softly.

The fact that she appeared rather lost irritated the hell out of him. "I think we covered that."

Her eyes narrowed slightly but she said nothing.

"He locked onto her," Calum repeated. "And had we let them talk a bit more I might've learned from where he projected himself."

Irritated, Devin asked, "Again, why not just lock on then show up as the beastie he is?"

"It's a way of scrying using dark magic. Typically doesn't work but because Isabel was weakened by both thinking you were Lucas earlier and her volatile emotions in general, he unfortunately made a connection."

"I'm sorry," Isabel murmured and sat on a nearby rock.

As she appeared so discomforted, Devin found himself being torn between continuing to question Calum and going to her side. The need to protect won out. "Does he know exactly where she is? If so, how long before he gets here?"

"He can only go off of what he saw around her and anything she divulged which wasn't much," Calum said.

"Thanks to me."

Calum nodded, his eyes on Isabel.

"So why were you opposed to me interrupting their meeting? Seems I gave him less time to take a peek around," Devin provided.

"As previously mentioned, given some time, I might have been able to back track his astral link," Calum said matter-of-factly.

The same old dealing-with-all-things-Calum irritation flared. "Yeah, at her expense! Or did that not occur to you?"

"Sometimes we must suffer momentary discomfort to accomplish the greater good." Calum's eyes flickered with scorn. "Isabel needed only to tolerate him for a few more minutes so that I might find where he was and therefore better prepared for when he might arrive. You let your emotions cloud your judgement, Devin."

Hell. Calum was right. Regardless, he didn't need to know that. "You could've enlightened me within the mind, huh Calum? Why didn't you?"

"Would you have believed me?"

"Aye!" Devin said. "I've dealt with astral projection before."

"Have you?" Calum asked, genuinely curious.

That's right. Calum didn't know the details of what Devin had already endured due to the curse laid upon him. Devin's eyes wandered to Isabel. Now was not the time to enlighten him.

"We'll talk more tomorrow, Calum," he said.

To his great relief, Calum understood and left. While Devin definitely still had issues with the man, he continued to prove himself a far more compassionate person than Devin would've ever expected.

"Please, you go too," Isabel said. "I want to be alone."

Not going to happen. Walking over, he sat on the rock next to her. Isabel immediately got up and started walking toward the house. Okay. She really was having issues. Again, he didn't blame her. Devin decided it best to leave her alone with her feelings. She'd been dished a lot of information today and he'd probably have better luck with her after she had time to cool down and think things through. About to head toward the fire, he stopped short when she turned and came storming his way.

"No, I want to talk about this n—"

Isabel kept speaking but he couldn't hear a word. Oh no, not now! A second passed before he could hear her again. Stopping directly in front of him, she said, "I've not spent my life crying over my sad circumstances and do not intend to do so now. I'm strong. I handle what's thrown at me no matter where I might be. I'll tell you everything you want to know. I'll trust completely in my future 'self' when it comes to you, Devin."

Though elated by her determination and sudden trust would she still feel the same way one second from now? Glancing over her shoulder, he pointed and asked, "That doesn't look right to you, does it?"

Isabel spun and made an indistinguishable sound. Backing up, she bumped against his chest. "The house," she stuttered, "the house has a roof... and window panes... and walls!"

Holding her upper arms, he inhaled the scent of her hair and said, "Welcome to the twenty-first century, m'dear."

"Oh my goodness." A shiver ran down her body and she whispered, "Am I the future me?"

Devin laughed softly and turned her. "You tell me. Do you remember everything that happened to us through the remainder of the house being built? Do you remember everything we shared together?

Eyes round as saucers Isabel shook her head. "No, I only remember up until the moment we just traveled forward together."

"Wow," he said. "This situation gets odder and

odder."

Another shiver rippled through her and it occurred to him how frightened she must be.

"Listen, I'm here with you. You are completely safe. Neither I nor my cousins will hurt you. We'll only protect."

"Oh no!" Isabel exclaimed. "Lucas." Pulling away from Devin she stared up at the house. "He's trapped in there as a wolf." She backed away. "There's no way I can go in there. He'll get me!"

The front door swung open and Andrea stepped out, followed by the rest of the team. This time it hadn't taken them long to sense he'd returned.

Andrea smiled. "Isabel, so glad you've returned."

"Returned?" she asked.

"Yep. Remember how I told you about your future 'self?' Well, she already met my family." Turning his attention to his cousins, Devin quickly explained that Isabel was her eighteenth century self this visit and introduced everyone yet again. "Keep in mind, the twenty-first century and all it has to offer is going to be a little bit of a shock to her."

"Say it isn't so," Seth replied with a charming smile, never taking his eyes off of her. "You're in the best hands. I, for one, will make sure no harm comes your way."

A shy smile blossomed on her face.

"She knows what we are," Devin interrupted. "In fact, she learned everything an hour ago, so let's take it easy."

"Lucas really can't hurt me in there?" Isabel asked again.

"Who's Lucas?" Dakota asked.

"The wolf," Devin provided.

"Not with all of us around," Leathan answered Isabel's question. "Besides, last time the wolf made an appearance we worked a lit—"

"Last time he made an appearance?" Isabel asked, alarmed.

Devin shook his head and scowled at Leathan. "Lucas didn't actually make an appearance. Not like you remembered him. Besides, we combined all of our dark magic and definitely managed to leash the beast."

Even as Devin said it he didn't quite believe his own words. He hoped. Glancing at each face he looked for some sign that things had remained quiet in his absence. "How long was I gone this time?"

"Not sure," Andrea said. "You were with us when you went to bed. It's almost 6:00 AM now, so it depends what time it was when you traveled back."

"What! You've got to be kidding me. Not even twenty four hours have passed?"

Andrea shook her head.

So it was mere hours ago when he and Isabel's ghost had.... Clearing his throat, Devin looked at Isabel. "I'll keep you safe. I promise."

When her eyes met his, Devin was pleased to see a mixture of trust and renewed determination. He sensed that Isabel was taking off her mask and resolved to show him the woman she really was beneath the proper English façade.

Almost to prove his point her response held a distinct southern twang. "So who would like to show me the house?"

Before Devin had a chance to respond, Seth looped his arm through hers and ushered Isabel toward the house. Bloody American had the gall to glance over his shoulder and shoot him a I'm-still-in-this-race wink before they vanished inside.

CHAPTER THIRTEEN

Isabel stood at the window and watched the sunrise crest. The house had aged but it remained lovely. Not surprisingly, it was laid out as Devin had described. As she ran her fingertips over the curtains, Isabel couldn't help but feel an attachment. Why, she couldn't be certain. Maybe because she knew she oversaw its building. Or maybe because she supposedly haunted it for so long. Either way, there existed a definite mental connection... perhaps even physical.

"You really are stunning," Devin said softly.

Turning, she found him leaning against the doorway, hair wet and brushed back. His come-hither eyes roamed her face. Isabel's heart caught in her throat. As with the house, Isabel felt an inexplicable connection to him.

In fact, she could easily believe that they fall in love.

"Thank you." Isabel smiled. She had to admit, the 'shower' had felt wonderful. And the soaps and shampoos Andrea had given her to use, amazing! Regrettably, she'd had to put her dress back on instead of trying on one of the more current fashions. She'd worn pants before and the idea of doing so again held great appeal. Turned out, they might travel back in time unexpectedly so best to remain dressed for the period.

Isabel breathed deeply when Devin joined her at the window. He smelled fresh and soapy, masculine.

Gazing up, she once more lost herself in the grayish green swirls of his eyes. Without thought, she reached up and touched the side of his face. So smooth.

"Freshly shaved," he murmured. "Not a look you've seen a lot of."

"I really am sorry about the way I treated you at the river. I was so scared. Still am. There's so much… happening."

"Water under the bridge. This situation's tough all the way around." He smiled and winked. "But no more spitting in the face, okay?"

Nodding, it occurred to her she didn't have to play the part she'd perfected. Isabel was no innocent school girl. Devin was from a time that was obviously far less strict. She wanted to embrace the real her… the real him. They were courting after all, weren't they? Isabel cupped his other cheek and pulled his lips down to hers. When his mouth slanted and his arms snaked around her waist, Isabel melted. His kiss felt so different from Lucas'.

Far better.

If he used his magic on her this time, she didn't care. But Isabel had the feeling he didn't. That he had no need. When their tongues meshed and he pressed her hips against his, Isabel felt a sharp surge of desire. Devin's low groan told her he felt the same.

"Breakfast's ready. Oops!" Andrea vanished from the doorway the moment she appeared.

Isabel smiled and broke the kiss. "I like her. She's nice. I probably should be embarrassed she caught us like this but I'm not. It's strange."

Nuzzling her neck, Devin offered a haphazard grunt of agreement or disagreement. She couldn't tell. His lips against her neck and his arousal pressed against her belly stole all thought. It had been far too long since she'd had a man.

Lucas.

His name in her mind brought sour thoughts and she pulled away. "We should go eat. Something tells me I'm about to taste food beyond my wildest imagination."

Devin winked. "Comfort food I'd say."

Grinning, Isabel's eyes fell to his erection but she said, "Blueberry pancakes!"

Eyes wide, he grabbed her hand before she could escape to the kitchen. "Not so fast, lass."

The way he said it with an incredulous drawl and that sexy Irish lilt, Isabel knew she'd just taken them to the next level with a simple glance. But she couldn't help herself. Besides, it felt natural with Devin. The act of intimacy didn't frighten her at all where he was concerned. If anything, she felt eager almost, strangely impatient.

"Yes?" she asked innocently.

"After breakfast, you and I need to talk. Perhaps a walk?"

"Of course. I'd love to."

"Good. Now go get something to eat. I'll be there in a minute."

Isabel nodded and headed for the kitchen. As she walked down the short hallway, she couldn't help but wonder if her ghostly self was watching. If Lucas was watching. The same wonderful smells she'd ignored when so close to Devin became stronger. Coffee and warm blueberries at the forefront. A homey scene greeted. Instead of using the formal dining room, the group sat on stools around a center countertop. When she entered, Andrea instantly jumped to her feet.

"Would you like some coffee, Isabel?"

"Yes, thank you."

Dakota patted a stool to her right and smiled. "Come. Sit."

Isabel sat down. They made her feel comfortable instantly. As Andrea slid a cup of coffee her way, Dakota plunked a plate in front of her. Leathan handed her a container with cream, a bowl of sugar and spoon. Seth placed some eggs and bacon on her plate, offering a wink alongside. Smiling slightly she nodded. No doubt, he was very handsome but not nearly as attractive as Devin.

"If you don't mind, I'll serve the pancakes."

Isabel watched Devin enter and open what they'd explained was a modern day oven. He pulled out a plate full of flat, round cakes.

Serving her first he said, "I cooked them while you were showering." With a spatula, he slid one onto her plate. "As promised love… a pancake."

Despite the fact he'd just placed such a scrumptious smelling cake in front of her, Isabel could only focus on one thing. He'd called her 'love.' As she stared at the plate, she couldn't help but like the way the one little word made her feel.

"I think you'll like it," Devin said softly. When their eyes met and held she knew he wasn't referring to the pancake.

"I think you're right," she replied.

They continued to stare at one another.

"Well, are you going to try the pancake or what?" Seth asked.

Isabel blinked and looked away. Before she could begin to cut it, Seth said, "Please, allow me."

Plopping a dab of butter on top and pouring a

little syrup over it he grinned triumphantly. "There, now that's the way a pancake should be eaten."

Isabel could've sworn she heard Devin mutter 'meddlesome Americans' as he served everyone else pancakes. No one seemed to have heard it so she made no comment. Taking her first bite, she closed her eyes and moaned. Delicious!

When she opened her eyes all the men stared. Dakota elbowed Leathan. "What?" he asked. "She eats food like you."

"Aye, she does," Devin said, his attention solely focused on her lips.

"What are the odds?" Seth agreed, his eyes doing the same dance as Devin's.

"I'm sorry. I don't understand," Isabel replied, embarrassed.

"No, no, ignore them. Enjoy your pancake," Andrea pleaded and frowned at Seth. "They tend to get caught up and act like idiots when women chew their food. Poor Dakota suffered the same punishment."

"We're only human... kind of," Seth said around a mouthful of pancake.

Isabel continued to eat, quietly this time. She couldn't help but wonder if Devin had also been as impressed with Dakota. Eyeing the very modern appearing woman, Isabel thought her extremely attractive. How long had she been married to Leathan? When her eyes once more found Devin, he was busy eating.

The next hour passed pleasantly. Conversation mainly focused on the interaction Devin had with Calum and talk of future paranormal investigating within the home. Isabel found it all extremely intriguing and found she was rather glad to be here now instead of her other 'self' and her ghostly self. Odd to know one has multiple bodies running around, alternate realities happening at once. One nugget of conversation saddened her though.

"I wish I could tell you I'd seen your husband in my time," she said to Andrea.

Nodding, Andrea sighed softly and started to clear the dishes. "Me too."

"We'll find him, sis. Promise," Seth said.

"I know."

Isabel offered to help but Andrea graciously declined. "Go keep Devin entertained. The more you two communicate the closer I think we'll all be to defeating this house."

As she and Devin exited the front door Isabel wondered why Andrea referred to the house as the problem when it was clearly her ex-fiance who was the true cause of all the grief.

"Because she likes you and doesn't want you to feel in any way responsible," Devin said.

Startled, Isabel stopped on the last step. "How did you know what I was thinking?"

Devin held out a hand. "It's written all of over your face. You worry too much."

I do? If so I always thought I hid it well. She took his hand as they walked across the lawn. Everything looked so very different. Gone were the endless workers. The tents. Instead, only a stretch of green lawn and taller pine trees.

She liked it.

From the man with whom she held hands to the modern house to the setting in which they walked. All of it felt right. How could it? This was a place of entrapment for her soul. A living nightmare if she were to believe all she'd been told.

The warm sun climbed toward the noon zenith. Dark, tumbling clouds rolled across the sky and threatened tranquility. Yet Isabel felt alive. Enjoyed the energy she felt boiling in the brooding storm. Grass seemed more verdant and vibrant beneath their feet. The pungent, crisp smell of pine billowed on the air and mated with the morning heat.

As they walked down a different path through the woods, Isabel knew that this was exactly where she was supposed to be. It was time to tell the truth to someone other than Calum. "He bought me."

Devin continued to walk and hold her hand. Instead of a look of disbelief or a burst of anger his features simply set themselves in a stern line. "Lucas."

"Yes. But he bought me to save me. Little did I know it at the time. Frank, my eldest brother, realized I was old enough to start making money. Given my looks, he decided that selling me into sex slavery would reap faster and much higher proceeds than whoring me out night after night."

Devin said nothing as they continued to walk but the set of his brow lowered, his hold on her hand tightened. Best to continue. "He put word out that I was up for sale. I've no idea if any others tried to purchase me. All I know is that Lucas showed up that eve at the docks. Money was exchanged and I suddenly found myself in the hands of a complete stranger. I've never been so scared in my life."

Breaking free of the forest they came to the very spot they found themselves so often. By the river. Isabel was amazed. It was but a trickling stream.

Bright orange blossoms covered the ground like a blanket. A spicy scent rose in the air. She leaned down and picked one of the delicate flowers, then held it to her nose. Closing her eyes she inhaled deeply. "These smell like Heaven. What are they?"

"Butterfly Weed," Devin whispered.

Opening her eyes, Isabel realized he stood close, mesmerized.

"What is it?" She asked. "You have such a strange look on your face."

"Do you like the smell better than that of the rose?"

She ran the petals under her nose again and smiled. "Actually, I do." She held the petal beneath his nose. "Smell. What do you think?"

Devin wrapped his hand around hers. Thunder rumbled in the distance. The air thickened with humidity. His proximity magnetized her every sensation. Isabel had never been more aware of another person in her life.

"I think it reminds me of you."

"Of me?" Isabel's eyes rounded in sudden comprehension. "This is the flower you told me was my favorite the first morn we met. How extraordinary!"

"Come," Devin led her to the edge of the stream where he pulled his shoes off and motioned for her to do the same. "Tell me the rest of your story, Isabel."

Ah yes. Shoes off, they sat. Pulling her skirts up, she showed off a good deal of knee and shin. Why not? She felt far freer in this time period.

Far freer with Devin.

"The minute my brother left, Lucas said, "You don't belong to me. Do what you like. I don't buy slaves. I don't buy people." I still remember the sound of the water splashing off of the pier. The smell of the bracken." Isabel frowned, running her palms over the cool grass. "I wanted to run. Break free. Until I realized I had nowhere to go. No one to run to. And, as an odd twist of fate, no one to run from."

Devin again said nothing. His palm floated over the grass next to hers. In his own way, if felt as though he were letting her know that he understood and cast no judgement. That he was just like her.

"So I decided to create a new identity and set out for a new life. Cutting all my hair, I dressed like a boy and caught the next ship up the coast until I arrived in Boston harbor."

"How'd you like it?"

She shrugged. "It was tolerable. Busy. After working for a bit, I was able to buy forged papers saying I was a British nanny. Voila, I once more became a girl and was able to pursue my main love, working with the disabled." Isabel sighed. "It was like being reborn."

His hand covered hers. "I understand."

"Do you?"

He nodded. "My da was deaf."

That stunned her. Really? But she didn't press.

"I'm sorry. What about your mother?"

"I don't know. She died in childbirth."

Oh Lord. "Mine too."

"I know."

"You do?"

"You told me."

Isabel took a deep breath. "I'm sorry for your loss but I have to know... am I simply repeating everything about myself you already know? If so, I find this all a bit…trying and hurtful in its own strange way."

"No, Isabel." Devin squeezed her hand. "While I do know about your journey up the coast I don't know this end of it. You never really had the chance to tell me your impressions. And certainly didn't share anything about Lucas's part in it."

One part of Isabel wanted to end this conversation now. Another part knew she had to go on, get this off her chest. "Lucas stayed close. He never pressured, never used his influence over me. After all, I was free. Instead, when I wasn't working he…" She had trouble speaking. Memories overflowed.

"He what?"

"He courted me."

Devin frowned and gazed ahead. Isabel clearly saw red flecks spark around his aura. He called on his dark magic, searched for something. "Tell me more."

Having had enough conversations with Calum, she wasn't afraid of Devin, understood better than most he was deep in thought. Trying to figure out a puzzle that bothered him. "Once well-established—based on my own credentials I might add—I realized it was time for a change. That I would likely do even better in Portsmouth."

"Did Lucas have anything to do with your decision?"

"Yes he did." Isabel tried to pull her hand away from Devin's but he would not release. "He thought Portsmouth a calmer city. One more adept to the visage I had built for myself. Classier."

"My arse," Devin muttered. "Go on."

"I ended my employment in Boston and boarded

a ship to Portsmouth. Once there, Lucas and I established a private residence and I gained employment with a very wealthy family with a deaf child."

The crimson aura crackled around Devin. "I need to know what happened at the end of your relationship. Everything, Isabel."

Biting her lower lip, she pulled free her hand and placed it on her lap. The sun snuck behind the approaching cloudbank. Leaves rippled in the light wind. "He became a good friend. Always there for me. Understood everything I was going through. How could I not agree to his proposal?"

"Did you sleep with him?"

Isabel sat up straighter. "Excuse me?"

"Sorry, perhaps I phrased that incorrectly. Were you lovers, Isabel?"

"I don't see how that's any of your business."

"Yes you do." Devin's expression didn't change. "It's relevant to dark magic." The gray flecks in his eyes darkened. "And it's relevant to you and me."

Isabel already knew the ramifications through dark magic. Calum had been sure to fill her in on all necessary details. Though she wanted to hold onto her pride, she knew things were well past that and hadn't she told herself hours before that she wanted to embrace this modern life. Besides, Isabel had been down the worst sorts of roads and came out stronger for it. She'd be damned if Devin would strip her of that. "Yes, we were lovers."

Devin said nothing for a few minutes but his aura looked like a plethora of bloody fireworks. His jaw ground back and forth slowly. Finally he said, "So you're not a virgin."

"No." She ran her big toe through the cool water. "Did you think I was?"

"No."

Well, he answered that fast enough! "Why?"

"Pancake comment?"

Isabel wanted to be furious but the minute he said it with pure aggravation sparking his silvery eyes, she burst into laughter. "Indeed!"

It was obvious he didn't share the same humor. "Where did it happen? How?"

He was jealous! Clear as day. Which sobered her immediately. "I don't see how it's relevant."

Devin stood in the water before her so fast, Isabel swore he never moved. With his height, he still looked down at her. Red pulsed around him. Nearly a living, breathing thing. She leaned back, trying to adjust to his sudden domination. Black clouds smothered the sky. Wind whipped the flowers to fury.

"You're scaring me, Devin."

"Did you know he could turn wolf when he took you?"

Despite her fear, aggravation rose to the front. And despite her aggravation, a tear slipped free. "What does it matter?"

Devin pushed up her dress, moved closer, fury obvious. "Are you kidding me?"

Blinking, Isabel tried to understand what was happening. At the same time, she didn't really want to. Devin was furious but the anger had more to do with another man touching her than whether Lucas was wolf by that point. Should she tell him the truth now? Or wait? What difference would it make? Maybe the truth would make Devin see things as clearly as he needed to. "Yes, I knew he changed."

His brows lowered three times quickly, as though he suffered a twitch. Then his lips pulled back. For a split second, Isabel thought perhaps he'd taken the bite. But the strange visage vanished as quickly as it came. Instead he seemed enraged. Devin's aura burst bright red and he lurched forward. Somehow, she ended up on her back amidst the Butterfly Weed. Jet black clouds blanketed the sky behind him. The tall pines seemed to grow taller. His bright grayish green gaze turned to a painful silver hue.

"Devin," she whimpered.

Isabel sensed it was far too late for pleas. Her skirts were around her waist, legs spread wide on either side of his heavy, seething body. She blinked and his clothes were gone. Isabel grinded her teeth and tempered the fear. Even as she did, his lips were against her neck. His fresh, soapy smelling hair brushed her face. *Breathe. I need to breathe.* But it was impossible. Was she going to pass out? Isabel grasped at the ground and seized handfuls of flowers. When his lips covered hers and his pelvis ground against hers, Isabel brought the fistfuls of Butterfly Weed up against his hips and gasped.

"You knew." His words sounds agonized as his lips traveled down her neck. "And you let him touch you."

Her lips throbbed, left bruised by his sudden and violent kisses. *I knew. I did. But there's so much more. I trusted him.* She tried to speak but he spread her legs further, his fingers crawling up her inner thigh. The pines overhead started to bend in the wind. A heavy raindrop hit her cheek and rolled down like a tear.

"What gives you the right to judge?" she

breathed as one long, thick finger pushed inside of her. Isabel tried to fight Devin. Tell him how wrong he was for thinking this of her—for doing this to her. But it was impossible to talk. When his lips covered hers once more and his free hand roamed the side of her breast, Isabel fought back.

With passion.

Chest tight, heart beating out of control, the feel of his finger sliding in and out of her, the brush of his thumb over her clitoris made Isabel thrust. Want.

"Do you wish I were wolf?" Devin murmured close to her ear. "Like him" He nipped her chin. "Or is warlock better for you?" The red around him seemed to crawl around them both. Every inch of it heated her skin. Though he only touched her front, a fingertip slid lightly up her spine while strong hands clasped her backside. Isabel arched, needing release.

A low dark chuckle came from Devin, "Do you think it will be that easy?"

Isabel struggled for air as she stared up. Anger and resentment boiled off of him but she saw past that. He was hurt. She tried to speak. Tell him that he was so much better than Lucas. She learned quickly that warlocks were far different than werewolves. Werewolves acted off of baser animal instinct. Warlocks acted off of pride and extreme human intelligence. A very dangerous combination. However, they shared one same trait.

Once aroused, they couldn't be stopped.

Devin's finger slowed, twirled, plunged. His smoky intense eyes locked on hers. In, out, in, out. Her nipples throbbed. Isabel licked her lips unable to look anywhere else but into his eyes. It was all his power now. Rain began to fall more steadily. The heady, spicy perfume of the flowers rose around them. His wide shoulders and chiseled muscles flexed.

"Do you want this?" he asked.

Was that a question meant to confuse? Did it really matter? Fingers caressed every part of her body. The top of her dress pulled down of its own accord. His eyes never leaving hers Devin leaned down, took an erect nipple into his mouth and sucked deeply. Groaning she closed her eyes. "You seduce me," she whispered.

"Do you want this?" he repeated.

"What if I say n—"

Isabel shuttered as he swiftly removed his finger and began pushing the tip of his erection into her. A vein in her temple began to throb. She'd never felt anything so intense.

"Do you want this?" Devin whispered.

Her mouth moved. No sound came out. He pushed further. She gasped.

"Isabel," he whispered next to her ear. Taking her fistfuls of flowers he raised her arms until they rested by her head. The crimson aura around them vanished. Rain fell heavier. A clap of thunder roared overhead. "No more magic. Do you want this?"

"You ask me now?" she choked. "When halfway in."

"Aye."

Never more shell shocked, she gazed up at him. Somehow, his honesty, the fact he'd pulled away his magic, that he was willing to stop now aroused her more than his violent warlock take-over. The truth was she'd never needed it more. Lucas had been nothing next to this. "Plea—."

Devin pushed so hard, so deeply that words no longer existed, vanished into thin air. Her fingernails dugs into the flowers, squished them between her fingers. Her legs rose to meet him, thighs around his waist. Rain covered their skin in hot delicious slickness. Pebbles beneath ground into her body so strongly that pain met pleasure as he thrust. Stretched, filled, Isabel tried to gain purchase on his slick skin. Strange animal groans started to come from her throat.

"So beautiful. Perfect," he murmured as he thrust deeper, moaned louder.

Isabel felt his lips everywhere. Smelled the scent of his skin everywhere. With a new roll to his hips, she arched up. Something odd was happening. A deep seeded tingle in her core. "Devin," she whimpered.

"Right here, love." His words followed another electrifying spark. One strong arm snaked beneath her legs and pulled higher with each thrust. "Right. Here."

A strange sound came from his throat nearly the moment her body bucked, thrust and lost ground. The pain, pleasure was so intense she held on for dear life. Stiff, throbbing within he released a strangled shout. Isabel felt so much at once.

She floated.

In bliss.

Pulsing and lost and in such extreme pleasure, Isabel didn't know who or where she was for a great deal of time. When at last awareness started to infiltrate so too did the soapy fresh scent of Devin's hair, the masculine smell of his skin and the now super spicy scent of well heated Butterfly Weed.

"I'm sorry," he said softly, still nestled deep

within her sweet heat.

Had Isabel been any other woman what he'd pulled this afternoon might have been a true affront. But she wasn't any other woman. Life had dealt her realism. And now—in more ways than one—the supernatural. How did she know he felt that way? But Isabel knew without doubt that he was feeling these emotions. She also knew she had the right to get mad, to shove Devin away, cry abuse and demand retribution.

But to whom? And was it really abuse?

Isabel herself was the only judge she had left and truth told, she knew deep down that she'd never met another man like Devin before and would never find another like him. She also knew that if she demanded retribution right now, Devin would do his very best to see himself punished.

Which essentially proved he was truly the good man she knew he was.

Best to be a woman about this.

"You will never touch me again." Their eyes met.

"Of course." Yet he still did not pull free from her body.

"You will never get so jealous of Lucas again."

"Of course." He shifted slightly. Isabel tried to ignore the sharp thrill of pleasure.

"You will move. Now."

When he pushed forward, Isabel squeaked and knew her eyes rolled back in her head.

"You didn't say which way to move."

"Out," she gritted between closed teeth.

He moved out halfway. "You didn't say how far."

Best to try to be an old fashioned woman about this. "No I didn't. I expected you to be a gentleman."

Devin's lips lowered and grazed hers lightly. His tongue slowly licking her upper teeth mere seconds before his teeth grazed her lower lips. Isabel's eyes drifted somewhere between open and shut. Arousal flared and moisture pooled below. Thankfully, her legs were still immovable. Perhaps it was best to be a modern day woman about this. "I expect you to do the right thing."

"Hmm." He nibbled the far right side of her neck. His fingers gently pinched a nipple. "Are you sure?"

"Yes," she whispered. If anyone had decency outside the supernatural, it had to be Devin. Even as she said it Isabel felt his member expand within, stretching her sore muscles.

Scooping his strong arms beneath her limp legs, Devin grinned and gently kissed the corner of her lip. With a sharp thrust he said, "I always try to do the right thing."

CHAPTER FOURTEEN

Why the hell didn't I do the right thing?

Not the first thought he wanted to have after releasing in Isabel for the second time. *Balls to the wall buddy, you're a real asshole.* Carefully pulling out he fell to the ground beside Isabel and draped his arm over his forehead. The heavy rain had turned to a light drizzle. Turning his head, Devin's eyes traveled over her. Full breasts led to a tight little waist and the most amazing set of legs he'd ever seen. Her wet hair blended with the flowers. Her chest rose and fell rapidly. A thin layer of steam burned off her body into the hot summer heat.

Devin had never seen anything so bloody fine in his life.

Never felt anything so incredible.

What had he done?

"You don't need to apologize," she whispered.

"Aye, I think I do."

Shaking her head, Isabel slowly sat up and looked down at him. "No, you really don't. I'm a full grown woman." She wiped damp hair away from her face. "I'm not upset."

Despite what she said, a pale hue underscored the rosy blush he'd put in her cheeks. Lips he'd kissed were swollen and overused. He sat up and ran the back of his forefinger down her upper arm. "I never wanted it to be that way our first time."

He shook his head. *Damn cliché, Devin.* Not to mention he'd bedded her without a condom. Real smooth.

"Again, we're both adults," she replied.

"Regard—" Devin stopped talking. If he had hackles, they'd be raising. Something was very wrong. Drizzle still fell. A light wind still blew. Yet something had changed. Eyes narrowed, he scanned the forest.

Crunch. Twigs snapped. Before he had a chance to respond, a massive wolf stepped into their small clearing. Its coat was a rich blue, black. The same color of Lucas's hair. Its eyes shone a deep, dark yellow. It was the same wolf that haunted the Georgian. Devin sensed rather than saw Isabel freeze. Like a predator stalking its prey, the wolf slowly lumbered forward, dangerous gaze locked on Isabel.

Hell no. Devin summoned dark magic moments before Seth appeared. Like an oily whip, his cousin's magic streamed toward the beast as it lunged in her direction. Isabel screamed. Seth's magic caught the beast around the middle and snapped it in half, leaving nothing but a sputtering cloud of otherworldly residue.

"Damn!" Seth crowed. "I needed that!"

Devin had Isabel re-clothed with a flick of a wrist. Not before Seth enjoyed a good eyeful. One he didn't particularly try to hide. Clothed again, Devin stood and pulled a trembling Isabel up with him. "Are you alright?"

Wide-eyed, Isabel merely nodded. Though her lower lip trembled, she threw back her shoulders and stood on steady feet.

"My apologies bursting in on you two like that," Seth said, blue eyes twinkling. "But man did I need a little excitement. This haunting has been boring as hell."

"Not on our end." Devin didn't take his eyes off Isabel. "Are you sure you're okay?"

Nodding, she looked around. "It was a ghost. The wolf?"

Seth nodded and grinned. "Yep."

"And what brought you out this way to begin with? See the ghost wolf leave the house?" Devin asked, scowling.

Seth arched a brow. "You kidding me? I hoped to see a little something else."

"Asshole," Devin muttered.

"What did you hope to see?" Isabel asked before figuring it out and saying, "oh," absently.

But somehow Seth's charming smile and carefree attitude managed not to offend. Typical.

"You're not getting this one, Seth. All mine," Devin said. Though he referred to the wolf both he and Seth knew who they were really talking about.

"We'll see," Seth replied easily and strolled over to the stream.

Devin wondered if Isabel was taken in by him like every other hot blooded lass. Seth was the poster boy for the all American male. Uncouth, with a live-on-the-edge attitude, he managed to reel them in. Females flocked to him like bees to honey. And Seth had always been very thorough about providing for all his 'bees.'

Not this one.

"I'd say it's time we focus more on ghost hunting in the house. Isabel needs answers. We all do." Devin said and took her hand. Thankfully, she didn't pull it away. He thought for sure she would.

Seth kneeled and splashed water on his face.

"Nothing's going on there. Never does unless you and some form of Isabel is present." He stood and turned. "Like I said, boring as hell."

"So I should expect more," Isabel said. "Much more," she continued when Seth looked at her like she had three heads.

"Things are bound to get interesting but remember, we'll protect you." Devin squeezed her hand. "I'll protect you."

"Yeah. Great job with the protection this time, cuz. Gonna go take a nap. The ol' 'magic' takes it right outta me." Seth winked and started down the path.

Devin ignored him and turned to Isabel. Taking her hands in his he looked into her wary eyes. "We've got to see this through. Release everyone from Calum's curse."

Isabel nodded. "I know."

"It's okay to be scared. This is a messed up situation."

She released a small burst of nervous laughter. "Oh, I'm scared but I know there's no choice. I've…we… have to go forward with all of this."

Devin studied her face. He didn't miss the fact she wouldn't look him directly in the eye. Her eyes sort of fell on his lips, cheek, very indirect. Fine. He got it. And he deserved it. He wanted to take more time and explain to her that all of this was new to him too. It wasn't easy being what he'd become. But somehow that explanation sounded weak. Life dealt people hardships. His hardship was coming into magic. Not as hard as what most people endured.

Not nearly as hard as what Isabel had endured in her lifetime.

"We'll get through, promise," he said.

"Don't make promises you can't keep."

Devin bowed his head. "Can you at least accept that I will always try to protect you?"

"Yes," she whispered. "I have no choice."

Not what he wanted to hear but what had he truly expected her to say? She was no fragile flower. With one last glance at the crushed Butterfly Weed, he turned and pulled her along. "Come, let's go teach you about ghost hunting."

Though she didn't quite smile, a certain pressure released that had hung between them and they headed back. When the house once more loomed ahead, Devin felt they'd crossed their own personal dimension and were perhaps somehow better equipped to tackle the warped issues ahead.

As they walked across the lawn with the sun falling behind the Georgian he suddenly wondered... would they end up together when this was all over? Or would they have freed all and she would have died in the eighteenth century and he remained here. Sonofobitch. How else could it go? Devin worked hard to keep his emotions from his face. Yet somehow as they walked toward the house he knew with certainty her thoughts mirrored his.

Popping her head out the front door, Andrea smiled. "Just in time for snacks!"

Devin smiled. Seth must've told her he'd used magic. Food time. His belly grumbled in response. Andrea hadn't let him down. Lined up on the coffee table in the living room was a wide variety of cheeses, meats and crackers. Leathan and Dakota studied an open laptop. Seth—true to form after implementing magic—snoozed in a chair.

Diving in, Devin started eating. Interesting that the driving hunger hadn't hit him immediately. Then again, how much magic had he really used?

"Please eat, Isabel," Andrea urged.

"No, thank you," Isabel responded.

Cheese wedged between two crackers, Devin looked her way. "Are you sure?"

Nodding, Isabel's eyes were on the laptop. "The pancakes were filling."

True. Devin forgot they ate earlier. After munching down his cracker sandwich, he took a long swig of soda then sat down in front of the other open laptop, patting the couch. "Come sit, Isabel. Let me show you how we're keeping an eye on the entire house from this one computer."

"Computer," she murmured and sat.

"A machine that enables us to do all sorts of things." He turned it on.

"First working computer was invented by an Englishman named Charles Babbage in the 1800s," Leathan said absently. "First consumer computer in 1976. First laptop in 1987. First form of the internet was launched in February of 1969, then known as ARPANET. Non-consumer computers of course. Only linked four universities. World-wide web went live in 91."

Dakota chuckled as she walked into the room and plunked down in a chair next to Leathan. When she looked Isabel's way she explained, "He's a history buff. Always amazed by what he knows."

"Internet? World-wide web?" Isabel repeated softly.

Devin squeezed her hand. "I know it's a lot to take in. Technology has come a long way since your time. The world-wide web is a global system of interconnected computer networks."

Andrea rolled her eyes. "It basically means that everyone can hop online and connect with people and sites around the entire world."

Isabel's mouth hung open. This was totally freaking her out.

"Listen, why don't we start by looking at what the laptop is doing right in this house? Plenty of time to learn more about the net later." Devin clicked the mouse.

Eyes wide, Isabel studied the four rooms that popped up on the monitor.

"Look there." He pointed at the one in which they sat. "That's obviously the living room." Devin waved at the camera so she could see him waving to the computer monitor. "There are cameras in every room that record what's happening. Each camera can do a few different things, one being the ability to detect thermal heat signatures. The theory holds that we can catch spirits or ghosts that way."

Thankfully, Isabel appeared more interested than afraid. She watched avidly as he pointed out the dining room, kitchen and hallway. Clicking to another screen he showed her some of the upstairs rooms.

"Have you caught my ghost on camera yet?" she asked.

Sharp images of hot ghostly sex popped into his mind. Devin cleared his throat. "No, not that I know of."

"I did catch you on camera though," Andrea volunteered. "Devin, where'd you put the picture?"

Awe hell. "Not sure," he mumbled.

"Probably wore it down to nothing by now," Seth

said, eyes still closed.

"Morning sunshine," Dakota said.

One eye popped open and looked at the clock on the mantel. "Afternoon." Yawning, Seth opened the other and stretched. "How long was I out?"

"Maybe 20 minutes," Andrea said.

"Nice. It's less and less each time." Seth crossed one leg over the other, ankle to knee. "I've been practicing hard to have the magic affect me less. Seems to me a warlock who naps after using magic is far too vulnerable."

Dakota laughed. "One with his bare ass up in the air isn't all that much better off."

Leathan winked. "Hey, nothing says I can't still wield the power while taking care of—"

"Enough." Andrea shook her head. "Last thing I want to hear about right now."

Devin popped another cracker in his mouth and again realized he'd felt a little less dependent on the food this time. Was it because he'd used less magic or because he too grew as a warlock? Then again, he'd denied the gift for the last year where Seth had embraced so who knew.

"What picture?" Isabel interjected.

Hell, he'd hoped the topic switch would've distracted her. Apparently not. "Just a picture that someone took of Tim and Andrea... and you...sort of."

Andrea's eyes narrowed on him. "Let's see. You've had enough time in the present to shower and dress. Seems to me those pants have pockets. My bet is the picture is right back in one of them."

Devin too narrowed his eyes. Andrea shrugged and winked.

Isabel's azure eyes met his. "Do you have the

picture, Devin? I'd really like to see it."

Damn family cornered him. With a sigh he reached into his right pocket, pulled it out and handed it to her. Taking the picture, Isabel stared... and stared. "It is me, isn't it?" She whispered. Then it fell from her limp fingers.

He snagged the photo and put it back in his pocket. So what if that was strange. Even with her sitting here next to him, a flesh and blood woman, this picture had somehow become part of him. At least in this dimension.

Isabel eyed the room, then the laptop monitor. Fear flickered for a moment before a steady resolve leveled her gaze. "It's hard to imagine I'm here in person and as a ghost. Frankly, it's discomforting and... a little baffling."

"I'm sure," Leathan concurred. "But I have to admit, you're handling it very well, lass. Not an easy thing to be tested by Calum's curse."

"Speaking of," Seth piped up. "When do you think he'll pop in again?"

Leathan shrugged. "If it's anything like the last haunting, more and more the closer we get."

"Get to what?" Isabel asked.

Devin took another swig of soda. Happy as hell Isabel seemed to be taking this in stride. Even happier she hadn't honed in on the worn down picture. Then again, she was beginning to understand the extent of his feelings toward her so he supposed it really didn't matter.

"The crux of the haunting," Seth provided. "The point the beast is unleashed." He nodded toward Devin. "And he hopefully kicks its ass."

"Oh," she whispered.

This time he didn't miss the slight tremble of her hands.

Thump. Scratch. Slam.

Everyone looked up at the ceiling. Devin and Leathan simultaneously pulled up the bedroom above on their laptops.

"Speak of the devil," Leathan muttered.

"Devil one and two," Devin agreed.

Isabel leaned forward and cocked her head. "Is that who I think it is?"

Devin nodded as he watched Adlin and Calum circle one another in the room above. "Wizard and Warlock. Both ghosts. Seems their residual interaction in this particular house is to be nothing less than comical."

To prove his point, Calum threw some sort of black fireball at Adlin. Adlin cleanly caught it, rolled it like a snowball until it shone white then whipped it back. When it hit Calum, the warlock melted into a puddle until he seemed to melt through the floor. Isabel squeaked when the drips started to fall from the ceiling into the living room.

Within seconds, drips turned to pouring rain, until Calum was once more a whole man who stood in front of them. Dusting off his top hat he scowled and tossed another black ball at the ceiling. For a split second a hole opened and Adlin fell through. Though he appeared out of control for a moment he gained his bearings and landed neatly beside Calum.

"You refuse to listen to reason," Adlin scoffed.

"Your reason claims Anna is within my reach." Calum placed the top hat on his head. "And that is plain ridiculous."

"Calum!" Isabel cried and stood.

Calum turned abruptly. His jaw dropped. "Isabel?"

Nodding avidly she went to embrace him but caught only air.

"So sorry, love. I'm but a ghost," he explained with a frown. "But I see you are not. How curious!"

"Is it really so curious considering the mess you've made of things?" Adlin mumbled.

"Calum," Isabel rushed on. "Mere hours ago I left you in the eighteenth century. You had only just learned that Devin was your ancestor. Lucas had appeared as an astral projection. You said he was scrying and locked on to me."

Calum blinked rapidly. "I did?" Putting a forefinger to his lip he shook his head. "Are you quite sure?"

Eyes round, Isabel put her hands on her hips. "Are you not the ghost of Calum O'Donnell? Did you not live his mortal life?"

Devin had to give her credit. She thought on her feet and didn't back down.

Calum looked at Adlin and cocked a brow. "Could it be I forgot parts of my life?"

Adlin snorted. "As likely as me forgetting I'm Scottish."

"Well, man, I'm injured."

"As you should be."

"Excuse me?" Isabel said.

"One moment, dear," Calum said, attention completely focused on Adlin. "I've no reason to lie to Isabel. She's a good girl. Always looked after her I did."

"Did you? Then why is her eighteenth century self in the twenty-first century and her ghost trapped here!" Adlin bellowed.

"Indeed!" Calum turned his attention back to Isabel. "My girl, what is going on?"

"You tell me!" She cried.

"Aye, you tell her," Adlin agreed.

"Now, now," he said to Adlin. Even as the two started on another tirade they began to fade.

"No!" Isabel shook her head and tried to grab onto Calum. Even if she could grasp him it was too late. They were gone.

Seth burst out laughing. Isabel turned in his direction. "What do you find so humorous?"

Shrugging he said, "What don't I find humorous? Save losing my brother-in-law. This is the house of comical horrors."

"Seth, you really need to get a grip," Andrea said.

Rage started to bubble inside Devin. The more Seth laughed the more the rage grew. Suddenly his laughter sounded louder, became his sole focus. Obnoxious scent filled his nostrils. The room narrowed down to Devin and Seth. Somehow he moved closer without flexing a muscle. Somehow he covered distance with a mere thought.

"Keep it up. Laugh," he threatened.

Seth's laughter died. Black flared to life in his eyes. Lips pulled back. "Back off."

Thump. Thump. Devin couldn't tell if he heard his heart or Seth's. Fury swallowed his every thought. Seth didn't stand a chance. With a cry of rage, Devin lunged.

"No. No. No!" Andrea cried.

"Devin! Please stop!" Isabel yelled.

"Hell no!" Dakota added.

Before Devin understood what was happening he fought both black and blue light. It all but blinded. He struggled and staggered back. Roaring with rage, he pushed forward. The black light receded slightly. The blue light brightened.

Then he saw red.

Devin flexed his fingers and growled. Strength filled his limbs. Pure power. Unlike anything he'd ever felt. Stalking forward, he focused on the black light. On Seth. "Come here." Deep, dark, different, Devin felt his voice vibrate in his chest. "Come."

Seth stood, braced his legs. A wicked smile erupted, eyes wild, thrilled. "Ah, now here's some real action. Have at it, fuck nuts."

"No. Please." Isabel moaned.

Devin didn't stop to wonder why wind blew in the middle of a Georgian living room. No reason to wonder why the air turned to ice. He wanted blood. Seth's blood. Hackles rose. Not waiting another second, he lunged and ripped through the blue light.

Now it was all red and black. Devin and Seth. An inhuman roar broke from Devin. He bared his teeth. *I'll rip out your throat. You're no competition. Isabel's mine.*

Smack.

Devin reared back in pain. *What the hell?*

Smack.

Falling to the ground he tried to bite at the attacking creature. As before the blue and black light surrounded him. This time he couldn't fight it.

Smack.

Everything went dark. Cold.

Life felt very far away.

"Please. Wake up. Please."

Such a soft voice but still so very far away.
"Devin. Please."

Pain seared when he tried to open his eyes. Holy hell. A cool cloth touched his forehead, cheek, neck. Isabel's gentle voice once more said, "Devin, please."

Trying again, he found the harsh light a little less blinding.

"Do you want me to blow out the candle?"

Candle? He shook his head and croaked, "Water."

Like the angel he knew she was, Isabel put a cup against his parched lips. Bringing his hands to the cup he first sipped then gulped. When finished, he laid back and said, "Thanks." Vision clearing somewhat, Devin realized he was in his room at Andrea's. Only a small candle burned on the bedside table. Nighttime had fallen. "What happened?"

She brushed back hair from his forehead. "From what I've gathered you experienced some sort of possession."

What? He tried to sit up. The room tilted. Devin fell back against the pillow. "No."

"Yes." She set the cup aside.

Devin remembered everything clearly. There came no bits and pieces of a forgotten moment...not really. It certainly hadn't felt like possession. Then again, what did possession feel like? He thought back to Leathan's experience with it. How furious he'd been with his cousin. "Oh no. Seth. Leathan. I fought them, eh?"

Isabel shook her head, blond hair shimmering in the candlelight. "Not you. Never you."

Devin closed his eyes, wanted to puke. The bloody wolf. When he opened his eyes a mixture of sympathy and concern lit her eyes. "Did I hurt anyone?"

"No one was hurt." A strange sadness entered her eyes. "Except for you. There's no way it didn't hurt you," she whispered.

Swallowing hard, he wiggled his toes and fingers. Everything was there. But all wasn't there. He'd lost time. Been possessed. How had that affected Isabel? Watching Lucas in wolf form do what he'd done? He reached up and stroked her cheek. "What about you? Are you alright, Isabel?"

"Seems you're always asking me that."

"And I always will. At least until we're free of this mess."

Isabel leaned her soft cheek against his hand. "It is a mess but—" Her eyes closed. "This house also feels somehow like an embrace. As though it cares for us and hopes we free its walls of Lucas forever."

Her words startled him. This Georgian... an embrace? Brushing his finger over her velvety lip he closed his eyes. Aye, set aside the fact it was one of the haunted houses entrenched in Calum's Curse and trapped the beast set to destroy him, this house also held the feel of Isabel. He knew he would never look at it again without seeing the way she overlooked its being built. The way she strolled every day, hands clasped behind her back, beauty not the least hidden by her stern demeanor as she approved and disapproved various parts of its construction.

Somehow, in the midst of all the evil trapped here, she and he had found a nook. An unexpected haven that while housed his nemesis, also embraced all he loved.

Isabel.

"Come. Lie down." Devin gently pulled her down until her body lay flush against his. Her head tucked into his neck. He stroked her hair and whispered, "I'm so sorry about all of this. Every last part."

Her slender hand found its way onto his bare chest, fingers slightly curled. "Don't be."

It occurred to him that he only wore boxers. Devin figured he'd be thanking his cousins tomorrow for getting him to bed. Hell if he could remember anything after wanting to destroy Seth. No doubt, he'd hear about that too. Breathing deeply, he continued to stroke Isabel's hair and for no particular reason he could name addressed the one subject he swore he'd steer clear of. "Do you like it in this time period?"

She lifted her head, eyes sad. "Do you suppose it matters?"

"I'm hoping," he replied evenly. "Whether here or there, I want to be with you, Isabel."

Isabel reached down, grabbed something then pulled it up onto his chest. Devin saw the picture of her ghostly self between her delicate hand and his skin. Her blue eyes were warm. "Andrea told me about how you treasured this picture." She smiled softly and whispered, "It's been quite handled, Devin."

"That is has, lassie," he whispered in return. "And what think you of that?"

When her lips met his, Devin wasn't sure how to handle things. Only hours before he'd taken her like a rutting animal. Was she now giving him a second chance? Giving him the opportunity to show her he was capable of romance? God knew he was. Before coming into Calum's curse he'd had any woman he wanted for the simple fact that he knew what women wanted.

But this was Isabel.

And Isabel was no average woman.

Her tight nipple prodded his chest through her oversized t-shirt. Damn! How could he not have realized she was only wearing one of his shirts? Nothing beneath! Bloody werewolf ghostly possessions had his mind not recognizing he had a goddess dressed in next to nothing in his bed.

Devin kissed the side of her neck and asked, "Is it too soon?"

Moaning, her hand rode up his chest and her leg covered his. Lord, he loved eighteenth century women with twenty-first century attitudes. He flipped Isabel beneath him, legs spread. This time he would do it right. This time he wouldn't be a crazed warlock who needed to prove his manhood. The erotic friction between his clothed cock and her wet, hot cleft nearly drove him past coherent thought.

The candle flickered.

Devin smiled.

The wolf was here again. Lucas.

When he turned his head, yellow eyes glowed from the corner of the room. Blue and black crackled around him and Isabel. Ah, his cousins had protected him and for shame, Devin didn't particularly care if they had or not. He knew he should be scared or furious. That he wasn't should have once more forewarned him that he wasn't thinking clearly.

"What is it?" Isabel asked but he crushed her question with a hot, intense kiss. One he knew the wolf watched. One he knew drove the wolf crazy.

Soon, however, the wolf didn't matter and Isabel stole his every thought. If Lucas stalked, watched, Devin considered this a worthy revenge.

He sat up, straddled Isabel, locked eyes with her then slowly, inch by inch, pulled up the T-shirt. Enjoyed how her rosy pink nipples tried to burst free from the thin white material. How her eyes drifted to mere slants and her full moistened lips fell apart in a gush of soft, relinquishing breathy air. Leaning down he ran his teeth over her cleavage, laved his tongue thickly over each eager nipple. Chin thrust up, throat bared, he nibbled up the center, nipped so hard at one point that she gasped and thrust her hips.

"Devin," she choked. "Too much."

"Isabel," he responded and rolled her onto her side—facing away—then ran his fingers lightly down the side of her belly, over the delicate protrusion of her hip bone. So smooth and soft, every delectable inch. He adored the way his hand covered half her waist and how the tight muscles of her backside nestled up against his groin.

Do it right. Romance her. You know how.

Even as he repeated the words in his mind, Devin pulled back her head and nibbled her ear. Isabel moaned. Devin pulled the T-shirt down over her shoulder and nipped. Isabel groaned. Spooning her tightly, he buried himself in her sweet hair and breathed deeply.

The candle flickered again. The air grew colder. The wolf was near.

Did she know?

Body on fire, he ran his hand over her belly, down between her legs. If she knew of the wolf,

Isabel said nothing. When she pushed back against him, Devin groaned. This was right. He must be doing it right. There was no help for him either way. With a savage growl he ripped away his boxers, lifted her leg and entered in one smooth thrust. Isabel arched and cried out. He pulled her close, offered no escape. Pulling out slightly, he thrust again, harder.

"Oh!" She gasped and exploded around him, her body a chasm of intense, hot, gripping need.

Hand grinding into her hip, Devin rode her orgasm with renewed fervor. Wrapping his free arm around her middle he trapped her as he took and took and took. When her hands grasped for escape on the bed sheets, he moved faster.

"Devin!"

Too late, she exploded in another orgasm. This time her inner muscles seized so strongly that Devin was forced to relent. Crying out, his body bucked and locked within hers. New sweat poured from his body. As slippery as things became he didn't let go.

She was his.

Panting heavily Devin tried to hold on to reality but the pleasure was so extreme. Her tight little body so bloody perfect. If and when his orgasm spent itself, Devin had no idea.

He passed out.

CHAPTER FIFTEEN

"Are you there?" Isabel whispered. "Please. I need to talk to you."

No response. Her ghost was nowhere to be found. Just the low flicker of the candle and warm summer wind blowing the curtains into the room. She rolled onto her side and studied Devin. Deep in slumber, he was gone to the world.

Reaching up, she ran the tip of her finger over his eyebrows. She liked the way they angled up, as though he were an optimist. As though no matter how hard life, he saw it for the better. His eyelashes were long and thick, nearly tangling at the corners. Framing those pale, greenish gray eyes of his, Devin didn't need to possess the unnatural allure of magic to be so utterly handsome.

With a small smile, Isabel studied his body. Long and lean. She loved how his slim hips tapered into legs that weren't too muscular but just right. How his shoulders weren't overly beefy but strong, wide and sure. And all those muscles in his chest and abdomen. So tone and fit. Truly, she'd never beheld a better looking man.

Cuddling down next to him, Isabel felt safe. Why, in this house, she had no clue. As she pulled a blanket over them she knew well why…Devin. He'd had an unbelievable effect on her. While it seemed she only closed her eyes for an instant when she opened them bright sunlight streamed through the windows. Devin was no longer in bed nor was he in the room.

Isabel climbed out of bed and pulled on the strange leggings Andrea had loaned her. Sweatpants? Very comfortable. But was this outfit appropriate? Truth told, she had little else to choose from until Andrea provided her clean dress. She could only hope that they didn't end up back in the past anytime soon. If so, she'd have some serious explaining to do. Padding down the stairs she followed the delicious smells coming from the kitchen. She stopped at the door and smiled. Devin was stirring something in a pot and sniffing the contents.

"It smells delicious," she said.

Turning his head slightly, he offered a crooked smile that nearly made her knees buckle. "I knew you'd be up soon." He made his way over, pulled her into his arms and gave her a long, thorough kiss. When at last the kiss ended, he merely held her and rested his chin on the top of her head. "I messed up again last night, didn't I?"

"What?" Isabel looked up at him. "I thought it was wonderful."

Stroking her cheek he said, "Did you? It didn't go nearly how I intended it to."

"Pray tell, how did you intend it to go? I felt it all rather satisfying."

"Is that all," he said, a glint of humor in his voice. "What I meant is that I intended the encounter to be far more romantic."

"Ah." Isabel kissed the palm of his hand. "It felt perfectly romantic to me."

"Did it then?" Devin wrapped his hand around the back of her head and angled her mouth against his in another deep, passionate kiss.

Pop. Blurp.

"Damn." Devin released her and made it to the stove in one long leap. He pulled the pan off of the burner and stirred its contents vigorously. "Looks like it'll make it."

"It better!" Andrea said, walking into the kitchen. "Nobody makes sauce like you."

Staggering in with a bleary look in his eyes, Seth grumbled. "That better be a spaghetti lunch you're cooking."

Isabel sat at the island and welcomed the cup of hot tea Devin slid her way.

"Definitely smells like it," Leathan said. "Never knew an Irishman who could cook a better Italian meal."

Andrea gave Devin a kiss on his cheek and ruffled his hair. "Glad to see you cooking away again, cuz."

Devin winked. "Eh well, feeling a bit more like my old self."

"Bet you are," Seth muttered and poured a cup of coffee. He eyed Isabel with what she could have sworn was remorse.

"Tell me you made the garlic bread too." Dakota sauntered into the room followed by Leathan.

"Of course!" Devin opened the oven. "Just started to heat."

"Nice."

Everyone once more sat around the kitchen island. Isabel thought for sure she would feel uncomfortable in this particular setting with virtual strangers but like yesterday, it felt so right. Meant to be. All of these people. This house. And as she'd so desired, home cooked meals were being cooked for her. It all felt perfect. But would she feel the same if she had the memories of her ghost?

"What time did you wake up?" Andrea asked Devin.

"A few hours ago. Took a walk then decided you'd all be ready for lunch when you finally got out of bed." Smiling at Isabel, he stirred the contents of the larger pot.

She couldn't help but smile in return. It felt like she walked on air. Was she falling in love with Devin? Taking a sip of tea Isabel tried to ignore the tight feeling in her chest. It was far too risky to love Devin when it was so entirely unclear how this story would end. She thought about what Devin said last night about wanting to be with her. Perhaps living in this time period. It was hard to say. Things were so very different here. Yet she'd always been good at adjusting to new places. And with Devin there by her side. Just maybe...

"I can't believe we all slept so late," Leathan murmured around a mouth full of coffee.

"I can," Seth muttered into his mug. After a good long sip, he glared at Leathan. "Why do you look so damn refreshed this morning?"

Leathan grinned at Dakota. Winked at Seth. "Worked off my hangover before it had a chance to kick in."

"Sounds like you deserved some drinking time," Devin said, grim faced.

"You better believe it," Seth grumbled.

Devin poured hot water and noodles into a sink strainer. Steam rose, fogging the window above the sink. "Guess it's about time someone filled me in on the details of last night."

Seth arched a brow at Isabel. "You didn't tell him?"

"Some of it," she said. Then we became distracted. He doesn't need to know that though. But somehow she gathered he already did. Seth struck her rather intuitive... and dangerous.

Devin leaned against the counter, eyes skirting between his cousins. "I want to apologize to everyone for what happened." Clearing his throat he continued, "Especially you, Seth."

"Hmph." Seth downed the last of his cup. "Is what it is, cuz."

Frowning, Devin turned and refilled his cup, then Seth's. "Not sure why I keep going after you."

Seth shrugged. "Seems I just can't stop living in death's shadow. When I'm not seeking it out, it's trying to find me."

"Seth!" Andrea said. "Don't talk like that."

Isabel noted the disturbed look that passed over Leathan's face before it quickly vanished. Voice upbeat, he said, "I see Devin's got the dining room table set. Let's get this food in there and eat."

Everyone agreed wholeheartedly. Within minutes they sat down to a table heavy with bowls of spaghetti, sauce, meatballs and garlic bread. Before Isabel had a chance to assist, her plate was full and she was surrounded by three big men eating with astonishing gusto. Andrea chuckled and motioned for her to eat.

The minute Isabel took the first bite of Devin's meal, she thought she'd died and gone to heaven. "This is amazing!"

Devin sat beside her. "Not bad for an Irishman, eh?"

Isabel shook her head and sunk her teeth into the bread.

"I have to thank you for returning 'our' Devin to us, Isabel," Andrea said. "He hasn't cooked like this in far too long."

"I haven't been around to cook like this," Devin defended.

"True, but we all hope that'll change," Dakota said.

Isabel glanced at Devin and didn't miss the contentment that warmed his eyes. Sitting back, she glanced around the room and again thought of walking through this house a few days ago when this room had no walls. When Devin talked of home cooked meals. She liked the way he made this house come alive. In fact, for a while there Isabel had completely forgotten that this house was extremely haunted by both herself and Lucas. A shiver ran down her spine.

When Devin's strong, reassuring hand found her thigh beneath the table she knew they were thinking the same thing once again. She also knew that this was the right time to talk about last night's events.

"I take it you do not recall what stopped you... Lucas from hurting Seth?" She asked Devin.

Devin didn't seem surprised that she broached the topic. He squeezed her thigh lightly and pulled away his hand. "No, I don't. I'm assuming it was Leathan and Seth's magic."

Leathan took a swig of his drink, shook his head and looked at Isabel. "Maybe a little but I'd say mostly it was Isabel's ghost."

Devin's eyes widened and he focused on her. "Really?"

"Yes." Isabel worked at a wobbly smile. "She was something."

"You are something," Devin said. "Why didn't you tell me last night! I would have... I mean I wouldn't have–"

She put a finger to his lips and shook her head. "It wasn't something you needed to concern yourself with last night. Lucas had drained the life out of you."

"Not all the life apparently," Seth commented dryly.

Devin's eyes narrowed on his cousin. "Have some tact."

"He's right," Leathan said. "Too much. Even for you, Seth."

Seth's eyes darkened but he said nothing.

"My ghost is strong. And very mad at Lucas... the wolf," Isabel said to Devin. "Though I'm not surprised in the least."

"Was it caught on camera?" Devin asked.

"You didn't already look to see?" Leathan said.

Devin shrugged. "Nope. I got up and took a walk. Needed time to think."

Andrea looked between Isabel and Devin, a small knowing smile on her face. "Totally understand."

"Well I don't," Seth said. "We still have a puzzle to figure out here."

"He's right," Leathan said to Devin. "One way or another this house seems to have multiple dimensions that suck you and Isabel back and forth. Not to mention it still has Andrea's husband. Don't get me wrong Devin, I'm glad as hell to have you back to normal but from here on out we all need to focus on investigating every chance we get. Especially when you're in this time period."

Appetite gone, Isabel noticed everyone had finished their food. They certainly ate fast. Standing, she started to gather everything and bring it into the kitchen. Andrea followed her lead. Dakota meanwhile left the room and returned a minute later with a laptop computer which she plunked down on the end of the table.

When things were cleared off, Andrea urged her to join them at the table. Though she'd much rather wash the dishes, Isabel sat down. The idea of watching what happened again last night was less than appealing. Regardless, Isabel wanted Devin to know that she would remain by his side through this. She wanted Devin to know that she was as there for him as her ghost seemed to be. In a strange way, she and her ghostly self were a team.

When Dakota turned the screen to face them, Isabel was once more amazed by what she saw. The living room popped up on the screen. There she sat next to Devin and around them everyone else exactly as they had been. It was incredible! She sat here watching the past unfold once more. Yet why find this so astounding when she had recently traveled three hundred years into the future in the blink of an eye?

Devin leaned forward and watched the screen intently when it became apparent he was getting irritated with Seth the night before. Isabel couldn't help but inwardly cringe as the nightmare once more unfolded on the laptop.

Seth burst out laughing. Isabel turned in his direction. "What do you find so humorous?"

He shrugged. "What don't I find humorous? Save losing my brother-in-law. This is the house of comical horrors."

"Seth, you really need to get a grip," Andrea scoffed.

Devin got up and stalked toward Seth, his gait strange, uneven almost. His nostrils flared. "Keep it up. Laugh," he threatened.

Seth's laughter died. Black flared to life in his eyes. Lips pulled back. "Back off."

Isabel watched, once more fascinated as Devin's body seemed to warp and transform into something half man, half wolf. Somehow Lucas's ghost wolf merged with Devin's human form. Though gruesome, she found it morbidly fascinating. As she did last night, Isabel tried to swallow but was unable. With a sudden cry of animal-like rage, Devin lunged.

"No. No. No!" Andrea cried.

"Devin! Please stop!" Isabel yelled.

"Hell no!" Dakota added.

The same black slickness she'd seen at the river erupted from Seth as he tried to fight off his cousin. Devin staggered back. Roaring with rage, he pushed forward. The black light receded slightly. Leathan stepped forward, blue light pouring from him to fight Devin.

But the wolf, Devin, flung away the crippling power and rippled with rage, a red aura swallowing his form. "Come here," he growled at Seth. Voice different, dark and cruel, he repeated. "Come."

Seth stood, braced his legs. A wicked smile erupted, eyes wild, thrilled. "Ah, now here's some real action. Have at it, fuck nuts."

"No. Please." Isabel moaned.

Wind blew through the living room. Everyone's breath fogged as the room turned frigid. An inhuman roar broke from Devin's chest and he lunged at Seth. Suddenly, something materialized between Seth and Devin. Devin fell back in obvious pain. At first whatever attacked him appeared a pulsing mist. Devin tried to bite at it. Soon the mist turned to the form of a woman. Herself! Shocked Isabel watched in horror as it screeched like a banshee until the wolf jumped free from Devin's body.

Yellow eyes narrowed, the great ghostly wolf stalked away from Devin's body, tail swooshing back and forth. It looked at her ghostly self and somehow spoke. "You." Then it swung its attention to her. "And you. Mine."

Licking the saliva from its jowls the beast turned and ran into the wall where it vanished. A terrible chill ran through her body. Isabel began to shake violently as she stared at where the wolf vanished.

"I'll get you through this. I promise. But you've got to be strong."

Isabel tore her eyes away from the wall and stared at the remnants of her ghostly self. All she could do as her ghost vanished was shake her head. *Please don't go! I have so many questions for you!* But speech was impossible and her ghost slowly faded away. Tears started to pour down her face. All she could do was stare blindly at Devin's unmoving form on the floor. Was he dead? Had Lucas killed him?

"Isabel, sweetie." Then she was surrounded by Devin's arms. "You should have told me about this last night. I obviously wasn't the only one attacked by that bastard!"

Isabel blinked rapidly, suddenly realizing that she'd started to cry in front of everyone. It was no longer last night. Nothing remained of it but this terrible video. Frustrated, she pulled away from Devin and quickly wiped away her tears. She'd sworn to herself last night that if she let Lucas affect her than he'd essentially won. Not to mention she appreciated what her ghost had said to her. Stay strong. If her ghost had managed three hundred years in this house alongside the pure evil of Lucas than she'd be darned if she wouldn't see this thing through and rid the world of this beast.

Devin's steady gaze met hers. What bothered her most was that Lucas meant to destroy Devin. The pain he'd already inflicted on this man made her want to twist a knife in Lucas's gut. Isabel felt a certain strength in that realization. Isabel wanted to kill the wolf. Lucas. Mainly because she loved its nemesis.

The realization came swiftly. She did indeed love Devin. With all of her heart. But now wasn't the time for soft moments. It was time to fight. The only way to do that was to help these paranormal investigators turned warlocks any way she could.

With new resolve she turned her attention to Leathan. "Lucas has one weakness. We all know what that is. I'd say it's time to hunt him rather than the other way around."

CHAPTER SIXTEEN

"A séance? I can't believe we're doing this."

"Well why not?" Dakota rolled her eyes at Seth. "Kinda plays into the whole ghost hunting thing, don't ya think?"

"Sure," Andrea said and pulled all of the chairs into a tight circle.

Devin shook his head, still amazed that this whole thing was Isabel's idea. Sometime between watching the video nine hours ago and now, she'd become an avid ghost hunter with a steely determination he couldn't help but admire. Did he wonder about her forthcoming and brave attitude? Yes and no. He knew she had it in her but worried that all of this was happening way too fast. How much change could one lass take?

"If I'd known we were going all 'teenager' I would've brought my Ouija board," Seth teased.

"You know you love it," Leathan responded.

Devin laughed. "He does, doesn't he?"

"Oh yeah!" Andrea said. "The Ouija board. All he wanted to play with since the age of three."

"You really do have a thing with death, don't you?" Dakota asked.

Seth grinned. "Bet your ass."

Devin sat in a chair and shook his head. "If you guys along with Isabel's ghost somehow protected us from Lucas last night then why is it again we're trying to summon the damn thing to us?"

"I'd say it's because Isabel's had enough of

running," Dakota said. "Can't say I blame her."

"She's a lot tougher than I ever thought a woman from that time period would be," Andrea said.

Devin well understood why. "Good thing I'd say."

"Aye." Leathan adjusted one of the cameras for at least the fifth time. "Her aggression is just what we need. No point sitting back and waiting like we did before. We're investigators and warlocks. Seems to me we'd do good to follow Isabel's lead."

"Amen to that." Dakota sat in one of the chairs, her attention turning to Devin. "I'm really happy for you, hun."

"Me too," he replied. "She's great."

"She's perfect for you," Andrea said.

Devin was about to agree when Isabel appeared in the doorway. Dressed once more in her eighteenth century clothes with her hair streaming in long, pale curls down her chest, her beauty left him speechless. Maybe it was the fact the room was lit with candles. Maybe it was the fact she appeared so elegant and graceful. But Devin knew better. It was her attitude.

As always, her narrow shoulders were thrown back, chin held high. Isabel once more oversaw this house. Just as she had since its very foundation was laid. He knew in that exact moment, no matter where she ended up, Isabel belonged to this house just as surely as it belonged to her.

He walked over and kissed her on the cheek. Tucking something into her hand, he urged her to sit. Isabel opened her hand and gazed down at the small Butterfly Weed in her palm. With a small smile she nodded and closed her fist. Sitting in the circle of chairs Isabel looked around at everyone. "I will not lie. I'm scared. But I have been scared for a very long time."

Andrea reached over and squeezed her hand. "It's alright. We're here with you."

"Do you think Calum and Adlin will join us?" She asked.

"I wouldn't count on it," Devin said. "They've seemed less dependable this haunting than normal."

Isabel nodded and glanced around the circle. "Do you know exactly how I should go about this?"

"In that you're summoning your own ghost to enter your body, afraid not, lassie," Leathan said.

"Maybe just asking the woman of the house to enter might help," Andrea provided.

Devin didn't like this at all but kept his mouth shut. They needed to make ground and Isabel no doubt was the best way to do that. Squeezing Isabel's hand in reassurance, he nodded.

Jaw set, she closed her eyes and spoke softly. "Isabel, are you here?"

Everyone waited. Silent.

Isabel repeated, "Isabel, it's me… you, from the past. Please, I give you permission to speak through this body. Talk to the people in this room."

Everyone waited.

Silent.

Still nothing.

"Isabe—"

"Are they doing what I think they're doing?"

Isabel blinked. Obviously confused.

"Fools!"

This time when Calum and Adlin appeared they didn't bother pouring through the ceiling. Instead, they glared down at Isabel like two kindred devils derived from the same cesspool. This time they weren't focused on one another.

Isabel blinked faster, eyes fluttering so quickly Devin felt panic clutch his insides. Was ghostly Isabel coming?

"Stop this now!" Adlin roared. "She'll be hurt."

"As he says!" Calum's words moved all their chairs back a few feet. "Isabel should not be your soldier in this!"

"Shhh." Isabel's eyes stopped fluttering and her chin rested on her chest.

Adlin and Calum seemed to rise up, peer down, somehow surrounding her without moving.

"Where am I, Calum?" Isabel whispered. "Where are you?"

Calum's eyes narrowed. "Right here, m'dear. You have been invited into your mortal body, Isabel. Do not fear."

Isabel's head snapped up. Devin's jaw dropped. Her eyes were no longer a radiant violet but now a deep, chocolate brown. Her lips no longer soft and velvety but somehow curved and plush. "Who is Isabel?"

Calum staggered back. Adlin appeared amazed.

"Who is Isabel?" She repeated. "Calum, where are you?"

The candles flickered when Calum rushed forward and fell to his knees before Isabel. Peering up, heart in his eyes, he whispered, "Anna?"

"Sonofa—"

Andrea grabbed Seth's arm and shook her head sharply.

"Where are you?" Anna said again. This time her voice seemed further away, the anguished tone more obvious. "I miss you."

Calum miraculously took Isabel's hand, bowed his head and rambled, "I'm here. I miss you. I am so very sorry. Can you forgive me? Please tell me where you are. I miss you. Please forgive me. If I could do it all over again I would have never left. I thought I did the right thing. So very wrong. Please forgive…"

They all watched as Calum's ghost, tears running down his face, vanished. As did Adlin who stood over like a silent sentinel.

Silence.

Seth finally broke the silence. "Holy shit."

Devin immediately went to Isabel and shook her. Enough of this. Last time he'd let her play martyr.

She frowned and blinked, her eyes once more violet. "Did my ghost enter my body? What did I miss?"

Devin pulled her into his arms and said, "No she didn't."

He sat on the couch, pulled her onto his lap and held tight. Bloody bad business they were in. Why had he even entertained the idea of any spirit entering her body? Bunch of crap. Last time he'd let her go all hero on him. "You okay?"

"You've got to stop asking me that," she mumbled.

Pulling back, he let her up for air. "No I don't," he said. "You won't be doing that again."

"Doing what?" she asked and tried to sit up. He pulled her back.

"Doesn't matter."

She frowned. "Well, something obviously happened. Were the cameras running?"

Snort. Chuckle. Full fledge laugher.

Devin dragged his attention away from Isabel to find his cousins laughing. "What the hell's so funny?"

Andrea shook her head. With a smile, she sat next to Devin and Isabel. Touching his arm she said, "It's okay, cuz. She's not scared. She's one of us now!"

Huh? Were they out of their minds?

"Well, did you catch whatever happened on camera?" Isabel repeated.

Devin frowned and looked at her. Isabel shrugged.

She wasn't scared in the least. All she was worried about was whether they'd recorded the encounter. His little Isabel had turned into quite the paranormal investigator. Damn! "Not sure love, we haven't had a chance to look yet."

Seth already had the laptop out. The scene replayed even as they spoke. Isabel watched intently. When it was over she sat back, eyes a little glassy. "I can't believe Anna made contact. Poor Calum. But good too I suppose."

"So you know the story between Calum and Anna?" Andrea asked.

"Parts of it." Isabel peered around the group. "Probably not all of it. I knew that he'd been married to her and had a child. They were very much in love but things went wrong and he had to leave her with her family in Scotland. Then he came to America. He never went into details about what went wrong. But he did share many lovely stories about their time together."

"I think I speak for everyone when I say we'd like to hear a few of those stories sometime," Andrea said softly.

Isabel nodded. "Of course." Attention turned Devin's way she said, "He left her because of the curse, didn't he?"

"Yes and no." Devin took her hand. "Though she didn't seem to remember it tonight, Anna eventually shunned Calum in life. When he turned to dark magic he became a different man. It seems however, perhaps the afterlife released her from heavy thoughts and she's only remembered the good they had together."

"Strange seeing Calum act like that," Seth said.

"He's definitely not the guy we thought he was," Devin agreed. "Not sure why he ever turned to dark magic."

"For his family," Leathan reminded. "Thought he could gain more wealth and power and better support them. Little did he know the consequences."

"I still can't believe that the man who saved me from a destitute life is the same monster sent from a nineteenth century coven to destroy Calum's descendants," Isabel said. "How did Lucas time-travel? How did he ever know that I would eventually be protected by the same man's bloodline for which he searched?"

"I've been giving this some thought," Devin replied. "We know that Calum can time-travel with aide from Adlin. Calum hides each warlock stone somewhere in the world. He then travels to a given time period and builds a house. Once a house is built, he lures the monster set to destroy each descendant to the home where he traps it. As we all know, only the stone can release each said beast."

"Yeah, we know all that," Seth said.

"So I'd say we need to focus on what's different this time. First off, the beast was lured way too soon.

The house isn't even built yet," Devin said.

"And that would be because the wolf made contact with Isabel and found Calum sooner, presumably never lured by Calum to begin with." Leathan said. "But I don't believe in coincidences."

"Neither do I," Devin agreed. "Which leads me to believe that the wolf somehow found Calum sooner and used Isabel as bait."

"But how would I possibly be considered bait?" Isabel asked. "After all, Calum's primary goal was to trap the threat to his bloodline. Despite what a good man he is, I can't imagine Calum ceasing such to help a perfect stranger."

"Initially, we couldn't either," Leathan said. "But now I'm not so sure. Seems to me if he was aware of the wolf tracking him, he was most likely keeping a very close eye on the beast."

Andrea nodded. "And under that assumption, Calum could have very well stepped in and taken you under his wing, Isabel. No matter how kind Lucas was to you."

"Now that I think of it." Isabel glanced uneasily at Devin. "Calum did conveniently approach me shortly after Lucas tried to kill me. I was petrified and alone and in desperate need of escape. A girl can go through a lot and her life and stay strong. This... Lucas... was just too much."

"We all reach our breaking point, sweetie," Dakota said. "Sounds like you persevered much longer than most would have been able to."

"Damn straight," Seth seconded.

"So Calum approached you and offered you a job overlooking the building of his house. Why? Were you even remotely qualified for such a job?" Leathan asked.

"No, Calum was honest with Isabel up front about most everything," Devin said. "At least from his stand point. Calum back then didn't know what ghostly Calum knows. And as you already gathered Isabel doesn't know nearly as much as her ghost does, unfortunately."

"Hence the need for her to make contact and fill in the details," Isabel added. "I keep trying. Calling to her. Nothing."

"She was a lot more active before," Devin said.

"Was she ever." Seth winked.

Eyes narrowed, Devin studied his cousin with suspicion. He'd looked everywhere for the camera recording from the night Isabel's ghost had visited him and initiated sex. Nowhere to be found. Leave it to Seth to wait this long to hint at the damn thing. Thankfully, Isabel made no comment. He'd filled her in on most of it anyways. Did she really need to know about that? Hell if he knew his conscience wouldn't bother him though. Regardless, another time maybe.

"Okay, so we're assuming Calum did the right thing and took care of Isabel. Fair enough." Andrea looked at Devin. "So now the greater mystery is the stone, talisman that's connected to Devin. The stone that will set Lucas free from this house. When Isabel with all the memories traveled here with you at the beginning Devin, she wore that stone around her neck." She looked at Isabel. "But you don't have it yet. So it stands to reason you'll be finding it soon. My question... after all Isabel knows now why on earth would she keep it if she knew it would ultimately lock her in this house with Lucas?"

"The million dollar question," Seth muttered.

Devin brushed some hair away from her face. "It obviously meant a great deal to her. She somehow connected it with the... way we felt about each other."

Isabel blushed. "True, I'm a romantic. However, I'm also a realist. I couldn't imagine any scenario in which I would keep a stone with me that would trap me alongside Lucas for hundreds of years."

"Love and monsters make people do crazy things," Dakota said.

Leathan smiled. "Aye, so true, lassie."

"Still," Isabel said. "We're missing essential information. I must have had a very good reason. One beyond love."

"I'd like to know what the hell—" Seth stopped talking. "Wait a sec. Did we ever verify at the Victorian whether Calum hid the stone before or after he built each house?"

Dakota shook her head. "Nope. Not that I know of. Didn't really matter in that case."

"I'm starting to think every little detail matters in Calum's curse," Leathan said.

"Ditto that," Seth said.

"Okay, so evidently he hides the stone afterwards which probably makes sense. He seals the trap using the stone," Devin said.

"Could have easily been that the stone is a spare key, dark magic and all," Seth said.

"Don't be an arse," Devin returned.

Seth pointed a thumb at his chest. "Who me? Easy killer, just making a point. Nothing in any of this is predictable."

Andrea frowned at Devin this time. "You really are quick to go after Seth this haunting. Something we might want to look closer at while we investigate."

Devin shrugged.

"She makes a good point," Leathan said. "But we'll worry more about that as we go."

"Not much to look at," Devin stated. "He wants Isabel."

Seth cocked an eyebrow. "So that means you have to go after me at every turn? We're supposed to be best friends."

"I see you aren't denying that you want her," Devin said.

"Why should I?"

"Enough!" Isabel said, looking between the two. "I would think it rather clear I have feelings for Devin."

Surprise made Devin's brows rise. Isabel wasn't one to hold back. Her proper little skin had been shed and he liked the hell out of it. Loving her was one thing. It came naturally. But truly liking her? Easily becoming a no-brainer.

Dakota sniggered. "I was going to say let's set the testosterone aside for a night but you outdid me, Isabel. Perfect."

Seth said nothing. But his cousin didn't dwell on anything too long. Especially women. Easy come, easy go.

Devin sat back as the conversation continued and appreciated the warm softness of Isabel's hand in his. The pillar candles had burned down about halfway, casting low-lying shadows around the room. Did Isabel's ghost lurk somewhere in those dark corners? Did she feel betrayed by the feelings he had for her in solid form? Or did she understand? He imagined she would. After all, this Isabel was her original self. The one he was supposed to fall in love with all along. This was the most important version. At least he hoped.

There still remained so many questions. The stone. How Isabel remained trapped in the house. The scar. Glancing at her, he reveled in her perfect profile and smooth skin. This Isabel had no idea she would be scarred. Should he tell her? No. Would she be able to handle it? Obviously. But how did it happen? Devin knew that there must be great violence in her future. And most likely in his because he had no intention of leaving her side, no matter in what form she existed.

"I'm tired. Up most of last night with Seth," Leathan said. "Who wants to take the night watch?"

"I will," Devin volunteered.

"Are you sure?" Andrea asked. "You were up before all of us this morning."

"Positive. Too much on my mind. Might as well ghost hunt."

"I'll stay up too," Isabel said.

Seth stood and stretched. "Sounds good to me. I'm off."

Leathan and Dakota stood as well. "See you in the morn, cuz."

Andrea yawned. "You two want something to eat before I crash?"

Devin smiled. "No, we're good. Get some sleep."

Once they'd left Isabel promptly pulled her hand from his, sat up straighter and turned hard eyes his way. "So when did you plan on telling me that you'd made love to my ghost?"

CHAPTER SEVENTEEN

"I ah… you don't understand… I… didn't." Devin stood and got busy fast adjusting one of the cameras. Finally he turned and crossed his arms over his chest. "I really had no choice in the matter."

Isabel eyed him, lips firmly set. "No choice?"

"None," he declared. "She… it…. You seduced me."

"Is that the best you can do with your explanation?"

Devin's eyes searched hers. "You have to understand, she… you were so beautiful."

"And?"

A vein ticked in his forehead. "Sometimes a man loses control especially if…"

"Especially if what?"

Devin seemed undecided for a moment before he crossed the room and pulled her to her feet. Taking both of her hands he said softly, "Especially if he has strong feelings for her."

Oh, she couldn't do this any longer. A giggle erupted.

Devin frowned. "What?"

Isabel rolled her eyes and shook her head. "Did you really think I was upset with you? She's me… well, my ghost! If anything, I'm flattered. We did not even know each other that well then."

A quick flash of shock crossed his features before Devin growled and scooped her up. Somehow in the blink of an eye she was beneath him on the couch, long skirts a tangled mess. Encaged between his arms, Isabel laughed.

"You're trouble, you know that?" He nuzzled the side of her neck. "I just can't seem to peg you."

"Peg me?" Isabel stopped laughing when his hand rode up her leg. "Oh I think you've pegged me."

This time Devin chuckled before he rose up on his elbows, expression suddenly serious. "I'm sorry. That experience was nothing like the real thing."

"Shhh." Isabel grinned. "She might hear you."

A small smile blossomed on his face. For a fraction of a second Isabel felt something dark surface in him. It was that same alluring magic she'd experienced before. In the foundation at the beginning. In the forest yesterday when he took her. Devin's black magic seemed to fluctuate around him. It pulsed and caressed her as surely as his hands and lips. Isabel's hips surged up. Tried to meet it... Devin.

As he nibbled her earlobe and ran his hot palm up between her legs Isabel wondered if she had by nature an attraction to the beast. Had being with Lucas knowing he was a monster made her more in tune with the darker side, made some small part of her need it desperately?

"Um, it's called the night watch for a reason."

Both sat up abruptly when Seth walked in and grabbed his drink.

"Night, Seth," Devin said.

"Later." Seth left.

"He's probably right." Isabel tried to ignore her aroused state. "We really need to focus on what needs to get done here. We're too easily distracted."

"Mm Hmm." Devin sat back and crossed one leg over the other. "I'll bet I know who made sure you saw that video."

"Seth's your cousin. He only has your best interests in mind."

Devin snorted. "Sure he does."

"So you two really are normally close?"

"Aye." Devin shrugged one shoulder. "Seth's always been the wild one. Total dare devil. Lad really shouldn't be alive right now. Regardless, we've always gotten on well. I think this curse is changing us all and not for the good."

"I think that depends on how you look at it," she said. "If you three work together well this curse might bring you closer."

Devin studied her. "You might be right. It's just hard. I've denied this magic for a year where Seth and Leathan embraced it. Who knows, Seth might have issues with that fact."

"True." Isabel placed her hand on his knee. "Or you might be acting like any man would when another man shows interest in his woman."

His shrewd gaze cut to her core. "Well said, sweetheart."

A sharp thrill raced through her veins. When a slow burn covered her cheeks, Devin's eyes lit with a strange sort of possession. Reaching up, he ran the back of his forefinger over her cheekbone. "I like making you blush."

Isabel very rarely thought about her looks. Typically throughout life, they'd only caused her trouble. She'd always made a habit of toning down her feminine appearance. Yet right now with the way he was looking at her, she was glad she'd been born attractive, that a man like this would look at her in such a fashion.

A candle flared and spit. Its light flickered across Devin's face, lit his gray green eyes. His brows slowly came together as he clutched her chin. When his face began to blur she clutched his arms. "Devin," she whispered. "Stay with me."

Even as she said it the candlelight warped around the room, twisting and turning until it became the fire in the middle of a lawn in front of the Georgian. Isabel grasped at the air and fought off panic. "Devin?"

"Right here."

Sitting on the ground, she twisted around. He was right behind her. "Oh, thank God!"

"No." He stopped her before she embraced him. "We're back, Isabel. Your employees are right over there." Devin stood, pulled her up and turned her away.

It took all of her willpower not to turn back. Looking at the men around the fire and the framework of the Georgian she said, "No time has passed here, has it?"

"Doesn't look it." Devin put his hand on the small of her back. "Good thing I'm wearing the right clothes, eh? You'd best join them at the campfire or retire to your tent."

Disorientation took over. How odd it was to be back in her era after traveling to the future. "I'll go to my tent." She looked over her shoulder, up into his eyes. "I wish you could be there with me."

With a small grin he said, "Imagine the look of shock on your poor make-believe mistress's face."

"You're impossible." Grinning, she walked

away. Even as the distance grew between them she knew Devin watched. Odd how it felt like they'd been involved so much longer than they really had. As each heavy step separated them, Isabel felt emptier. Glancing at the house, she had the sudden urge to run back, grab his hand and spend the night within its wall-less structure. Somehow—despite all the bad—it was good... at least for them.

When Isabel made it to her tent she looked back one last time. Devin had joined the men at the fire. All laughed. Everyone had been working hard and making good progress. They had much to be proud of.

Minutes later, as she lay looking up at the tent roof, Isabel debated whether she should confront Calum now. But what exactly would she confront him about? He had done her no wrong. If anything he saved her from sure death. They had become friends.

After a restless night, it was with this thought firmly in place that Isabel found herself strolling down the woodland path with Calum the next day.

"Of course we are fast friends, Isabel," Calum assured, top hat removed, black hair glistening in the sunlight. "And I'm so sorry that my blasted circumstances seem to have sucked you in such as they have. I could have never imagined this."

"Of course you could have! Did you not take to dark magic? Did you not witness things you thought impossible when you did so?"

With a heavy sigh, Calum shook his head. "One can see many things and still not imagine all the future holds for him."

Isabel had told him she met his ghost in the twenty-first century. She had not told him that he made contact with Anna. Based on the heartache she witnessed there seemed no reason. It was a path he and his love had to travel. Right now she was far more concerned with her and Devin's path. "Where is the stone, Calum?"

Hands locked behind his back, he continued on his leisurely stroll. "I don't have it."

"Of course you do. Where is it?"

"What was it like? The Georgian in the twenty-first century? Breathtaking I'd say!" He declared.

"I told you it was lovely." Isabel frowned. "I won't be deterred. I must know where that stone is. It would comfort me greatly to know it was far from here."

"Then it is."

She stopped short and exclaimed, "Calum, that stone has the power to trap me in the house for hundreds of years."

"No, only I have the power to do that."

"So the stone has nothing to do with trapping the beast?"

"I never said that."

"Then it does."

"Highly unlikely."

"Ugh!" Strolling ahead she threw her hands in the air. "I heard Adlin was like this but you? This is a new side to your personality, Calum. One I am not sure I like."

Within seconds, Calum was walking alongside. "I still can't believe you met that old bugger."

Isabel pointed from him to her as she walked. "We would have never met if it wasn't for that old bugger. He helped you travel through time."

"Very true. However, I still consider him a thorn

in my backside."

"Seems to me he has your best interests at heart."

Calum stopped. "The time hopping has addled your brain, child. That wizard is problematic. Never says what he means. Never means what he says."

"Much like you," she pointed out.

"How wrong you are! I always come straight to the point."

Putting a hand over her head, Isabel groaned. "Tell me, Calum, did you come to my aide because you'd been tracking Lucas and wanted to protect me?"

"I came to your aide because you were a woman in need of help."

She faced him, hands on hips. "Yes, you've always said that. Why didn't it occur to me sooner than you'd been watching Lucas all along? I guess despite my hard upbringing I trusted too much. Needed to. I suppose I did believe in coincidences." Fury started to bubble up. "And I led Devin and his cousins to believe that I knew of the curse. Calum, you told me you knew magic and knew how to trap the beast. You said nothing of your connection with Lucas. You told me he hunted you because you had me, because you had the ability to imprison him. You said he needed to destroy you! It was all one big lie!"

Isabel turned and stormed down the path. While in retrospect the whole affair was not so terrible the fact her friend hadn't simply come clean from the beginning bothered her a great deal. When Isabel got to the river it occurred to her Calum wasn't following.

"Of course I'm following you."

She turned and found him leaning against a nearby tree. "Really, Isabel, why the dramatics?"

There was something dangerous surrounding Calum. Somehow it reminded her faintly of Seth. Those two were definitely related. "You don't like the truth do you, Calum?"

"What is the truth, Isabel?" He pushed away from the tree. "How is it that you feel you know it when even I do not?"

Now was not the time to show weakness. "You know more of the truth than I, Calum."

Sauntering her way he said, "Do I? Are you quite sure?"

Isabel felt the magnetism radiating off of him. Calum possessed his own allure. Not romantic in her case. But watching him right now, approaching like a stealthy panther, Isabel couldn't help but wonder about the love between him and Anna. And, quite frankly, the sex. "Do not turn this around, Calum. You did not tell me everything. I want to know why."

About a foot away, he stopped. His blue eyes turned black, then blue again as he contemplated her. "Because it would have been too much for you to handle then. Not now. But I'm not sorry. I only had your best interests at heart." He put an icy finger under her chin and tilted back her head until their eyes were aligned. "Tell me, would you have come had you known that Lucas was my beast to trap. For all I seemed like a saving light in your life, would you have come had you known how completely immersed in dark magic I am? How truly evil I am capable of being?"

Fear shot through her body.

"Gotta say, the word Warlock doesn't feel like a perfect fit. How about sorcerer?" Devin stalked from the forest. Where Isabel had moments ago compared

Calum to a stalking panther, Devin definitely possessed his own unique dark strength. His, however, held the sharp tang of denied domination. Devin's deceptive gait and sharp eyes bespoke a creature who longed for the blood of his prey.

Calum slowly pulled his hand away and turned toward Devin. To the untrained eye, it might appear a confrontation over a woman. Isabel knew better. This was a meeting of two very different types of magic...both equally lethal. These men didn't deal with testosterone. No, what fueled them was far greater.

"Not in the mood for your antics right now," Calum said softly. "Haven't we already been down this road? You know who's stronger."

Black and red met in a large, sizzling arch between the two.

"Not the time and place," Calum repeated.

Devin's lips pulled back. Isabel studied his expression, again astounded by a certain familiarity. Wolf. Somehow it was part of him or overtook him. She couldn't be sure. One thing she did know... she wouldn't lose him to Calum's magic.

"He's right," she said calmly.

The aura's continued to spark off one another. Devin's eyes met hers. "Could be I'm going nuts but didn't he just threaten you?"

Yes. "No. At least not in any way we need worry about." Isabel turned her attention to Calum. "Know that you have lost my trust. I remain your friend only because I believe there's still good in you."

She took Devin's hand. "Please, come. There's work to be done and I'm needed."

Devin and Calum continued to stare at each other

until Devin finally turned away and walked with her. Phew! Though hard, Isabel didn't dare look back. If there was always one thing that existed between her and Calum it was an equal respect for one another's self-constraint and the innate ability to know the other's boundaries.

"The minute I think I get that guy, maybe he's good, he's pulls that sorta crap," Devin muttered as they walked down the path.

"It's the only way he knows how to react," Isabel said. "Now that I know more about his story I see his actions are mostly designed to protect himself from further hurt."

Devin shook his head. "How can you say that after he betrayed you? How can you protect him?"

Isabel bit her lip. "Because that is my magic."

He cocked a brow.

"Well, you and he possess real magic. You came into it recently and it totally rearranged your whole life. Meanwhile, I've been living real life since the day I was born. In my case, not a nice place. I grew up hard. Learned how deceptive, cunning and manipulative human nature can be. Despite all that, I made a point to look for what good there is. All of this is my magic. People lie. But there's always a reason. The real trick is being able to look past it, understand why people act the way they do."

"Sounds like good old fashioned reasonable deduction to me. Common sense."

Isabel winked. "That's right. Trust me, most people don't possess it."

Devin stopped and pulled her down to sit on a nearby rock. "You have every right to be mad at Calum. He betrayed your trust."

Warmth flooded her cheeks. Until this very moment it hadn't occurred to her that Devin heard everything. "I am sorry I did not tell you and your cousins I knew of the curse. I simply felt so divided. There still remained a certain loyalty to Calum. I wanted to talk to him first." She fiddled with her skirts. "Assuming I'd be talking to him again."

Stretching his legs, Devin lifted his face to the sun. "Isabel, you didn't betray anyone's trust. You simply decided to trust a friend. No harm in that." His head dropped forward, eyes met hers. "Besides, this whole experience has been one strange thing after another. After all, I slept with your ghost."

Hand over mouth, she hid her smile and nodded.

Prying her hand away, he cupped her head and pulled her lips to his. This time she pushed her tongue forward. His tongue met and swirled. Fluid flooded between her legs. Isabel wanted him again. Needed it.

A warm wind blew down the path. Leaves rustled. Devin left her lips until his mouth fell next to her ear and whispered, "I want you. Now."

"Can't do "

He smothered her denial with a kiss and wrapped his arms around her waist.

"Missus might be bathing."

They pulled back at the voice. Footsteps rode the wind down the path.

"True. Ain't such a bad thing, eh?"

"Nah. But she doesn't need us watching."

"Yeah, I know."

"Missus!" John hollered.

Isabel jumped up, straightened her skirts and waved for Devin to stand. He offered a wicked smile. "Awe, c'mon, they know. Pretty sure they tried to get us together."

Isabel worked at her best stern expression. "Regardless. It's inappropriate."

"Missus!" Andy hollered moments before he and John appeared on the path ahead.

"Yes, right here," Isabel smoothed her hair. "What is it?"

John and Andy stopped and offered two fairly toothless grins. "Sorry missus," they said in unison.

Back straight, shoulders level, she breezed past them. "Sorry for what? Come. Work to be done."

"Yes, ma'am."

Isabel had no idea if they looked at Devin or made any sort of expression behind her back. Not her problem. They should have never found her out in the woods with a man to begin with. Never mind a man who worked alongside them! If she heard 'Irish have all the luck' muttered on the wind, Isabel chalked it up to her imagination.

The sun fell exceptionally bright over the house this morning, illuminating the wood in its white light. Isabel stopped for a second to appreciate the beauty. When John and Andy stopped alongside she kept a purely speculative look on her face.

"The men are mulling about," she stated.

John cleared his throat uncertainly. "Yes, missus."

"Why?"

Andy made an odd sound but responded nonetheless. "Waiting on you, missus."

Isabel closed her eyes briefly then opened them. She was in charge here. This was her responsibility. Since she'd woken this morning the very last thing she'd done was give any sort of direction. Her mind had been awash in needing to talk with Calum. How to further understand everything that was happening. Glancing at Andy and John, Isabel realized she'd abandoned something she was very proud of. Despite the untruths between her and Calum and the real reason she was here, Isabel had led the building of this house well.

She didn't intend to stop now.

"Walls are going up!" She announced and strode forward, Andy and John fast on her heels.

"Yes Ma'am!"

And so they did.

One week later, Isabel wiped away a damp tendril of hair and walked through the first floor of the Georgian. Late day sun splintered through the building as men worked hard. Late August heat hung heavy. The scent of freshly cut wood permeated the air. A smile threatened to stretch her face but Isabel tempered it. Managers— especially women—didn't smile. If she let one go during work hours it might make her appear weak. Instead she chewed the corner of her lip. In reality, these men respected her. A little smile most likely wouldn't hurt a thing.

Walking into what would eventually be the dining room Isabel was glad she hadn't pushed Calum to add more to this house. It could be because she'd traveled to the future and seen that it remained this size. Or it could be because more than ever she wanted this project completed. Isabel wanted Lucas trapped. She paused in the kitchen where the center counter island would eventually stand. How she missed it. Them. The future.

Slam. Slam. "Good headway."

Isabel turned and stared down at Devin. Shirt off,

sweat pouring down his chest, he hammered a board into place. She licked her lips and nodded. "Indeed."

Crooked grin executed especially for her he replied, "Indeed."

There were always so many things to say between them but luckily during the moments they couldn't speak, he understood just by looking into her eyes. "Right on schedule. House should be finished in the autumn."

When he stood, she did her best not to step back. Devin had a way of overpowering without moving an inch. All the hard labor building the house had only added to his physique. The sunlight had darkened his skin even more creating a near breathtaking combination with his dark auburn hair and pale eyes. Without another word, he nodded and left the room. Isabel watched his tight backside vanish down the hallway.

Taking a deep breath, she worked to control the heavy thud of her heart. He had promised to remain completely professional. Good thing. Isabel needed this house built well. If she gave in to their ever blossoming romance right now her leadership skills would be non-existent.

Thank God for nighttime!

Professionalism no longer existed. At every opportunity they stole away. Only for long walks and talk of course, perhaps some intimacy. No more. Isabel sighed. Why was she being such a prude? She wanted it. He wanted it. But she'd kept it at bay. No doubt they both knew the truth. Isabel was back in this era. And in this time period Lucas was coming. Calum was watching.

Constant fear.

Stepping outside, she eyed Calum's tent. He hadn't left the grounds since last week. She didn't imagine he would until the house was built. The game had changed. They hadn't spoken. Isabel figured he simply didn't trust her anymore. How had things become so turned around? He was the one who had betrayed her! Sort of. Despite what she'd said to Devin, Isabel remained aggravated. She could admit to herself that this anger was for Calum to know of, not Devin. Calum was her friend first. Somehow telling Devin she was furious at Calum seemed a betrayal to her friendship with Calum. Ugh! She'd spent her younger years remaining passive, then remade herself into a strong individual who knew she could accomplish anything if she set her mind to it.

This rift between her and Calum needed to be rectified.

Isabel strode across the lawn to his tent, felt ready to fight him tooth and nail. "Calum, it's Isabel." Not waiting for a response, she pulled the flap aside and entered. Dark coolness greeted. She had to take a few moments to let her eyes adjust.

At last she could clearly see Calum sitting behind his desk scribbling away furiously in his journal. Isabel plunked down in the chair across from his desk. "We need to end this."

Calum kept scribbling away.

Isabel would not be disrespected. "You tell me the truth, Calum."

He kept writing away.

Fine. Isabel had sworn she wouldn't do this but...

"What would Anna make of this behavior?"

The pen slowed until it stopped. Calum carefully

set it aside, closed the journal and sat back. When his bloodshot gaze rose to hers Isabel gasped. It appeared her friend had aged ten years in one week.

When he spoke his deep voice rasped, "You tell me the truth, Isabel."

Throat closed, Isabel knew he'd been in a great deal of pain this past week. But why? For all she wanted to keep the inquisition in her court she said, "What truth, Calum? You know everything."

Lips thin and tried, Calum bowed his head. "You're right, I should give you a truth first." His dark gaze rose to hers. "The minute I touch you I can divulge your every experience. I think Devin's description of us being sorcerers was at the very least adept. Creative, but adept."

Isabel shook her head. "I don't understand."

"Anna," he mouthed silently.

Blood froze in her veins. Not because Calum looked so terribly evil right now but because behind that dark nature dwelled something unattainable and vulnerable. Something in great need of release.

She chose her next words carefully. "What of Anna, Calum?"

Hot wind gushed through the tent when he leaned forward. The roar of his voice made the ground tremble. "You had contact with her in the twenty-first century!"

Oh no. Isabel counted from one to ten in her head and struggled to keep her disposition level. Implemented everything she'd learned over the years to protect herself. Grinding her teeth she kept her eyes locked with his. To look away would be her end. Yes, she must be honest. "I did not tell you because I did not want you to hurt. Apparently, my discreetness was for naught."

The air inside the tent chilled. Black shifted around Calum's form like a bubbling cauldron. "You should have sought me out immediately when you returned from the future. This information belonged to me!"

As magic swirled around and Calum glowered, something snapped inside. Would every man she came to trust in her life eventually turn on her? If he was any example the answer was yes. Isabel was tired of being afraid, tired of the unpredictable nature of man. Standing abruptly she said, "No, this information belonged to me, Calum! I was the one thrust through time. I was the one who had to make due. Not you. I am eternally fed up with being the one that has to disguise who I am for the simple sake that I live in a man's world." Tapping an angry finger on his desk she glared down. "As of this moment, I resign. I am no longer in your employ. I am leaving."

CHAPTER EIGHTEEN

Devin watched Isabel storm from the tent.

Growling, he waited until she was a good distance away before he entered. Calum sat behind his desk, a shrunken husk of a man. Yes, still vital but appearing very weak, extremely defeated. When had he last eaten?

"What?" Calum croaked.

"What?" Devin asked. "Really? You need to ask that?"

Calum's head rose, his dark eyes narrowed. "Get to your point. I'm tired."

Devin sat. "As you should be."

"I don't owe you an explanation."

"I, above all, you owe an explanation." Devin sighed. "I am of your blood. I'm… family." He threw the arrow. "I descend from you and Anna."

Calum's eyes flickered away in pain. "And for that I'm sorry."

"Sorry? Please. You're not sorry in the least. It's killing you that you haven't gotten to know me better. Yet you haven't, have you? I would imagine that's because you've got a sense of order in your head. You have a job to do and all the details that pop up along the way are elements of a situation better left alone."

"What you think of me is the least of my concerns," Calum said.

"Exactly." Devin crossed his arms over his chest. "I'll make sure Isabel doesn't leave if you tell me one thing."

"Isabel won't leave. She's bluffing."

Devin chuckled. He couldn't dispute the fact. "Then why don't you go out on a limb and answer my question anyway."

"Depends on what it is," Calum grumbled.

"You have all the facts. You know Isabel will be trapped in the house you're having built. What are you doing to do to prevent it from happening?"

A bit of the old Calum seemed to resurface as he sat back, a contrite look on his face. "How could I possibly prevent something that has already come to pass?"

Devin groaned but maintained a semblance of calm. That is until he spoke. "Okay, let me rephrase. Where is the bloody talisman? Up your god damned arse?"

Jagged bolts of black lightening shot from Calum's body. Devin didn't care. He felt the same crimson lightning bolts shoot from his body.

"The stone is none of your concern. Apparently Isabel is, so I suggest you go deal with her. Use your remarkable charm to ensure she stays," Calum growled.

Devin steepled his fingers and shook his head. "You just don't get it, do you?"

"I understand everything," Calum assured. "It is you, my offspring, who knows nothing."

Should he leave now? Devin wanted to stay and wring the life out of Calum but knew if he did Seth might not be protected in the future. After all, this man still needed to build another house. So he stood and paused for a measure. At last he said, "The stone is very much my concern. It's supposed to trap the creature set to kill me. As to me ensuring Isabel stays? You can bet your life on the fact I'm going to leave this tent, find her and do everything in my power to convince her to get the hell out of here."

Devin turned and walked away. About to leave the tent, he froze and said over his shoulder. "I'd think as her friend you would want to do the same."

He stepped out into the late day light and squinted. The Georgian appeared proud at the hour. As though—with only two floors worth of walls erected—her chest was already puffed in pride. Figures. Seemed to be the way of all around here. What was that about pride cometh before the fall? About the last thing a paranormal ghost hunting warlock should be thinking but hell. Looking up at the sky he shook his head then continued walking.

Time to find her.

Night was less than an hour off. The sun hung low in the sky. In a way that made half the world yellow... the other half black. His surroundings were steeped in that odd mix of pre-twilight before sunset that no one ever mentioned because for most, it meant nothing. It wasn't all that beautiful or striking when compared to what nature was capable. However, at this moment, Devin felt acutely aware of everything, of this in-between time. The pines smelled more pungent, somehow crisp in the somewhat oppressive humidity.

As he searched the grounds, Devin was amazed a whole week had already gone by. Would they travel back to the future soon? They'd yet to see any sign that Lucas drew near. Yet Devin suspected the man would find his way here, sooner rather than later. He hoped he was wrong.

When he couldn't find Isabel on the lawn or anywhere in the house he suspected she'd ended up in her tent. Careful that no one saw him, Devin snuck around the backside. After all, it'd look entirely inappropriate if he went in.

"Isabel," he whispered. Scratch. Scratch. Devin ran his nails over the canvas. "Isabel?"

"Devin?" she whispered back. Next thing he knew she stood behind him. "Are you trying to spy on me?"

"If I were you'd never know it." Grinning, he pulled her into his arms.

Hand to his chest she pushed him away. "Not here! Are you mad?"

"At times." He nodded toward the woods. "Let's go for a walk. We need to talk."

"You're right. We do."

"This way." Leading her into the woods directly behind her tent, he figured they'd walk through the forest until they made it to a part of the path well away from the house.

The tree cover made the woods considerably darker. While some might consider it spooky, Devin found it rather romantic. He took her hand and said, "I'll be leaving with you."

"So you heard that, did you?" Isabel said. "Well, I'm not really leaving. I was simply furious with Calum. I wanted him to think I was leaving."

"He didn't believe you." Devin helped her around a tree stump. "And neither did I for that matter. But you know what? I think it's a good idea. If you and I leave, how can you end up being trapped in the house? I can protect you as easily as Calum. We go and he can stay and build this house."

Isabel sighed. "So we're assuming that Lucas has completely lost interest in me then. Somehow I doubt that. Thinking logically, isn't the only real plausible reason that Lucas is heading this way is for me? As I've learned, the beast wants Calum's bloodline, not the man himself."

"Aye, Lucas definitely wants you. True. But I can't help but wonder if even though the beast is supposed to go after the bloodline and only comes this way because of Calum's magical lure. What's to say Lucas won't change his mind when he gets here and kill Calum even if the coven gave him strict orders not to?"

They stepped onto the path and kept walking. Isabel frowned. "So if you and I leave, Lucas will do one of two things. Keep on the scent leading him here and try to destroy Calum or decide to track me instead."

"Yep," Devin said. "But just maybe by the time he arrives here we'll be long gone."

A flock of bats flew overhead, darting in and out of the trees. "Do you not desire to stay here and protect him? After all, he's your bloodline. That and if he's killed Lucas won't be trapped. That might change everything in the future. You might have already been killed! Given that possibility you and I will never meet. I don't think this is a good idea, Devin."

Granted, he'd thought of that. But protecting Isabel right now seemed so much more important. "You think well, Isabel. I'm just really worried. I don't want to do the wrong thing and lose you. I'd rather die than take that chance."

A haunted expression dimmed her eyes. "I am

staying, Devin. I think that you and Calum are stronger together than apart. I also believe this is how it's meant to be. One way or another, I'm supposed to end up trapped in that house."

Devin knew he couldn't make her do something she didn't want to. And most likely, she was right. Calum and he would be much stronger fighting the wolf together. The stronger they were the better he could protect Isabel as well.

"It's full tonight," she murmured as they left the forest and entered the clearing on the river.

Devin stared up at the pregnant moon sitting above the tree line. Damn. They'd been watching it grow all week. Lucas would turn tonight. Would that make it easier to track them? Though it shouldn't as he'd only been here in astral form... but what if it did? Save what he'd seen haunting the house, Devin knew little of the beast and had purposely not asked Isabel about it. Now, as the swollen orb peered down, Devin had a strange feeling he should. That it was important they shared all the information they could.

"Ouch!" Isabel smacked her arm. "Mosquitoes."

Devin winked. "Now that's something I can fix." With a flicker of concentration he surrounded them with an invisible wall of scentless bug repellant.

"How?" she asked.

They sat on a rock at the edge of the river. "Sometimes dark magic has its good points. Put up a little wall they wouldn't like."

"That is convenient." She smiled. "I think you're going to come in handy."

The minute she said it they both grew silent. To talk about their future was a tricky, presumptuous thing. "Isabel, tell me more about Lucas." He paused a second. "About when he changed into a wolf."

A shiver ran through her body. Apprehension made her shoulders go taut. "Must I?"

He held her hand in his lap and spoke softly. "I think it would be a good idea. I think any truths we can tell one another might help with everything we're going to go through."

Nodding slightly, Isabel whispered, "You're probably right." She gazed up at the intimidating moon and waited several moments before continuing. "When the moon first started to rise that night, Lucas was particularly... amorous. As the moon climbed higher, his nature started to change. He became edgy, restless. When he left me to go for a walk I worried. He seemed so out of sorts. Not himself at all. Convinced he might do something out of character I followed him into the woods."

When she stopped talking, obviously in pain, he squeezed her hand and waited patiently for her to continue. When at last she spoke her voice was strained. "I remember how the moonlight illuminated everything. How handsome Lucas appeared braced against the tree. Odd how a man can appear so attractive when in the midst of such intensity."

"So he was starting the change?"

Isabel nodded. "I didn't realize it at first. I just thought him deep in thought. I still remember the smell of the ocean salt drifting on the wind, the trees blowing overhead. It was such a poignant moment. One I wished to share with him. I felt the need to release him from such heavy thoughts."

"So you revealed yourself?"

She shook her head. "No. I was about to when I noticed something wasn't quite right. His face suddenly appeared... different somehow. His shoulders became wider, more curved, his legs more muscular. I'm glad I noticed these things as the next moment he clutched his midriff and staggered away from the tree. Within seconds he was crawling on the ground crying in pain. In rage."

"I'm surprised you didn't run to him," Devin said softly.

"No. I knew there was something terribly wrong. Something... inhuman was happening." She bit her lower lip. "The cries of pain continued. His body began to transform. Bones cracked and grew and changed. He was part man part beast when I turned away. Then all I remember is running. Running until I could no longer feel my feet. Running until there wasn't a breath left in my body. As it turned out I'd only run until I was under the blankets in my bed. I never slept. Only waited. My heart pounding in my ears. At times I couldn't tell if it was my heart or the sound of the wolf's steps as it climbed the stairs to my room. That was the longest night of my life."

Devin pulled her closer, wrapped his arm around her shoulder. "I'm so sorry you went through that, love. I'm assuming it never came."

"No," she responded. "Lucas returned home the next evening, the same man he'd always been. Gone was the rage and discontent. As I soon found out when I confronted him about it all, those personality traits were symptoms of the upcoming transformation."

"I'm surprised you didn't leave, Isabel. It seems like the most logical thing to have done."

"Love isn't logical," she whispered. "And I did love him. At least I thought I did. Men had always proven themselves to be monsters one way or another. I suppose I figured at least his monster only came out once a month."

While it stung that she talked of loving Lucas, Devin couldn't deny her the feelings she'd once felt for the man. "What happened next?"

"Despite the fact that I was determined to be supportive, I think I changed. Either that or he did because I knew his secret. Lucas somehow seemed darker to me. Our relationship became strained. And strangely enough, I began questioning my feelings toward him. Had I ever truly loved him or had I simply been attracted to the kindness he'd showed me in a world where genuine kindness tends to be a rare commodity?" Isabel looked at him. "It was much different with him than it is with you."

"Good. I think," Devin said.

"Yes. Very good."

"Tell me the rest of your story, Isabel."

"There's little left to tell. The next time Lucas changed, he tried to kill me."

"That seems like a lot to tell," Devin said.

"It's really not. The next full moon I stayed home. As far as I know, Lucas went back to the woods to turn. I suppose I figured if I was safe at home before I would be again." Her body began trembling in his arms. "I could not have been more wrong."

"So he came to you as a wolf," Devin said.

"Yes," she whispered. "He was ravenous, like a rabid beast. The fear I felt the first night could not compare with the fear I now felt. It all happened so fast I was lucky to get away alive. But then again, as I later found out, someone helped me."

Surprised, Devin asked, "Calum?"

Isabel nodded. "Somehow he fought off Lucas or at least slowed him down so I could escape. It was the next morning that Calum approached me. You know the rest of the story from there."

So Calum had saved her? Again his predecessor proved himself a worthy man. "I'm so sorry you had to go through all of that, Isabel. Must say, you're one brave, lass."

"Not really." Her shaking subsided. "I was petrified."

"But you stayed with him after seeing him turn. That couldn't have been easy despite your love for him. You gave him more of a chance than most women would have."

With a shrug she pulled away a little. "I suppose I felt a bit bad for him. I think sometimes that might have been where his anger came from. He knew I pitied him. How terrible is that?"

"Not terrible. From what you described, it sounds like he goes through a great deal of pain when he changes. Not to mention it's got to be a terrible way to live knowing you're a werewolf, even if you are a part of some evil coven." Devin put his thumb beneath Isabel's chin and tilted up her head. "I'm so sorry about the rage I felt when you told me you slept with him after knowing he changed. I was wrong to have responded like I did. Take you that way."

Her wide eyes softened. "You needn't apologize. Sometimes jealousy can be the highest form of flattery."

Staring at her face in the moonlight, Devin felt humbled. She was amazing. "It blows my mind how you still manage to remain an optimist despite everything you've gone through in life."

"With a solid dose of realist," she reminded before his lips met hers. This time the kiss was slow and easy. When he pulled away, she said, "I think I can remain optimistic because there are so many out there that live a more difficult life. I think of the deaf children I've worked with."

"Through all of this I completely forgot you worked with the deaf as well. What are the odds that we'd share that?"

Isabel grinned. "It sometimes makes me wonder if there isn't a grander design in this whole situation. Strangely enough, it gives me hope. Perhaps we're meant to share a life together. Help the deaf together."

"That'd be nice, wouldn't it?" He didn't give her a chance to respond but pulled her close for another deep kiss.

This time Isabel ended the kiss. "Odd how it seemed the sun never really set tonight but the moon certainly rose." Her eyes roamed his face. "We should get back to the camp."

As the humidity settled into evening, the smell of Butterfly Weed grew stronger, its spicy scent only leant to the rampant arousal he felt. It'd been far too long since he'd slept with her. "You're right." He stood and held his hand down to her. "Come."

She allowed him to pull her up the path. About halfway between the house and the river he veered off. "I want to show you something."

"Oh, I don't think this is such a good idea, Devin. People will wonder."

"Do you honestly think that no one has a clue at this point?" Grinning, he led her deeper into the forest. "Some things are obvious in any century."

"Where are we going?" She asked.

"Not too much further." A few minutes later he stopped. To the common eye it simply appeared a thicker part of the forest. "I've been doing a little exploring since traveling back to this century." He sniggered. "Lotta time to kill when there's not much to do after work. Twenty-first century definitely has its perks."

"I hope I have a chance to experience those perks first hand," Isabel acknowledged.

Devin didn't want to think about her not remaining with him somehow. Here or there. Tonight wasn't for worrying about that though. Tonight was theirs to experience some of the good side of his magic. At least he hoped she'd see it that way. Turning away, he faced the closest tree.

And split it in half.

CHAPTER NINETEEN

Isabel couldn't believe her eyes. He'd destroyed the pine! Or had he?

"I only opened a door," he said. "Go on, check it out."

Eyeing the massive split in the branches of the pine, she spied a faint glow coming from within. As she walked closer she realized there was just enough space for one person to slide in. Completely trusting Devin, she cautiously slipped between the gaping pine branches until she stood underneath the tree. Devin came in behind her and the branches closed behind them.

"Pretty amazing, eh?" he said.

"Devin, this is incredible!" They essentially stood in an igloo formed over time. The mammoth pine overhead had no branches for at least twenty feet. After that they were sparse on the inside and so dense and old at the outer edges that the tree's lowest branches blanketed the ground. Isabel looked up and up into the tree, amazed by how the bright crystalline moonlight somehow shone down through the top creating a cathedral affect that held her mute in awe.

"Intense, isn't it?" Devin whispered from behind, wrapping his arms around her midsection. "Look down."

Isabel looked to her feet and gasped. "The pine needles are glowing!"

Devin's hand drifted up and caressed her breast while his free arm pulled her against him tighter.

Pleasure warmed her blood. "It's been too long, Isabel." He nuzzled the side of her neck. "Please."

Isabel felt wanton. Free. Pushing her backside against his arousal she said, "Can we be found?"

"Not easily," he whispered into her hair, nibbling her earlobe, then the tender backside of her neck. With a swift talent she could appreciate his hand pulled down the front of her dress and allowed her breasts to spill free. She moaned when his work roughened hands cupped and stroked both. Her nipples ached with need. Within a second her dress and undergarments were pulled down and tossed aside.

Devin spun her so quickly she fell back against the tree trunk. Cupping her face, his lips covered hers in rough, needy passion. Isabel breathed deeply through her nose and smelled the rich aroma of pine...the musky scent of her own desire. As his hot lips traveled down her neck Isabel's head fell back against the tree. *God, I want this man. Around me. With me. In me.*

When his large, warm hands kneaded her backside and his liquid hot lips clamped down on her overly sensitive nipple, she cried out and looked down. Isabel had never seen anything so erotic as the sight of her heaving chest, full breasts and Devin kissing his way down her belly.

On his knees, Devin's hands left her backside and grasped her hips. She watched as he gently caressed her slightly protruding hip bones. Leaning forward he flicked his tongue feather light over the soft area between her hip and belly. Her lips fell open. Her inner muscles clenched. He certainly had talents far beyond Lucas.

Pulling off his shirt, Devin looked up, a wicked grin on his face. Had he heard her thought? When his gaze fell from her eyes and slid down her body it felt like warm maple syrup had been poured over her sensitive skin. I feel every nerve ending. It's so intense. Isabel let her head drop back against the tree once more and closed her eyes. Felt every little caress on her body as though it were the first time a man had touched her. I feel worshiped. For the first time in my life. A tear slid down her cheek.

When his hands cupped her backside again she felt lighter. "Devin!" She gasped as sharp pleasure rocked her forward. Hands fell to his strong shoulders and Isabel tensed. His talented tongue licked, laved and probed between her legs. Pleasure washed over her in thick waves and Isabel had no choice but to lean against the tree for support.

With every twist and turn of his tongue, Isabel spun higher. He's killing me right now. This is it. Her toes curled, leg muscles tensed, buttocks clenched. Still his tongue roamed until it went where no tongue had gone before. Waves of clenching pleasure rippled up through her belly and chest, down her arms. Even her scalp tingled with pleasure. Almost. Almost. Then, as if a sword of red hot desire stabbed straight up through her body, Isabel arched, unable to look anywhere but up through the tangled branches to the pulsing moon above. A strangled sob broke from her chest as an orgasm blew through her entire being.

The pleasure felt so intense that for an unnamable amount of time, she lost herself, floated somewhere beyond her body, became so much a part of the pleasure and pain that nothing else mattered. Higher and higher.

It took several more seconds to realize Devin now stood, his long, thick erection eager, ready. He held her pressed against the barely abrasive bark, legs high. "Isabel," He whispered. "Love."

Pulling forth every ounce of strength she had, Isabel managed to wrap her arms around his neck. Her legs remained useless. With a long groan, he slowly pressed deep inside of her. Thud. Thud. Her heart beat up through her throat. Her core sparked and ignited in renewed need. Devin's strong arm scooped down beneath her backside and lifted while he braced the other arm beside her head. Instead of the rushed sex he'd offered before this time he moved at a far more leisurely pace.

Isabel cried out as he easily drew forth her pleasure once more with each smooth, practiced stroke. Clenching his shoulders tighter and tighter, Isabel wrapped her now eager legs around his torso, met him at each excruciatingly mind blowing thrust. When her movements began to match his Isabel sensed Devin losing control.

"Bloody perfect lass," Devin said between clenched teeth.

Devin's restraint snapped. His vigor went wild. His thrusts fast and furious. Pleasure spiraled up so sharply, Isabel froze for fear of its intensity. I'm going to blow apart! When Devin cried out and tensed, Isabel lost all air and shivered into a vicious string of spine tingling orgasms that ricocheted through her body. Pulse after pulse after endless pulse.

After a very long time Devin whispered, "I'll never be without you."

It was only then that Isabel realized Devin was

now on his knees with her against the tree. When had he gone down? When had she? Their bodies were soaked with sweat. His hair fairly drenched.

Running her hand through the wet locks she looked into his eyes and said, "No, you won't."

Devin ran his finger over her lower lips, beneath her chin. "I've never—"

His entire body tensed. Gooseflesh crawled over her skin. Startled, Isabel realized Devin had implemented his magic and they were both dressed again. Leaning close to her ear he whispered so softly she barely heard it. "Say nothing. Don't even breathe if you can help it. Danger."

With the flick of a wrist, the moonlight streaming in from above was muted as branches slowly moved overhead. Silence fell heavy. Every little fine hair on her body rose. What had Devin sensed?

Snap. A small branched broke beyond their alcove.

Devin moved slightly, positioning his body so that he protected her but faced outward. Trembling, Isabel knew something was very wrong.

Grrrrr.

Devin remained very still. Isabel's heart thudded harder and harder. A wolf had growled. From the sounds of it, a very large wolf. Lucas. He'd found her.

A furious roar erupted before a wide swath of pine needles vanished. All that remained was a gaping doorway in the wall of pine. Cool air blew in. Yellow eyes gleamed through the night.

"No!" Isabel screamed. Too late. Devin lunged forward, red sizzling off his body. Scrambling out after him, she grabbed a short stick and ran after the tumbling forms of the wolf and Devin. When they fell apart, both came to his feet.

Lucas, a massive black wolf, stalked around Devin. Devin, glowing a fiery red, snarled right back. There's no way he could fight the wolf, could he?

"Lucas," she pleaded. Anything to get his attention away from Devin. Would the wolf know her as Lucas did? Patting her chest she said, "I'm right here my love. You found me."

Swinging its massive head, yellow eyes stared. Fear curdled in her stomach but Isabel continued talking. "I'm so sorry I ran from you. It was a mistake. Do you understand? A terrible mistake."

Fangs bared, the great beast started to lumber her way.

"Yes, that's right," she said. Skitter. Thud. Slam. Her heart beat out of control, its sound thrumming so loudly in her ears she could hear nothing else. This was it. Lucas had her. Maybe it was for the best things ended this way. With Devin safe. One less monster to deal with. Palm slick with sweat, she clenched the stick and banked her fear. This stick needed to meet its mark.

"Terrible mistake, my arse." Red lightening arched out from Devin toward the wolf. Lucas dodged. Enraged the wolf ran and lunged. Isabel cried out as Devin fell beneath the great beast.

Isabel ran and jumped onto the wolf's back. With a quick jab, she sunk the stick deep into its right shoulder. Yelping, it flung her off and scraped one massive paw through the air. Pain wrenched the side of her cheek as its claw raked down the side of her face.

Stunned, Isabel waited for the beast to jump on her and end it but black fire burned through the trees and struck the wolf. It let loose such a cry of agony that Isabel thought Devin had somehow defeated it. Sitting up, she watched as the wolf ran into the forest. Calum appeared out of the night. Though she tried to blink it away, blurriness kept marring her vision. Though she rubbed her eyes, Isabel felt warm fluid gushing down her face. Ignoring it, she stumbled to her feet and staggered toward Devin. Why wasn't he moving?

Culum crossed her path, leaned over, picked him up and threw him over his shoulder. "Isabel, are you well enough to follow?"

Nodding numbly, she glanced back one last time. No sign of the wolf. It'd vanished. Trying her hardest to put one foot in front of the other, she followed Calum through the woods. Please don't let Devin be dead. Please God. But all she could focus on was his limp form hanging over Calum's shoulder.

When they were nearly to the wood's edge, Calum said, "I've put up a protective barrier around the men tonight. One I should have already had in place. You and Devin will stay in my tent with me."

Isabel didn't dare debate. In fact, she had to admit she preferred to stay with them both tonight, especially with the wolf out there. A few candles lit Calum's tent, casting lonely shadows here and there. With the flick of his wrist, two more cots appeared. He laid Devin down in one. With a loud sigh he shook his head. "Not good."

Still wiping her eyes, Isabel peered down in horror. A huge gash marred his collarbone. Blood poured down his chest. "So pale." She sat on the edge of the bed and took Devin's limp hand. "My God. It looks as though he was bit."

"You both need to be tended," Calum said softly.

"No. No. I'm fine." Standing, she swayed slightly but walked over to Calum's linen trunk where she fell to her knees and started pulling out clothes. "We need hot water. Alcohol. A thread, needle."

Calum's hand fell on her shoulder. "You don't need any of that, child. I'm a warlock."

"Fine, then summon some boiling water." Isabel continued to rummage through his chest. "And find the strongest alcohol you have, none of that weak wine."

"Isabel. None is needed. I am a warlock," he repeated.

Stopping, she glanced over her shoulder, suddenly furious. "Then where were you tonight?"

Head hung, Calum shook his head. "It happened faster than I expected. I'm so sorry."

Only then did she realize he wore black robes. Much like a monk might wear. Isabel had never seen him dressed like this. She stood slowly. "This is how you dressed in your coven, isn't it?"

Calum appeared much stronger than he had earlier but she didn't miss the dark circles that remained beneath his blue eyes. "Yes. These are the robes of my calling."

"Your calling?" Isabel closed her eyes briefly. When she opened them Calum remained standing in front of her, hands clasped calmly in front of him. "Dark magic," she whispered. "Evil."

Looking away, her eyes quickly traveled to Devin. The blood was gone. A clean, white bandage covered his collarbone.

"Not all evil," Calum replied evenly. "In fact, very little."

But she didn't listen. Isabel went to Devin and sat by his side. "He's alive."

"Of course he's alive, dear girl." Calum stood nearby. "He was lucky. Most don't survive the werewolf."

Isabel warred between being angry or grateful to Calum. Running her fingers lightly alongside Devin's bandage she asked, "He will heal with no problems?"

"He will heal. Come." Calum took her hand and pulled her to her feet. He held a cup to her lips. "Drink."

Isabel drank. The warm, spiced wine slid down her throat and quickly warmed her limbs.

"Now lie."

Isabel felt a warm calm slip through her veins. Exhaustion settled over her and she allowed Calum to lead her to her cot where she lied down. As he pulled blankets over her he whispered, "Now sleep."

So she did. In and out, slipping deeper into the shadowed corners of slumber Isabel swore she heard men talking. All she could make out before drifting off was one man saying, "You continue to surprise me, Calum."

And Calum responding. "I always will, Adlin."

Night became day. Cool water met her lips. She drank, and then slept. Day became night. Cool water met her lips. She drank, and then slept. When sunlight next warmed the canvas above, she awoke. Groggy and disoriented, she tried to sit up.

"Not quite yet," Calum said gently. Holding a cup to her lips, Isabel drank, grateful for the cool water.

Lying back on the pillow she smiled. Only then did she feel the terrible pain in her cheek. She reached up and touched a bandage. "What happened, Calum? Why am I in your tent?"

"You had an accident, Isabel. You and Devin. Do you remember?"

Memories flashed up fast. Lucas...the wolf attacking Devin. Devin! This time when she sat up, Isabel pushed past Calum. Devin wasn't in the other cot. "Where is he?"

"Here," Devin said softly.

Isabel turned. He sat in a chair near the corner of the tent, the white bandage stained slightly with blood from the wound beneath. Going to him she immediately started inspecting the bandage. "Are you okay?" She studied him intently for other wounds. For the most part he looked well. His muscled upper torso was too relaxed though, his position in the chair slumped, almost defeated.

Gently seizing her wandering, worried hand, Devin shook his head, voice strained. "I'm fine, lass. Please, sit."

"No. I'm worried. You look troubled. What is it?"

Calum sat behind his desk and poured wine into three glasses. "Please, dear. Do as he asks."

Isabel looked between the two. Any previous animosities appeared vanished, as though they'd never existed to begin with. Sinking into a chair, she took a glass of wine and sipped. "What has happened? Why do you both seem so serious?"

Calum looked to Devin. When Devin shook his head, he continued. "There have been some unfortunate changes."

Isabel frowned. "How so?"

"The wolf." Calum cleared his throat then

continued. "Has left its mark."

Isabel glanced at Devin. His smoky green eyes were unusually pale, his sensuous lips cut into a thin, grim line, the skin around his eyes drawn. "What does he mean?"

"Did Lucas never tell you how he became the beast he is?" Devin took a long swig of his wine. "Did he never mention the bite of the werewolf?"

She blinked and shook her head. "No. I asked but he gave no response. I let the matter drop."

Devin set aside his glass and said, "I was healed completely. The moon will be full again tomorrow night." He pulled away the bandage. Blood seeped in tiny ringlets from what was clearly a bite mark. "This wound knows the moon is nearly full."

Isabel abruptly stood. "It's been a mere day or two. Your mind's clearly addled!"

In a split second, Devin reached out and pulled her onto his lap. "You've been mostly unconscious the past month, Isabel. I woke up myself a few days ago."

"No." She tried to get up but Devin's arms became a vice around her waist.

"Aye," he said softly. "It takes longer in some cases for people to struggle through the effects of a werewolf." Devin pulled her closer, buried his face in her hair. "I've learned much in the past few days. I'm so petrified you're going to be afraid. I'm petrified I'll lose you."

Isabel stilled. "Lose me? No. Never." She turned in his arms and met his eyes. "You must know that."

A muscle leapt in his jaw. "Hear Calum out before you say that."

Ignoring sudden apprehension, she turned to

Calum. "Tell me then."

Calum's eyes darkened. "The bite of the werewolf is in itself a curse. In fact, many consider death a better outcome than the bite."

Blood chilled, Isabel could barely breath. "Make your point."

"The bite of the wolf is in effect how the species ensures its survival. He who is bitten by the wolf and survives carries the curse." Calum sighed. "He becomes the beast too."

Isabel stood abruptly and shook her head. "That's impossible. I've never heard of such a thing."

"Well why would you," Calum said. "It isn't exactly common knowledge."

"It's solid folklore in the twenty-fist century." Devin took another long swig of wine. "And I've learned without doubt that all folklore derives from truth."

Isabel tried to focus on his face. Her vision blurred. This was no time to swoon. Throwing back her shoulders she began pacing. The feeling passed. "I take it then that this is all pure speculation?"

"No, child." Calum poured more wine for Devin. "I sense the coming change in him."

Spinning, she glared at Devin. "Do you sense any changes?"

"Aye." He closed his eyes and rolled his head. "My senses are different. They strengthened when I became a warlock, but this..." His eyes met hers. "Is different. A man stands forty yards from me and I can smell on his breath what he ate for dinner the night before. A leaf falls from a tree in a forest and I can hear it brush by the limbs as it falls."

This can't be happening. I must truly be living a

nightmare now. Isabel released a shaky breath. She must view this in a logical manner lest her mind snap. "Do we think that this curse is confined to this time period?"

Devin rolled his wide shoulders, the muscles rippling beneath. "Somehow I don't think so."

"But you do not know for certain." She continued pacing. "Neither of you know for certain."

"When it comes to magic and curses nothing is ever certain," Calum conceded. "But a warlock, above most men, knows when something is not right with his body."

Isabel absently wiped away the tear she felt slip down her cheek and continued pacing. "So you're telling me that Devin will turn into a werewolf tomorrow night. That not only am I doomed to be caged in a house for three hundred years but the man that I love is a monster."

She froze the minute she said it. Putting a hand over her mouth she looked at Devin and shook her head.

One eyebrow arched. Resentment tinged his clipped response. "Oh yes, Isabel. I'll become a monster. Don't feel bad for saying so."

In that moment, Isabel warred between many emotions. Guilt. Fear. Pity. Regret. Desire. Love. But as she stood there staring at him it occurred to her that while these were justifiable feelings, she needed to set them aside and focus on his feelings. She remembered Andrea telling her about how becoming a warlock had affected Devin. How evil he's felt. How withdrawn he'd become. Yet he'd come out of that because of how he felt about her. And now he was facing something even more frightening.

Isabel should have trusted her instincts that night. They should have come straight back to the camp. Perhaps none of this would have happened had they done so. But as she'd so often learned in life, hindsight was positively useless. Trying to make the best of a situation or at least accepting a situation was the only way to handle things. Crossing to him, she knelt and took his hand.

"I've got to go check on a few things," Calum said and left.

Devin and Isabel stared at one another for an immeasurable amount of time. Finally, she reached up, touched his cheek and whispered, "I'm so very sorry, Devin."

He turned his head from her touch. "I don't want your pity, Isabel." Standing, he walked away from her.

Isabel jumped to her feet. "Please, Devin, don't go. We need to talk about this."

"There's nothing to talk about," he said vehemently. "The minute Lucas bit me he sealed our fate. I will turn at every full moon. As you did with Lucas, you'll try to stay with me, try to understand me until at last the distance grows between us. How could it not when you'll be constantly thinking that I will come to kill you every time I turn?"

Before she could respond, Devin strode from the tent. By the time she got to the opening he'd vanished. Isabel stepped back as tears began to pour down her face. He was right. She would always be wondering. Aimless and numb, Isabel wandered over to Calum's chair behind the desk and sat. Staring blindly, she kept replaying everything over in her head. There had to be some way around this. How could they have been through so much only to end up here?

Wiping away more tears, Isabel reached for a glass of wine and froze. Calum's journal sat on the corner of the desk. Instead of grabbing the glass she placed her hand on the book and slid it in front of her. Running her fingers over the title, Journal Two, Isabel couldn't help but wonder what he'd written. How he'd viewed all of this. Most of all, she wondered what secrets he kept. While she thought hindsight useless, Isabel couldn't help but be curious… if hindsight might be handed to her, why not take it?

Opening the journal, she began to read.

CHAPTER TWENTY

Devin strode restlessly through the house. The walls and roof were now intact. The men had accomplished a lot the past month. He couldn't help but be curious... was the project completed enough to trap a monster? *Should trap me as well!* Climbing the stairs, Devin ran his hand along the walls, trying to imagine it.

When he got to the third floor he leaned against one of the chimneys. All the workers had finished for the day and campfires were being lit outside. He slid to the floor, leaned his head back against the bricks and closed his eyes. Devin could almost feel the minutes ticking by, closing the distance between him and the full moon rise. He knew so little about what to expect. As much as he should be petrified right now, he wasn't.

All he could think about was Isabel. How he'd lost her.

Devin could still see the look on her face when she'd turned back to him in the tent. When she'd come and knelt at his feet. The terrible pity. Heartache. Loss. She'd said goodbye to him in that one long eye lock. He'd suddenly become Lucas in her eyes. A road she would not walk down twice. He didn't blame her. Isabel deserved to feel that way. But it didn't make the moment any easier. If he could've pulled her into his arms and said he didn't think he'd turn, Devin would've done so in a heartbeat.

But he knew he was going to turn. Very soon.

Swoosh. Devin heard the brush of Isabel's skirts as she left her tent. He smelled the sweet tang of her body's scent as she crossed the lawn, heard the anguished trip of her breath as she roamed the rooms below. Was she thinking of their time together in this house, both now and in the future? Or was she thinking of being trapped within its walls for the next three hundred years? Probably a bit of both. Devin listened to each step she took up the stairs. When she reached the third floor, Isabel didn't look at him but walked to the window.

Devin knew she knew he was there. He could hear it in the heavy thud of her heart, the scent of her increased blood flow. The dampness locked between her closed fists.

Long minutes passed before she finally spoke. "You are wrong about everything, Devin." She took a deep, steadying breath. "So very wrong."

Devin studied her profile. So beautiful with her hair semi-loose, pieces of its long, curling tendrils twisting down her back and over her shoulders. She had not removed the bandage from her cheek.

"I'm not wrong about a thing," he said.

Spinning, she leaned against the sill. "How can you think for a minute that I feel the same way about you that I did Lucas?"

"Because you do," Devin said evenly.

Isabel crossed the room and slid down next to him. They sat in much the same position they had that first night in the basement. "In truth, at first my thoughts compared you with Lucas. I saw no hope for us. But as I sat there reading Calum's journal I was quickly reminded about loves lost. About how fleeting it all is." She paused for a few seconds.

"Whether he had been the cause that led to his circumstances, in the end, Calum committed the ultimate sacrifice for love. He said goodbye to his wife and child forever to protect them. Keep them safe."

Devin shrugged. "I suppose that's the optimistic way of looking at it."

"That's the only way to look at it." Isabel took his hand. "Please do not push me away, Devin. You must know by now that I love you. My time here is limited. Lord knows what will happen afterward."

Devin closed his eyes. He hated not knowing. Not knowing when and if they'd travel forward together again. Not knowing if he'd hurt her when he turned into a wolf. But by far the worst feeling was whether he'd be able to protect her from Lucas when he turned. It was one thing being a warlock. He at least had his wits. But a werewolf? There were too many unanswered questions, too many gray areas.

He wrapped his hand around hers and opened his eyes. "I love you too, Isabel."

Leaning her head back against the chimney, she met his eyes. "I know."

"I'm not scared of turning." Devin looked past her to the darkening skyline. "I'm petrified of hurting you."

"I'll stay with Calum tonight. I'll be safe." A small sound of distress came from her throat. "I'm petrified of Lucas hurting you."

"I'm not. Looking forward to meeting him with equal strength."

"So you assume." Isabel sidled closer.

Devin knew she wanted to say more. That her true fear was that Lucas would attack him before he turned, or worse yet, while he turned. All he could hope was that all werewolves turned when the moon hit a certain zenith. He had no choice but to leave this encampment before. To risk her or any of the men's life for that matter was incomprehensible.

Lazy sawdust floated around them as the sun's very last ray slid over the sill and splashed across the floor. "What else did you learn from Calum's journal?"

Devin heard her heartbeat speed up for a moment before slowing down. "Nothing after the endless talk of Anna. It seemed Calum had been sitting in his tent that week before you were bit obsessing about years gone by. Sad really."

Isabel lied to him. "I could pull the truth from your mind if I wanted to. You know that right?"

"But you will not," she responded. "Because you respect me too much. Also, because you are resolved."

Devin lifted a hand and touched the corner of her cheek. "As you are to hide your wound from me."

A wobbly smile vanished before it had a chance to blossom. "Like you, I need time to cope with change."

His respect for her was too great to push. Even to say he'd love her no matter what she looked like would seem false to her freshly wounded vanity right now. Devin knew. He'd been there. Still, he couldn't help but think of what the 'in-between' Isabel had said about her ghost worrying what he'd think of her face. What a thing to cross time and dimension. Made 'wooing' a girl particularly tricky. "You know I'd love you no matter what you looked like, right Isabel?"

As forecasted, she shrugged him off and stood. Self-esteem was a fragile human thread, one he decided not to mess with again right now. Standing as well, he followed her to the window and looked down at the milling men below. The sun had vanished beneath the horizon and the full moon sat patiently above the tree line, its secrets eager to steel the night. Isabel's heart thundered in her chest. Devin had to give her credit for appearing so calm.

"How do you feel?" She murmured softly.

"You know exactly how I feel."

Isabel's eyes fell to his rampant arousal before returning to his face. Devin's nostrils flared when her juices began to flow. Isabel's throat rippled as she suffered a heavy swallow. "And you know exactly how I feel, do you not?"

The heat in her body rose. Musky scent began to waft from her pores. Devin struggled for air… calm. "Little time," he whispered.

Theirs was an unspoken challenge. An unvoiced decision. Would she walk away as she should? Would he let her go as he should? Isabel knew he experienced the arousal she'd witnessed in Lucas before he turned. Would she decide to let the wolf have her once more? Or would she decide to walk away. Devin knew it was out of his hands. Lust raged through his veins so harshly now, he could barely contain it. There existed no feeling like this.

Isabel's eyes turned to the moon and remained there for several seconds before they darted back to him. "Yes, Devin. Yes."

Her consent wouldn't have mattered at this point. The moon tasted like silk on his tongue. Isabel's sweat and scent created an ache that had to be filled.

Swinging her around, he pressed her against the wall, his front to her back. Devin snarled against her hair. Strange thoughts started to swamp his senses.

Mine. Mate. Impregnate.

Unable to control the low growl in his throat he spread her legs, pulled down his pants just enough, her skirts up and thrust inside her tight, steaming hot sheath.

Everything after that became incredibly acute. Her harsh cries of pleasure. His grunts of domination. In. Out. In. Out. The sharp scent of her musk running down his leg combined with the sound of dogs howling miles away. Grabbing her hair, he pulled back her head and nibbled her neck. Licked, nibbled.

"Devin!" She cried, her inner muscles clenched.

The sound was foreign to him. The creature he mated with his somehow, precious somehow. One last thrust. His seed pumped. Pleasure. Bliss. But time was running out. Pulling free, he yanked up his pants and stumbled toward the stairs. The walls closed in on him. Too close. He needed to get out of here.

Sweat poured down his face as he stumbled down, down, down. Crawling out of one of the back windows, he hit the ground. The cool earth rose up around him, the sky overhead felt free. The moon. Where the hell was the moon? He ripped off his shirt. Furious. Needing. Staggering into the woods, he fell against the tree and peered around. Where was the moon? This structure stood in the way, didn't belong. Felt foreign.

I need to get away. I need the forest around me. Freedom. So he began to run. Run until he could see the moon through the trees. Run until this cloying feel of need passed.

Arghhh! Pain ripped through his body so harshly he stumbled to the ground. It started in his face, as though nails were driven into every inch of his skin. Then his torso. As though sizzling fire burned it. Then his legs, as though he were being eaten alive. Fear and pain seized every part of his being. Where was he? What was he? Would this persecution last forever? Pain became so great that all he could do was wail. Cry. Scream. But nobody came. Nothing released him. Clawing the ground, he tried to drag himself away. Tried to make sense of complete confusion, complete and absolute terror.

Shhhhhh. Pain started to wane. Bit by bit. Shhhhhh. Finally, he lay still. Looking up he saw the wind blow through the trees. Shhhhh. Slowly, he stood and smelled the air. Ravenous hunger rumbled through his belly. Sniffing, he spied a dead carcass nearby. Fresh. Crawling on his haunches, he went to it. No danger was nearby. With lightening quick reflexes, he dragged it to cover, a rock with a small alcove beneath. As his teeth sunk into its warm flesh, he groaned in contentment. Eyes constantly on the forest around him, he ate his fill. Belly full at last, he sat back and rested his head on his paws.

Water trickled in the distance. A river turned stream. Someone whispered—the voice almost lost in the clicking of tree branches overhead. Primitive and low, an animal growled. Danger. Anxiety stiffened his spine. Another gust of wind blew. It carried scent.

Spicy. Fresh.

He knew this somehow. This was familiar.

Sprinting forward, he left his alcove and ran through the woodland. Every stone and stump was discernible—every twisting path, easy to navigate.

Eyes to the night, intent on his destination, he coasted around tree trunks, leapt over boulders, desperate to reach something.

The low growl grew stronger. Time was running out. Heavy breathing mixed with the wind. Thump. Thump. Its heartbeat mixed with his. Petrified and fast, pounding so hard and thickly it filled his throat.

Bursting free from the trees into a clearing he skidded to a halt.

Something knelt by a stream, its long curling mane a delicate fan over its back. Bright orange blossoms decorated the ground around it He inhaled.

Spicy. Fresh.

"I always wondered why they grew here." It fingered a blossom at its side without turning. "Butterfly Weed, my favorite flower."

Why did he understand it? He tried to respond but couldn't.

"Don't be afraid. Come closer. I won't hurt you," it whispered.

Hurt him? Unlikely. Why would it say such a thing?

Unmoving it spoke again. "Do you suppose these Butterfly Weeds became confused? Really, they're supposed to be fond of fields."

He took a cautious step forward. Danger was close. It should take care. Move. You are incredibly vulnerable to threat. Come to me. You are not safe. He sniffed. Putrid, flesh decayed. Too close.

"Can't say I blame them," it continued, soft voice mesmerizing. "I think I might grow here too. It's one of the most beautiful spots."

Not nearly as beautiful as it was— sounded. He needed to see its face.

Tilting back its head it whispered, "Look. I just knew that tonight I'd see them. A rare thing in Maine, but it happens."

Moving forward a few more steps he gazed up. A deep blue-green array of lights slithered across the night sky.

"Like I said," it continued. "Rare. But I had a feeling. You, them…magic?"

He took a few more steps. Wanted so much to talk to it—but could not.

"I'm glad you came."

What are you? Voiceless, he closed the distance and sat beside it. Head bent now, its mane hid its profile. Why did it hide?

"Things are different now," it murmured. Its slender paw cupped the pedal of a Butterfly Weed, its ivory texture delicate against the vibrant orange.

How so? Tell me! He edged closer.

"No, no, no," it said mournfully. "I wanted more time."

The moment it spoke another scent filled the clearing. Branches snapped. Standing, he walked around his newfound creature and stopped. Every nerve ending vibrated. Danger edged closer. The same low growl he'd heard before rumbled again.

Closer.

He growled.

So strong was his sudden need to protect this creature he readied himself for death. Licking his lips, he eyed the tree line. Blood. He wanted blood.

Another low growl rumbled from the night.

"Go now," it whispered urgently. "I am not worth it."

Not worth it? How could it think such a thing?

Pacing, he waited. Whatever came was nearly here, perhaps had always been. Watching. Waiting. He craved battle so strongly he almost strayed from his creature's side to seek out whatever lurked so cowardly within the darkness.

Crash. Snap.

A split second before he was able to react, his creature whimpered and crouched down further. Black and mighty, the darkness had limbs, jumping at them with a ferociousness he could never have anticipated. He crouched and sprung, met the beast in the air moments before it landed on his creature.

They rolled and rolled until water engulfed. He kicked and clawed. The cool water barely touched his skin as they thrashed and fought.

Where is your strength and might fool? You dare challenge me.

He knew that voice! But how? Ignoring the beast's words within his mind he sank his teeth into the pelt on its shoulder. Laughter rang. Yellow fangs crossed his vision. Still they rolled.

"Stop, no, please!" his creature pleaded.

Splashing, it pursued them.

Go back, he thought. *I will protect you.*

But as he battled the beast, he started to panic. Could he protect it? This monster was strong, powerful, and relentless. Mere minutes into the war he knew himself defeated.

"Let him go! You must!" his creature screamed.

Twisting to the right, he tried to shake the monster off. It clung to him, paws a vice grip, claws digging into his vulnerable flesh. Pain ripped and tore— a cruel unseen knife of destruction across his midriff. With a yelp he struggled to regain footing.

The sharp tang of blood filled his nostrils. The absolution of defeat a mere breath away.

"Get off him!"

Did it rip me in half? Why does the night blur? He saw his creature pounce on the monster determined to end him. "No," he pleaded. Nothing came out.

His head slammed against grass. Pebbles cut into his back. The edge of the stream cornered him. He scrambled. A fist size rock provided leverage. He pushed and flung forward. This gained him two feet of grass. Such pain! The creature bit and tore. Movement, coherent thought, became more and more difficult. Its screams sounded far off. A Butterfly Weed crushed beneath his nose, smeared into the ground.

There existed no more scent.

You dared challenge. You lost.

And he had. Even fury and vengeance held no appeal. Death however, lulled and pacified. No! How could he think such? Again furious, he lurched forward. Only to be dragged down once more. The beast's body pinned him, its growl close to his ear.

Its bite to his jugular—fatal.

Through the slim veil of night he watched his crimson blood drain and stain the grass. Pain fled.

His eyes slid shut.

A warm, gentle hand touched his neck. "Only we can do it together."

He lived? Prying open his eyes, he stared up. Blackness swirled around him. A creature stood over him. All pain had fled. His creature and the other beast had vanished.

"I am Calum. I won't harm you. Try standing," it

urged.

Flexing his muscles, he tried. And stood easily. Fear and the need to protect flooded his senses. Shhhhh. The wind blew through the leaves.

"Are you ready to protect your creature? Are you ready to protect Isabel?" It asked.

A heavy wet drop hit his nose. Damp filled the forest. Yes, he was ready. Darting into the woods, he closed the distance between his creature and him. He would save his Isabel. Nothing would ever hurt it again. When he broke free from the forest rain fell in heavy sheets. Light flashed overhead. Shaking his coat, he growled low in his throat and bared his teeth.

Calum was somehow already here. The enemy was about to attack his creature, Isabel.

Scrambling, he began running. He intended to die for Isabel.

CHAPTER TWENTY-ONE

Lucas watched…waited. Yellow eyes glowed and narrowed in the dark night. There remained two choices. Run and die. Or stand and fight. Inch by inch, Isabel backed away. Frigid raindrops hit her cheeks. Damp earth filled her nostrils. Fangs bared, Lucas seemed to smile. The beast knew she could not escape.

Think.

To die like this after everything seemed pointless, infuriating. Where was Calum? Had he not assured her protection, an easy transition? At the very least, some words of comfort. It appeared Lucas wasn't worried. He tossed his head back and forth, sniffing the air for trouble, before his hackles lowered.

Her heart thumped painfully in her chest. Isabel continued to back up onto the lawn. The fiendish creature enjoyed the game. No. I won't let it end here. She rubbed the ruby red stone hanging from her neck.

"I'm here. You will be just fine."

Hearing Calum's voice leant little comfort. Not daring to search him out she whispered, "I highly doubt it. Where have you been?"

Lucas growled—the sound a deep, dangerous rumble from within its immense barrel chest.

"I had to finish something," Calum said.

Rain fell heavier. Wind blew and bent trees. Distant thunder rumbled. Lightning flashed. The creature edged closer. She dared not speak again.

"It's time," he said. "I beg you once more. Please do not run toward the house. There's got to be another way."

Don't run for the house? Was he mad? Then again, he didn't know she knew that this was the only way. Something shifted to her left. She glanced. There was nothing there. Lucas pawed the ground, growled again. Eyes closed, she murmured a prayer to the Lord.

Opening her eyes, she clenched the stone tighter and started to run. An eerie blackness crossed her vision. The creature roared. She slipped on slick grass and fell. Petrified, she clutched desperately at the drenched surface.

A battle ensued behind her. Deafening keens rent the air as animal fought man. She stumbled to her feet and continued to run. But something happened. Despite her best effort, every step closer became a step further away. Clingy and wet, her skirts dragged around her ankles. Hair hung in her face, blocked her vision. Swiping the limp locks aside, she peered through the driving rain.

The house will keep me safe. The stone is my heart. One foot in front of the other she kept moving. Her calves stung. Her feet felt heavy. Somehow black and bright all at once, a strange light surrounded her. Suddenly, she no longer struggled. A strong wind shoved her forward.

Again, the Lucas roared, the sound furious and agonizing. What was happening? I need to slow down! But she couldn't. Too fast. I'll crash into it!

The air thinned. Her throat closed. I'm so scared. She tried to drop to her knees. Instead, her body hovered and flung forward so fast the house screamed up, a wall of sturdy wood that would surely kill her.

One final lungful of air rushed into her throat. "No!" she screamed.

As the house rushed up, time seemed to slow. Had she made the right decision? Would Devin remain safe if she sacrificed herself? But even as Calum's magic whipped her and Lucas the wolf toward the house, she knew she had. No matter how petrified she was about dying and becoming a trapped ghost, steeling Calum's stone and bringing it with her into the house was the only way.

Isabel covered her face as the house rushed up. This was it. She was going to die. Ughh! Pain rent her body as she crashed into the house. Bright light filled her vision then vanished. Falling sideways, she watched Lucas twist and turn within the oily black walls, struggling to find purchase with his slippery paws.

I need to breathe! Yet when she tried there was no air. Pain filled her chest cavity. Her eyes widened. Lucas's wolf eyes bulged as he too struggled for non-existent air. Suddenly, another wolf jumped in between them.

No Devin. No!

He too struggled for air, his strong limbs flailing in defiance. Isabel tried to reach out to him but he was focused on Lucas's dying wolf form. Raking her nails across nothing, Isabel tried. And tried. Her face began to feel swollen and heavy, lungs burned. Until lack of air turned everything gray.

Then black.

"Now, Isabel. Now!"

Isabel jerked awake at Calum's far off words.

How could she hear him? Jumping up she crawled to Devin's now lifeless wolf form and started to drag it. Despite the fact it had to outweighed her by half, in this reality, it came easily. Almost like a feather. Crying, she didn't look back but dragged and dragged within the walls until they were between the dining room and living room. At last she stopped, let go and turned back.

He was gone!

Blinking, she tried not to panic. Where had he gone? Looking around, Isabel realized she wasn't where she thought she was. No, by the looks of it, she was in a wall beyond the kitchen! Voices started to come through. Peering out, she realized she recognized no one in the room. To make matters worse, the design of the kitchen was entirely different. Try not to panic. You're a ghost now. Panicking will accomplish nothing.

To imagine haunting a house was one thing, to actually experience it, another. But life had always thrown curve balls at her. Best to focus on what she knew. Nothing was bound to make sense. Never say more than you need to. Look for the light at the end of the tunnel. God, where are you? Devin, where are you? Calum, where are you?

The next second Isabel knew as she watched Devin and Andrea talking in the living room. She kept trying to speak, but they didn't seem to hear. Different realities began to wash over her. Being sucked forward into the kitchen. Devin and his cousins were there. Everyone talking at once. Magic surrounded. The wall sucked her back in. At moments she was fighting Lucas, he was right there, then he would vanish. She couldn't keep track of one moment from the next. Somehow Isabel felt the pleasure of making love to Devin. Loving him. In the end, through all the brief flashes, all she knew is that she tried to be there when she could. However she had no real grasp on her actions save that she had to fight Lucas and protect Devin.

Confusion.

Disorientation.

"Now, Isabel. Now!"

Calum?

Then everything slowed and came to a stand-still. Isabel stopped.

Standing in the middle of the living room, she gazed around. It appeared to be the twenty-first century. Seth, Leathan, Dakota and Andrea formed a wide circle around her, beyond them stood Adlin and Calum on either side. Colors swirled and twisted so fast. Blue. Black. White. Green. But where was red? She fingered the stone hanging around her neck. Closing her eyes, she counted to ten in her head. When she opened them, they were all still there.

"Am I here? Are you?" She whispered.

None responded. All chanted. She shook her head and repeated, "Am I here? Are you?"

From nowhere two wolves materialized and began stalking each other between her and the outer circle. Devin and Lucas. Staring down at the huge black wolf and the equally large brown wolf, Isabel suddenly felt helpless.

Words started to float around her.

"Do you like it in this time period?"

"Do you suppose it matters?"

"I'm hoping," he replied evenly. "Whether here or there, I want to be with you, Isabel."

Devin? She remembered him saying that to her. Yet here he stood... a wolf. No matter, she'd watched him at the river. Such a gorgeous wolf. There'd existed no malice in his canine eyes when he'd come to the river. When he'd sat beside her. Isabel clenched her fingers. His coat had been so soft. His eyes so kind and protective. Devin in wolf form had not nearly the lethal capabilities of Lucas. They had always been two very different men.

Now they were two very different wolves.

A hot rush of air blew over. Isabel looked around, frightened. The wolves snapped at each other. Yellow glowing eyes met green glowing eyes. Teeth bared in deep aggressive growls.

"Devin, can you hear me?"

His wolf made no response.

"Lucas, I'm here. Now. Can you see me?"

The black wolf's eyes swung her way even as he sidestepped a swipe from Devin.

"Calum!"

Calum and Adlin, Seth, Andrea, Leathan and Dakota all stared straight ahead. All chanted. Light continued to swirl. Blocked in. Trapped. How did she get out? How did she end this?

"Now, Isabel. Now!"

Calum's voice once more slammed into her head. I'm trying. What do you mean?! Hand protective over the stone at her throat, Isabel wondered. She'd read his journal, knew that the only way to save Devin was to steal the stone. Hide it where it would never be found. But this same stone set Lucas free.

Shhhhh.

Isabel looked around. Where was that sound coming from? Suddenly calm she turned, peered beyond the walls of the house.

Shhhhh.

The wind. Why? In her mind's eye she was catapulted away from the house. Down the drive. Snap. She stood on a road. A long desolate road surrounded by pines. Snap. Isabel sat in a strange vehicle, moving quickly. Glancing to her left, she saw Devin. Not the wolf, but Devin.

The vehicle slowed. He got out.

"What are you doing?" She hopped out and came to him. Watched.

He leaned against the vehicle and pulled out a picture. It was of her. The way he looked at it broke her heart.

"Devin, I'm right here. Can't you see me, feel me... sense me?"

Something screeched in his pocket. He pulled out a small box and clicked it before putting it to his ear. "What, you don't like texting?"

Isabel couldn't hear what was said through the device. A strange chill overcame her. Was she witnessing something that had already happened?

"I dunno, habit not to I guess," Devin said.

Looking around, he shook his head. "The forest."

Tucking the picture in his pocket, he opened the truck door and slid into the vehicle. "You tell me how else to describe a long paved road with nothing but towering pines on either side."

Isabel jumped in next to him. Somehow she irrevocably knew that this was a moment in time. One she had to pay attention to.

Devin chuckled and started driving. "Turn right at the slumped pine tree. Drive a mile until you reach the really tall pine tree…you have reached your destination."

"Devin, please. Listen to me. I don't know where you are but you need to come back!" Isabel yelled. "Please, now. I need you!"

About to speak, he yelped and threw the phone aside. He blew on his fingers as if the device had burned him. A strange device flashed, its picture went fuzzy before it said over and over, "Turn left."

Isabel frowned at the thing and repeated, "Devin, you need to come back!"

Devin banged it with the pad of his hand. The vehicle leapt forward. He fell back. She fell back through the seat but managed to pull herself forward. The vehicle bucked and swerved. Hands on the wheel, Devin tried to bring it under control. It sped up. Started to fling back and forth.

"Come back!" Isabel repeated. What else could she say?

The feminine voice, though slurred and dying repeated, "Turn to the left."

"Now, Isabel. Now!" Calum's voice once more.

Suddenly, the vehicle slid to a stop. Isabel rolled forward, straight through the front of the machine and onto the road. Devin remained in his vehicle. Standing, she looked left and right, tried to gain her bearings. She'd never been here before. Had she? Left and right again. So familiar. Walking to the edge of the road, she looked at the dirt road that led to the house. She turned and walked across the road and stared into the woods.

Isabel knew this place. She had walked it many times. A strange sound roared to life. Turning she watched Devin drive his vehicle toward the Georgian.

That didn't matter. Something else did. Isabel turned back and continued to study everything.

"Now, Isabel. Now!"

Lord she was tiring of this. Sitting on a nearby rock, Isabel tried to figure out what she was missing. *What am I forgetting?*

Again words floated from nowhere...

"Sounds like good old fashioned reasonable deduction to me. Common sense."

"That's right. Trust me, most people don't possess it."

"You have every right to be mad at Calum. He betrayed your trust."

Isabel jumped up and looked down at the rock. The rock! Glancing back at the road then the drive, she realized... this had once been the original path to the river! Ready to run back to the house Isabel realized she had no one to run back to.

"Sounds like good old fashioned reasonable deduction to me. Common sense."

Isabel contemplated the words hanging in the air. Rather used to the snippets of speech left from the past by now. How would Calum relate this rock with common sense? Isabel sighed and sat down. They were dealing with a werewolf trapped in a house by a stone. Say the werewolf ever tried to search out the stone, he'd go by the senses given him. That would be acute scent and hearing. Or at least she thought so. Chewing her lips, Isabel scraped her fingernail over the rocky surface while she fingered the stone around her neck.

What was Calum up to?

Scent and hearing. Isabel lifted the stone to her nose and sniffed. As if a ghost could smell anything!

But did a rock have scent? One that could be tracked? Maybe if a human had touched it. But what if a warlock had touched it? Isabel studied the stone. Had it always been oblong? Had it always been a little misshaped?

"Sounds like good old fashioned reasonable deduction to me. Common sense."

Isabel swatted the repetitive words away. Though Devin had said them, now they belonged to Calum. Frowning, Isabel thought hard. The talisman trapped the beast. It was the only way to keep Devin safe somehow, trapped in one dimension while living out another. She rubbed her fingertips together. What was the connection? Why was everything in limbo? Stuck?

"Sounds like good old fashioned reasonable deduction to me. Common sense."

Standing, she yelled, "No more!"

Isabel turned and braced her hands on the rock. We're all trapped in this time dimensional game. She wasn't whole. Devin wasn't whole. Lucas had never been whole. What was left that wasn't whole? As she leaned forward, the stone around her neck swung forward, its crimson weight swinging back and forth in front of the rock.

The talisman. The rock. The talisman. The rock.

Isabel frowned and stopped the stone around her neck from swinging. As she'd heard her love phrase, Isabel whispered, "Sonofabitch."

Common sense slapped her square in the face. Better yet, it had been there all along. Maybe I don't have the whole stone. And a wolf could not hear or see a rock. What better place to hide the missing piece of a puzzle than within a rock… especially if it were part of a rock!

Isabel yanked the stone around her neck to eye level. Calum! Devious warlock! Eyes narrowed she started to study the big rock. About six feet by two feet, she began searching every inch, every little nuance and cranny.

Somewhere. Had to be.

But it was nowhere. She'd searched. Frustrated, Isabel started to pace.

"Sounds like good old fashioned reasonable deduction to me. Common sense."

"Enough!" She yelled. What was she missing? Isabel paced and peered down the road toward the Georgian. Toward a house she'd apparently been trapped in for three hundred years.

She froze.

Three hundred years. That's a long time.

Swinging back, she ran over to the rock and started digging around it. The soil moved. Thank God! Never knew in this ghostly state. Digging down a good five inches in the front she found nothing. Still hope. Crawling around the back she started digging.

And digging.

Until only one section of the rock remained. Brushing aside the leaves, Isabel started digging then stopped. About two inches down, something caught her attention. A blur of color. Could it be? Leaning closer, she rubbed away the dirt covering the rock surface. It was!

Nudged within a crevice of the rock was a piece of red stone.

With a yelp of excitement, she dug her fingernail into the surface and popped out the piece. Staring at the small stone in her palm, she picked it up slowly and held it next to the stone around her neck. Eyes narrowed she moved the stone around her neck into different positions. Hmmm. Isabel pushed the piece against the stone one way. No. That wasn't right. She twirled the stone. Tried again. No. Turning it a little more, she tried one more time.

Click.

It slid into place, molding together.

Eyes wide, Isabel stared at the perfectly oval stone.

Whoosh. A loud, eerie sucking sound rushed through the forest. She'd heard that sound before. Before Isabel could turn to brace herself, she was being sucked back toward the Georgian. As her spirit zoomed down the dirt drive toward the house, Isabel wasn't afraid of imminent death.

No, she looked forward to closure.

The stone was whole now. That meant something.

Her body suddenly slowed, hovering with twenty feet of the house before she fell to the ground with a heavy thud. Air rushed by so loudly, Isabel covered her ears. Crash. Boom. Intense sound vibrated all around. What was happening? Crash. Boom. Rolling onto her side, Isabel curled into a ball and wished she could crawl into the ground. That the horrible sound would stop.

As if her thoughts were answered, sudden silence fell.

"My love. My dear, sweet Isabel."

It was Lucas in human form…as she remembered him before the change.

Slowly, Isabel uncovered her ears but didn't dare move.

"At last," Lucas whispered.

When he crouched over her, Isabel wondered if she still remained trapped within the Georgian. His finger ran up her cheek. "I think things are now as they should be."

Be brave. Face this. I have no choice. Carefully sitting up, Isabel ignored the dull throb in her head, the subliminal ache. Looking up she met his eyes, unafraid. "We are alive again."

Crouching over her, he nodded. "Yes, I believe so."

"Where are we?"

Confusion passed over his face. "I am not so sure. Yet I suppose it matters little. I am with you."

"Do you remember why you came here?"

"Regrettably, yes." His finger once more brushed her face before his hand fell away. "Do you?"

Isabel could make little of their surroundings save they were very, very dark. "Yes. For me. Ultimately because you were lured."

Lucas nodded, eyes dark and sad, his masculine form tense. "Do you want to know why I saved you that night your brother sold you?"

"More than anything," she whispered.

"Because like me, you were resolved. And like me, you weren't defeated. A young girl in a world like this with no one and you knew that you'd survive. That no matter the circumstances, you'd somehow break free from the chains cast upon you. I saw all that in you even before we met on the pier." He breathed deeply. "I thought you spectacular."

Isabel was speechless. For several moments she simply stared at him. Finally she said, "Why were you in my time period?"

"You know why."

"You somehow tracked Calum that far," She replied.

Lucas nodded. "Each creature sent after Calum's curse is stronger and stronger. I tracked him as far as I could. To your time period at least. Then I lost him." His eyes fell to hers. "But I found something else... someone else. I became obsessed."

Frowning, she stared at him. "You were... are both warlock and werewolf. One with great power. Why value the courage of a mere human girl?"

Cupping her cheek he replied, "What makes you think I wasn't once a mere human boy?"

"But—"

"No," he whispered. "Let's leave it like this. Somewhat good. At least for you and I."

Isabel was about to speak when someone else spoke. "Step away from her."

Lucas' eyes started to glow yellow and the last of whatever good Isabel had seen there vanished. Standing in one swift move, he turned and said in a deadpan voice, "Seems I'm fairly outnumbered."

Scrambling to her feet, Isabel stood only to stumble back and land on her backside. Blinking, she tried to see more clearly beyond a few feet. Tried desperately to adjust to whatever reality she'd been plunked into.

"I'd say so, asshole."

Isabel knew that voice. Maybe. Why did it sound so garbled? Different? Before she could say a word, light sparked everywhere. Blue, black and most definitely... red.

Lucas stood across from Seth, Leathan and Devin.

A tornado of colors twisted around all. Seth's eyes glowed black. Leathan's blue. Devin's red.

Lucas's... yellow.

Each and every warlock appeared so large, so exceedingly threatening and deadly.

Another loud crash resounded when Lucas raised his arms in the air. Seth, Leathan and Devin flew backward, arms and legs flailing until they landed at least thirty feet away.

"What you forget." Lucas laughed, the sickly sound promising. "Is that I am far more powerful than the three of you put together."

Odd how Lucas seemed so compassionate one second and evil the next.

Scrambling to his feet first, Leathan's eyes narrowed. Isabel watched in horror as huge spiders poured forth, scurrying toward Lucas. Screeching, their legs moved them at an alarming speed.

Lucas chuckled and kicked them aside. The moment his foot connected with each beast, they melted away leaving a stench much like burning tar.

Almost as soon as Leathan released his assault, Seth's attack followed. Long thick venomous snakes were everywhere, their glittering eyes and slithering tongues eager. Lucas grabbed one by the neck and turned it toward the others. Hisssss. They wormed their way back toward Seth in ravenous fury. Apparently he was their new target. As Seth fought his own snakes, Devin started to chant. "Ten times sounds. Death to you. From every angle. I, a magician, able to send your."

Decies sonos. Mors ad te. Ab omni angulo. I. magus, mittere potestis tuum.

Lucas covered his ears and dropped to his knees,

screaming. Within a few seconds he fell silent. "You think to use sound against me? Destroy me that way?" A low rumble of tempered rage bubbled from within. Standing, he began to chant. "Three warlocks will be that fight against me. Fight if you can: But the whole three warlocks will be that fight against me."

Tria erit warlocks impugnántes me. Certa si potes: sed totae tres warlocks erit impugnántes me.

Even as the sun's purple pre-dawn shadow dusted the sky behind the dark green evergreens, Lucas' voice rose up and met with the black twirl of clouds above, pulling them down in a wide sweeping vortex.

Isabel watched in horror as the black cloud grew tendrils that rippled out and wrapped around each individual cousin. First Devin, then Leathan, then Seth.

Not for the first time since all this began, Isabel wished for a moment alone inside a church. This was evil and death and very, very wrong. For the first time, she recognized the language. Latin. How she knew, Isabel wasn't sure. Just that somehow it seemed holy while being used toward true evil.

But no matter how evil, it had Devin. And despite the warmth Lucas had shown, he would always give in to his baser nature. No longer the man he'd once been.

With a quick prayer, she tried to stand again. Luckily this time, her legs held. Shoulders back, head held high, she slowly crept up. Lucas was far too busy trying to destroy the others to notice. Closing her eyes, Isabel counted to five and tried to gain courage. Opening them, she didn't hesitate another moment... she attacked.

CHAPTER TWENTY-TWO

Attack! Now! Devin didn't need Calum's ghostly encouragement. The minute Isabel jumped on Lucas's back, he let loose his fury. Rage at every little thing this man's presence had meant to Isabel. Fury for the fact he'd succumbed to evil as he had. And for shame, fury that he'd loved Isabel so well and didn't do the right thing.

Yes, he'd heard every word Lucas had said to Isabel. Knew without doubt the man had found true love with her and turned from it for the sake of his coven's orders, for the sake of not taking a chance. As he stormed toward them, Devin wondered what he should do. How to handle it.

Furious. Disappointed. Overprotective. All these feelings blew through. Enabled him to gain the power to gently toss Isabel aside... to find himself face to face with a warlock far more powerful than he and not afraid in the least.

Peering at Lucas, holding him in the grip of pure rage, he chanted over and over, "Go to God. Be free of this curse." "Ituros ad Deum. VOCO maledictio."

Dark spirits began to dance behind him. Their faces warped and contorted in rage. Lucas stood taller, his gaze flickered to Isabel then back to Devin.

Devin continued to repeat the chant even as Lucas tried to fight him.

Crying in agony, Lucas finally fell to his knees, the spirits behind him eager, cackling. Suddenly the wizard Adlin's ghost appeared beside Devin and added his voice. "Ituros ad Deum. VOCO maledictio."

Lucas struggled, rising up then falling back to his knees again. Fighting because he knew his coven stood behind him, rising up because he tried to remain true to those who had so well deceived him. Roar. The wolf cried forth from his face, warping in and out.

From the night appeared Calum's ghost. His deep voice added to the chant. "Ituros ad Deum. VOCO maledictio."

All three said it over and over.

As they did Lucas's body shifted between man and beast, his cries of pain a heart-wrenching sound against the still Maine morning. The spirits behind caressed and nurtured the beast. They tried to remind him who he was. All he'd become.

Despite the fact he'd been man and perhaps kind at one time, he had chosen this path. He'd chosen evil over good and decided to be one of the creatures set to destroy Calum's descendants.

As the first ray of sunlight broke through the forest and traveled across the lawn, the spirits leapt back into the shadows, their long, skinny fingers trying to reach one last time for Lucas.

Still they repeated the chant. Over and over and over.

Another ray of sun splintered through the trees. Then another. Then another. Lucas peered forward, eyes narrowed into the sun.

"No!" The spirits cried at once, covering their ears.

As the last shadows were stolen from the early morning, so too were the dark spirits, their shadowed forms torn from sight.

Devin met Lucas' eyes. Dazed and confused, his lips formed few words without sound. "Ituros ad Deum." All fell back as his form disintegrated, shifting and reforming into smoke. Devin turned as it drifted into the light morning mist then traveled up a ray of sunlight until it last vanished from sight.

Isabel felt the shift. Knew inherently that no matter how dark he'd become, Lucas had been saved. He would not be thrust into hell.

Everyone stood on the lawn watching, waiting. But nothing else happened. "It's over," Calum said. "This part of the curse has been lifted. You are free, Devin."

Isabel released a small sob. When he looked her way, Devin realized it was not Lucas she looked after but her violet eyes were turned his way. Going to her, he pulled her up into his arms. Surrounded her in his arms. Protected her with his warmth.

How had they got here? When had they returned to the twenty-first century? The last he knew he'd been a wolf chasing her and Lucas into the house in the eighteenth century.

Everyone remained silent. A heavy silence hung over the front lawn. Pulling back, he looked down into her eyes. "Are you okay?"

The sudden apprehension and confusion on her face gave him pause. When a tear slipped down her face he repeated, "Isabel, are you okay?"

She shook her head slowly, closed her eyes and breathed deeply. Devin cupped her face and ran his finger down the scar on her cheek. She was here with him, somehow miraculously alive in the twenty-first century. "You're beautiful. You're here. We're together. All's well," he said.

Calum appeared beside them, voice quiet. "She can't hear you."

Devin glanced at Calum then back to Isabel. "Can't hear me? What are you talking about?"

Isabel shook her head and mouthed. "I hear nothing. I am sorry."

Though they weren't directly next to him, Devin suddenly felt the strength of his cousins. Though he continued to cup Isabel's face he said to Calum's ghost, "A temporary side effect of being trapped in the house?"

"No. A permanent effect," Calum said sadly. "To be trapped in another dimension, within a curse, and then freed alive... has its consequences."

Devin didn't hesitate; he released Isabel's cheeks and swung at Calum. His fist sailed through the ghost as did his body. Furious, he turned. "You jerk! Because of you she's scarred and deaf?" Devin lunged at him again, only to once more fall through air.

"Devin, no. Please no, my love."

He froze at the sound of her voice in his head. Turning to Isabel, he said, "Did you just talk to me within the mind?"

Nodding, she held out her hand. "I must have if you can hear me. I'm not afraid. It's alright. Please, I'm tired of all the anger."

"Tim?" Andrea's voice sounded from behind. Devin turned and saw her stagger toward the house. "Tim!"

They watched as her husband walked slowly out of the house. He appeared as though he woke from a nap. "Sorry," he mumbled. "One second I was talking to you, the next thing I knew I slipped and fell against the wall. Did I fall asleep or something?"

Running, Andrea nearly plowed him over as she wrapped her arms around his shoulders crying. Holding her he said groggily, "Still a little tired."

"I love you," She said again and again and walked with him back into the house.

Devin pulled Isabel into his arms once more and spoke within the mind. "I'm so, so sorry. You don't deserve this."

Isabel pulled away, shook her head and began to gesture with her hands. He stared, incredulous. "You know sign language?"

Nodding, a small smiled formed on her lips and she signed the words, "Those years before I left Virginia, I met a boy. He taught me a new way to communicate, a way in which we could talk to the deaf through hand gestures. That's when I first became interested in helping the deaf. When I first realized that people existed amongst us whom lived in a silent world."

Devin turned and glanced at Seth, Leathan and Calum. They shrugged in confusion.

Adlin piped in, "Sign languages have often evolved around schools for deaf students. In 1755, Abbé de l'Épée founded the first school for deaf children in Paris; Laurent Clerc was arguably its most famous graduate. Clerc went to the United States with Thomas Hopkins Gallaudet to found the American School for the Deaf in Hartford, Connecticut, in 1817. Gallaudet's son, Edward Miner Gallaudet founded a school for the deaf in 1857 in Washington, D.C., which in 1864 became the National Deaf-Mute College. Now called Gallaudet University, it is still the only liberal arts university for deaf people in the world."

"Sometimes, in cases like Abbé de l'Épée, they learn from others. Perhaps by knowledge learned and passed down from a very talented Virginian tutor. Walking over to Isabel he smiled and signed, "I was a cute little boy, wasn't I?"

When her jaw dropped then Isabel burst into laughter, Devin shook his head. "I've heard it said you were a devious wizard. Guess I didn't believe it until now."

Adlin winked and Devin caught a flash of his Maine vagrants, John and Andy in his wizened old ghost face. "Oh, you've no idea, lad."

"I am not afraid," Isabel said within Devin's mind. "This is a new life. A chance to start over."

"But I'm still who I am. A werewolf. I know it without doubt," he replied.

She touched his cheek. "But you're my wolf. You won't harm me. I know this without doubt."

Still, he felt tortured and conflicted, as though they still had so far to go.

"Well you do," Calum said.

Devin looked at Calum then back to Isabel and signed rather than speaking within the mind. "I want to know the truth. Why did you end up taking the stone into the Georgian with you? What did it say in Calum's journal for you to take such a risk?"

Isabel and Calum's ghost locked eyes for several moments before her gaze turned to his. "It was all rather simple in the end. And he wrote it in his journal for me to find. The stone was right there in his wooden trunk all along. And as we know, the stone traps the beast. But the stone also would lead me to you. Without one I could not have the other. As this particular haunting was locked in dimensions rather than clear set time, had I never brought the stone into the house you would have never come. You would have never freed me. In the same token, had you not come I would not have found the piece that ultimately freed both me and Lucas, and allowed you to defeat him."

Silence.

"Huh?" Devin, Seth and Leathan said at once.

Adlin rolled his eyes. "Calum's a devious, tricky warlock, he is. The old can't-have-one-set-of-circumstances-without-the-other trick. Brought them together good, you did." Turning to Calum he said, "Didn't think you had it in you. Well done."

Calum chuckled and nodded. "See, I'm not all that bad."

"Oh, you're bad," Adlin said. "This all could have been done much more directly."

"How so?" Calum scoffed as he walked alongside Adlin toward the forest. "This was a most direct approach."

"They're all staring at us with confusion. How was this the most direct—"

That was the last anyone heard from the two ghosts before they vanished into the morning mist.

All three remaining warlocks turned Isabel's way and signed adamantly, "I don't get it!"

Laughing, Isabel shook her head and signed back, "Is Andrea's husband free?"

Everyone nodded.

"Do I look okay? Do I look happy?"

Everyone nodded.

"Then didn't this story end well?"

Seth, Leathan and Devin all crossed their arms over their chests at the same time and frowned.

Raising her brows, Isabel signed, "I might be deaf but this is a reality in which I have some understanding. A reality I feel prepared to handle. With a man I know is ready to handle it with me. I'm not afraid to be in the future. I'm not afraid of change." She paused to let her words sink in. "But I suppose you need a clear cut happy ending."

Before anyone could say a word she wrapped her arms around Devin's neck, stood on her tip toes and kissed him soundly. Wrapping his arms around her, Devin lost himself in everything about her. In the amazing woman she was, is and would always be.

"I love you," He said within her mind.

Isabel only deepened the kiss and replied, "I know."

EPILOGUE

As they had before, Calum and Adlin once more walked between worlds, the tree roots and sky above. The serpents of the underworld swimming below. This time there was a little less animosity between them than at the Victorian. After all, they were beginning to count on the mere fact that they taxed one another's mind. That—as it turned out—was quite the stimulant for a deceased warlock and wizard.

"Don't blame Andrea and her husband for moving out. Can you believe Devin and Isabel moved in? They're going to foster deaf children apparently," Calum remarked.

"Seems so. Great thing," Adlin responded.

"Amazing how different versions of Isabel ultimately lead them to fall in love. And not once did her ghostly self or in-between self divulge too much information. Sharp tack that one. Somehow knew it might interfere with them ending up together if she said too much. Says an awful lot about her character despite the bizarre situation. I dare say I always knew she had it in her," Calum provided with pride. "Would make a good time-traveler. Did make a good time-traveler."

"Without doubt, a smart woman. As well as exceedingly practiced at being misled by others." His wry glance Calum's way escaped the warlock. "A sad thing to be sure. No doubt, Isabel is a woman who understands it best not to say anything until she has all her facts in hand. And to be faced with multiple dimensions." Adlin shook his head. "Something I'm not overly familiar with but duly impressed by. It worked out well indeed. Must have been a very strong pull between the two."

"Without doubt!" Calum nodded. "Have you any idea how difficult it was to stay silent through it all? On both ends."

"For you? Near close to impossible I'd bet. You left a lot to chance but it worked in your favor."

"Indeed!" Calum nodded and grinned, immensely pleased with himself. "Indeed. But as you said, the circle worked. All circumstances lead back around. Life in its own way always comes full circle."

"Karma," Adlin said. "Plus the Fates and destiny. Powerful mix."

Hands behind his back, Calum strolled along, smiling. "'Ituros ad Deum. VOCO maledictio' My lad did that all on his own. Quite brilliant."

"Indeed." Adlin nodded. "There is hope for your offspring yet."

Calum's brows rose. "Where did he ever get the idea to say, 'Go to God. Be free of this curse?' Stroke of genious. Sending the bloody werewolf's spirit to God would have never occurred to me."

Adlin sighed. "Of course it wouldn't. As far as you and I have come… we haven't really traveled far at all, have we?"

"Well, what do you mean by that?"

"I think you know exactly what I mean."

"Trust me, old man, I'm clueless."

"You said it."

The serpents swished around Calum's feet. The sun broke through overhead, covering Adlin.

"You connected with your love, Anna, in the

Georgian. Do you not recall?" Adlin reminded.

"What does that have to do with sending a monster to God?" Calum asked.

Adlin rolled his eyes and stopped walking. "Good question, Calum. As before, perhaps the battle is over for your kin. Perhaps not. Two creatures have come already. Do you not think the third will come for Seth?"

"Very good chance it won't!" Calum barked, admiring the swirling dance of the creatures beneath his feet. "It's locked up tight. Back to the matter at hand. Make your point about Anna, man."

"Well." Adlin tapped his toe and looked at the bright sun overhead. "With any luck your descendants might soon be free of the curse laid upon you." His wizened blue gaze glowed when it fell to Calum. "What will you do when and if you're freed from your vigilant otherworldly watch over them?"

Calum frowned and kept walking. "I suppose I'll be at rest." He contemplated this. "Sounds rather dull, eh?"

"True love is never dull." When Calum turned around, Adlin once more walked into the mist, slowly fading from his vision, but not before his words floated back.

"Freed love lives on forever. You, above all, need learn that."

Calum was about to tell him just what he thought of that when a few more words floated his way before Adlin vanished altogether. "A true Celt knows life and love is eternal. Anna waits."

Turning, Calum continued to walk down an endless path. Serpents swam after him. Darkness waited around every corner. Yet, Calum couldn't help but wonder. Would she wait an eternity? Did she even remember why she waited? For whom she waited? Better yet… could he suffer on forever not knowing if she did? Perhaps half the curse simply meant he loved too strongly.

And might never know if love truly had a happy ending in store for him.

THE END

WHAT'S NEXT?

Be sure to follow Leathan's story in *The Victorian Lure* (Calum's Curse: Ardetha Vampyre) and Seth's story in *The Tudor Revival* (Calum's Curse: Ultima Bellum)

Read the stories original to Adlin and Calum. Search for *The MacLomain Series* at Amazon, Barnes & Noble and Smashwords.

ABOUT THE AUTHOR

Sky is the best-selling author of seven novels and several novellas. A New Englander born and bred, Sky was raised hearing stories of folklore, myth and legend. When combined with a love for nature, romance and time-travel, elements from the stories of her youth found release in her books. Readers have described her work as "Refreshing" and "Unforgettable."

Purington loves to hear from readers and can be contacted at Sky@SkyPurington.com. Interested in keeping up with Sky's latest news and releases? Visit Sky's Website, www.skypurington.com to download her free App on iTunes and Android.

    Visit Sky at www.SkyPurington.com
    Twitter @SkyPurington

Made in the USA
Lexington, KY
19 January 2013